Acclaim for Julia Justiss's previous titles:

My Lady's Trust
"With this exceptional Regency-era romance,
Justiss adds another fine feather
to her writing cap."
—*Publishers Weekly*

The Proper Wife
"A spirited Regency-era romance that
far outshines the usual fare. Justiss is a
promising new talent and readers will
devour her tantalizing tale with gusto."
—*Publishers Weekly*

The Wedding Gamble
"This is a fast paced story that will leave you
wanting more…you won't want to put it down!"
—*Newandusedbooks.com*

JULIA JUSTISS

After twelve years as a vagabond navy wife, an adventure that took her from Virginia Beach to Monterey to Tunis, Tunisia, to Oslo, Norway, and back, author Julia Justiss followed her husband to his family's homeland in the Piney Woods of east Texas. Except for summer jaunts to New England to visit family and escape the brutal Texas heat, she's lived there ever since, in a Georgian manor house she built with her husband and three children. In between teaching high school French and attending ball games, cheerleading competitions and track meets, she pursues her first love—writing historical fiction. She loves hearing from readers—contact her at 179 C.R. 4112, Daingerfield, TX 75638 or via her Web site at www.juliajustiss.com.

JULIA JUSTISS

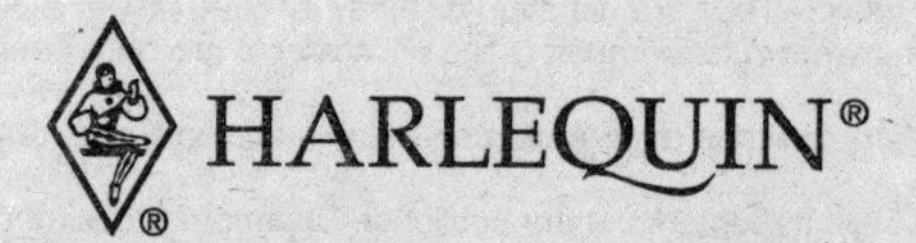

TORONTO • NEW YORK • LONDON
AMSTERDAM • PARIS • SYDNEY • HAMBURG
STOCKHOLM • ATHENS • TOKYO • MILAN • MADRID
PRAGUE • WARSAW • BUDAPEST • AUCKLAND

ISBN 0-373-83591-4

WICKED WAGER

This edition published by arrangement with Harlequin Books S.A.

Visit us at www.eHarlequin.com

Printed in U.S.A.

Dear Reader,

Writers are often asked how they get ideas for their stories. *Wicked Wager* began with a daily online serial I wrote for eHarlequin.com, "By Honor Bound," in which heroine Jenna Montague thoroughly routed the villain—one Anthony Nelthorpe.

When that story ended, I found I couldn't dismiss Lord Nelthorpe as handily as Jenna had. The dilemma of his character—torn from everything familiar and forced to remake himself in the cauldron of war after an upbringing that provided him with few assets to call upon—captured my imagination and refused to be dislodged. I knew sooner or later I would have to finish his story.

At the time I didn't know it would be Jenna's story, too. But after my wonderful editors, Tracy Farrell and Margaret Marbury, approved the project, I soon found that Tony's confrontation with Jenna was the pivot point on which his life had turned. His future could not be written without her.

What happens when they meet again three years later unfolds in *Wicked Wager.* Of all the stories I've written, Jenna and Tony's has turned out to be dearest to my heart. I hope it will touch your heart, as well.

Julia Justiss

To my son, Midshipman 3/c Mark Stafford Justiss
United States Naval Academy Class of 2006
And to his comrades in the armed services
of the United States of America.
I write of courage, honor and sacrifice.
You live it.

CHAPTER ONE

As Lord Anthony Nelthorpe, formerly captain in the 1st Royal Dragoons, stepped across the threshold of his London townhouse one foggy fall morning, a giggling, mostly naked woman burst onto the upper landing and fled down the stairs. A balding, half-naked man followed, eyes focused owlishly on his hand clutching the rail as he maneuvered the steps and then lurched off after her.

"So, Carstairs," Tony remarked to the retainer in threadbare livery who had opened the front portal for him, "I see my father is engaged in his usual pursuits."

"Yes, my lord," the man replied, his age-spotted hand trembling as he struggled to close the heavy door. Tony turned to assist him, remembering only at the last minute that this wasn't the army anymore, where a man in battle helped another man, regardless of rank. Carstairs would be as embarrassed as he was shocked, should his master's son and heir lower himself to assist the butler.

Curling the fingers he'd extended toward the servant into a fist, Tony turned away. "I expect the earl will be too...preoccupied to receive me this morning. At a more opportune moment, would you tell him I've arrived—and have some beef and ale sent to the library now, if you please?"

The butler bowed. "At once. On behalf of the staff, may I say 'welcome home,' Master Tony."

"Thank you, Carstairs." At his nod, the old man shuffled down the hall in the direction of the servants' stairs.

Mouth setting in a thin line, Tony watched him retreat, noting the hall carpet was as worn as the butler's uniform and dirty besides. Shifting his weight painfully, he limped toward the library, noticing as he went the layer of dust that veiled the few pieces of furniture and the ornate arches, which in his youth had sheltered exquisite Chinese vases set on French marquetry tables. Long gone now, of course.

Evidently Tony's esteemed father, the Earl of Hunsdon, still preferred to squander whatever income could be wrung from his heavily mortgaged estates on liquor and the company of lovelies such as the one who'd recently tripped down the stairs, rather than keep his house in good order.

Welcome home, indeed.

Gritting his teeth, he made himself continue the rest of the way down the hall, sweat popping out on his brow at the effort. The surgeons who'd put the pieces of his shattered knee back together had predicted he'd never walk again. He still wasn't very good at it, he admitted as he reached the library door and clung to the handle, panting. Thank God riding was easier.

A high-pitched squeal interrupted him, followed by a rapid pad of footsteps. The bawd ran into view, pausing with a shocked "oh, la!" when she spied him.

With matted hair dyed an improbable red that matched the smeared paint upon her lips and nipples, powder caked in the wrinkles of her face and beneath her sagging breasts, she was not an enticing sight, even had he been in better shape to appreciate the appeal of a mostly naked female. But then, with his ugly limp and post-hospital pallor, he was none too appealing himself.

Still, he'd seen his father unclothed, and Tony was twenty-five years younger besides. Not wishing to give the tart an opportunity to change targets, he ducked into the library, slammed the door and limped toward the desk.

With a groan, he collapsed in the chair. Well, Tony, despite the carnage of war, you made it home, he thought. No longer a captain, but once again Viscount Nelthorpe—whoever the hell that is.

Certainly not the self-absorbed, vain aristocrat so confident of his position in the world who'd left this house one drink-hazed night three years ago. Having lost more gaming than he could borrow to repay, he'd staggered home to ask his father for a loan. When that gentleman consigned him to the devil, with the threat of debtor's prison hanging over him, he'd had little choice but to leave his debts of honor unpaid and flee England, taking with him only the clothes on his back, his horses, and a commission in Wellington's Fighting Fifth Infantry—won in a card game.

Nothing like privation, terror, hunger and pain to give one a fresh perspective, he observed wryly.

Though he wasn't sure yet what he was going to do with that hard-won wisdom. Now that his eyes had adjusted to the gloom within the curtain-shrouded room, he noted the library was as dusty and unkempt as the hallway. Lord knows, he thought, puckering his brow in distaste, there was work enough to be done here.

A knock interrupted his reflections, followed by the entry of Carstairs. The butler carried a tray from which emanated such appealing odors that, for the moment, Tony forgot everything except that he'd not eaten since last night. Fool that he was, he'd thought to reach London before nightfall despite the slower pace necessitated by his recovering knee. Darkness having overtaken him on the road, he'd been forced to engage a room for the night and had not had cash enough to pay for his accommodations, dinner and breakfast, too.

Grimacing, Carstairs balanced the tray while he pulled a handkerchief from his pocket and hastily wiped clean a spot on the desktop. ''Begging your pardon for the conditions, Master Tony, but last winter his lordship let go all the servants but me, Betsy and one parlor maid—a good girl, but she can't manage all alone. Betsy's as fine a cook as ever, though, so you needn't be worrying about your dinner. She sends along her welcome, too.''

As he spoke, Carstairs removed the cover on the dish, sending Tony a drool-inducing waft of beef-scented air. ''Tell Betsy that, after what the army ate—or more often, didn't eat—in the Peninsula, she could give me no finer welcome home than this! As for the estate—I know you have done your best. I mean to do something about... conditions.'' Though heaven knew what, as he was nearly as pockets-to-let now as the night he'd run away.

But instead of returning the skeptical lift of brow a Nelthorpe's promise of improvement should merit, the old man's face brightened. ''We know if anyone can turn it around, you will, Master Tony. After all, you be one of the Heroes of Waterloo!'' After giving him a deep bow, as if he deserved the highest respect, the butler left.

Hero? he thought as he gazed after Carstairs with a self-mocking curl of his lip. *If you only knew.*

But surviving such a battle made one practical as well as philosophic. No sense letting the bleak memories spoil what appeared to be an excellent breakfast and some fine English ale. He'd wait until after he tucked into it to begin pondering his future.

Somehow he hadn't thought beyond the driving imperative to return home. After years of giving and taking orders in the army, followed by the day-by-day struggle to recover from his wounds, he found it disconcerting rather than relaxing to admit he had no plans whatever.

He must talk with Papa and determine just how grim their financial condition was—though judging from what he'd already seen, that looked to be grim indeed. Given the scene he'd happened upon as he arrived, any such conference would have to wait until this afternoon at the earliest.

With the ease of long practice, he submerged the sense of hurt that, despite having sent a letter informing his sire of his imminent arrival, his father hadn't bothered to remain sober long enough to personally greet the son he'd not seen in three years. So, what to do next?

He could write to tell Mama that he was back, but as she'd not corresponded with him in all the months he'd been away, he wasn't sure at which of Papa's remaining estates the countess currently resided. Probably the one with the handsomest footmen, he thought sardonically.

He'd ride to the park, he decided. The exercise of the knee muscles required for riding was beneficial, the doctors had told him, and paradoxically seemed to ease rather than aggravate the aching, as long as he didn't keep at it too long. And though this late morning hour was still unfashionably early for anyone in the ton to be about, he might spy an acquaintance with whom to share a drink at White's—where, he presumed, he was still a member.

His spirits lifted as soon as he'd climbed awkwardly into the saddle. The army must have changed him more than he knew if an excursion into the lingering smoke haze of a chilly London morning had more appeal than remaining in a cozy, if admittedly dusty, library with a snug fire.

Pax, the gray gelding given him by a grateful fellow officer whose life he'd saved at Quatre Bras, was proving an easy, even-gaited mount, though he lacked the spirit most cavalry officers preferred in a mount. But if God had any mercy to spare for the battered carcass of one

Anthony Nelthorpe, he thought with a shudder, he'd never again have need of a good cavalry horse.

As he rode down Upper Brook Street toward Hyde Park, a tepid sun began to break through the remaining haze. A happy omen for his return, perhaps.

Then he saw her—a slender lady mounted on a showy chestnut mare. Having watched her on innumerable marches from Badajoz through Toulouse, he recognized her immediately, though he was half a street away.

For a moment he halted, admiring as always her erect carriage and perfect form. Even on a sidesaddle, she rode as one with her horse, as if she naturally belonged there. Which, having spent the greater part of her life in the saddle, he supposed Jenna Montague did. Lovely Jenna—unattainable, unapproachable, his first colonel's daughter and the woman he'd once tried to coerce into marriage.

Except for when she found him on the field after Waterloo, Tony hadn't seen Jenna, now Lady Fairchild, up close since their ill-fated encounter at the abandoned monastery outside Badajoz. His fingers reached automatically to touch his throat, where beneath his cravat, he still bore the scar from the knife wound she'd inflicted while successfully resisting his misguided attempt at seduction.

The mark she'd left on his mind and heart had proved just as indelible.

As always, though he felt immediately drawn to her, he hesitated. Then he remembered that the man she chose to marry instead no longer stood watch, his steely gaze promising dire retribution if Tony dared to so much as approach his wife. Colonel Garrett Fairchild had died of wounds sustained at Mont St. Jean.

However, given that he'd nearly ruined her reputation, tricking her into meeting him without a chaperone at that deserted rendezvous, should he try to hail her, he'd probably receive at best a cold nod, at worst, the cut direct.

Which would it be? he wondered. Before he could decide whether or not to try his luck, she pulled up her horse before a handsome townhouse and handed over the reins to a waiting servant. No chance now of reaching her before she slipped inside—once more beyond his reach.

He watched until she'd ascended the stairs and disappeared into the entry. How differently might his life have turned out, had he secured her hand nearly three years ago? Her hand, the enjoyment of the curves concealed beneath her pelisse—and the rich dowry that would have allowed him to pay off his debts, abandon his nascent army career and return to comfortable decadence in London?

Instead he'd spent the following two years sleeping on the ground or in vermin-infested billets and foraging for provisions, his mind and heart branded with the searing iron of a dozen successive battles. Nightmarish vistas of smoke-obscured chaos, the smell of hot gun barrels and fresh blood, the screams of dying men and horses amid the din of rifle and artillery, haunted him still.

But over those years he'd also witnessed countless episodes of selflessness and self-sacrifice. He no longer believed, as his father had preached, that honor was a concept for schoolboys and fools. And he himself was no doubt a better man for having met the challenge of that hard, bitter trial.

Better, perhaps, but not of course the equal of Colonel Garrett Fairchild and the other truly courageous heroes who had perished in the woods and fields of Waterloo. In a supreme stroke of irony, two of the lost were the men to whom he'd owed gaming debts, their deaths effectively canceling Tony's obligations and freeing him to return to London without fear of being clapped into prison.

He kicked his horse into action and rode up to the gate. "Whose house is this?" he called to a young man in livery loitering at the foot of the steps.

"Viscount Fairchild's, m'lord," the boy answered.

So she was staying at the home of her late husband's family, Tony thought. Perhaps, even though she was likely to greet him with scorn, he ought to call on her. Garrett Fairchild had been a dedicated officer and an exemplary solder, and Tony did regret his loss. Besides, by the time he'd been lucid enough to carry on a conversation, he had been moved to a hospital, so he had never had the opportunity to thank Jenna for her care after the battle. Given the debt he owed her for that, he should deliver his thanks in person, even if she took that opportunity to administer a well-deserved snub.

Yes, he decided, urging his horse back to a trot, he would definitely pay a call on Jenna Montague.

CHAPTER TWO

ACCEPTING THE GROOM'S HAND, Jenna Montague Fairchild stepped down from the sidesaddle and looked with a sigh at Fairchild House. Riding in London's parks, though better than remaining at home, barely allowed for a decent gallop.

After three days in the metropolis, she was already wishing herself back in Brussels. Or Lisbon or Madras or anywhere near some vast open plain where she might ride for hours and escape the emptiness that echoed through her rooms, in her shattered heart, with Garrett gone.

Four months had dulled the agony of losing him to a barely tolerable pain. Unconsciously her hand slipped down to rest on the swell of her abdomen. Were it not for the child she carried, she wasn't sure she would have been able to force herself to return to the native land in which she'd lived exactly two months of her life, to reside as custom demanded in the house of her husband's relations whom she'd met only once, and briefly.

But with most of the casualties from June's battles either dead of their wounds or gone home to finish recovering, Jenna could no longer use the excuse of nursing duties to justify lingering in Brussels. With the future of Garrett's heir to consider, she'd been forced to leave the bittersweet comfort of the rooms they'd shared, the bed in which their child had been conceived, the simple grave in the rose-garlanded cemetery on the hill beyond Waterloo where she'd had his remains laid to rest.

Hoping Aunt Hetty had slept late today, so she might avoid the unpleasantness of dealing with the woman until afternoon, Jenna made herself walk up the steps.

The querulous feminine tones that reached her ears as soon as Manson opened the door told her that hope was not likely to be realized. Wishing Garrett had never invited his widowed aunt to move into Fairchild House, she put a finger to her lips to forestall the butler's greeting.

Silently she handed over her wrap. Perhaps she could creep by the front parlor and reach her room undetected.

But a board creaked as she crossed the landing and a moment later Aunt Hetty called out, "Jenna, is that you? Come in! We are planning Garrett's memorial service."

Swallowing her irritation, she bowed to the inevitable and reluctantly entered the parlor. From his seat beside Aunt Hetty, Lane Fairchild, one of the two cousins who had also accepted Garrett's invitation to reside at the family townhouse, rose at her entrance. The other cousin, Bayard, seated at a distance from his other relations, continued to stare out the window, apparently oblivious to her arrival.

Slighter and darker than his golden-haired first cousin, Bayard wore the abstracted expression that, she'd noted on her previous sojourn with the family, seemed to be his habitual mien whenever he was forced to remain in company. Probably he was mulling over one of the alchemy experiments on which, Cousin Lane had told her with faint contempt, he spent most of his time, hidden away in the basement room he'd converted into a laboratory.

And to which, if the pattern she'd observed held true, he'd soon escape. A privilege that, as Heir Presumptive and supposed head of the family, Aunt Hetty allowed him.

Lucky Bayard, Jenna thought with a sigh.

A thin, older woman wrapped in a quantity of shawls,

Aunt Hetty inspected Jenna with disfavor. "About time you returned. I cannot comprehend this penchant for riding! To promenade in the afternoon with the rest of the ton is quite proper, but to hare about at all hours with naught but a groom is simply not suitable in a viscountess."

"Now, Aunt Hetty, she has been a viscountess for less than a year and a Londoner for but a few days," Lane said soothingly as he came over to kiss Jenna's hand. "After a time, she will master the intricacies of ton behavior."

Giving her fingers a sympathetic squeeze, he continued, "How could anyone object, when the exercise seems to agree so well with you? The roses in your cheeks are as lovely as our Damask's finest late blooms. Manson, a dish of tea for Lady Fairchild, please."

"Prettily said, cousin," she replied, allowing Lane to lead her to a place beside him on the sofa and accepting the steaming cup the butler poured for her.

After the butler bowed himself out, Aunt Hetty sniffed. "Well, *I* think it's more than past time that Jenna gave due thought to her condition."

Stung, Jenna lost her grip on her temper. "I am quite protective of my 'condition.' After Waterloo, the doctors assured me most particularly that if riding eased my mind—and it does—I need on no account give it up. Do you really think I would risk Garrett's child?"

The peevish look on Aunt Hetty's face faded and Lane's expression turned shocked. "Do *you* mean to tell us," he said slowly, "that...that you are carrying Garrett's child?"

"Of course that's what—" she began. Stopping abruptly, she glanced at Bayard, still sitting distracted near the window. "I wrote Cousin Bayard several months ago, as soon as I was certain. He...he didn't tell you?"

"Aunt Hetty, did you know?" Lane demanded.

"I had no idea!"

"Well, this does put a new complexion on things," Lane murmured, pacing over to his cousin.

"Bayard," he said, giving his shoulder a shake, "did Jenna write informing you she was in a delicate condition?"

Bayard flinched, as if unwilling to be brought back to the present. "Oh, that," he said, jerking away from Lane's fingers. "Yes, she did. Of what importance is it to you?"

"It's of importance to any Fairchild! Dammit, man, she might be carrying the next heir!"

"Precisely. But since that eventuality would affect only me, I cannot see why you expected to be informed."

"Trying to play autocratic head of the family, Bayard? 'Tis a role that don't suit you."

"Boys!" Aunt Hetty reproved. "This is excellent news!" she said to Jenna. "After the despair of Garrett's loss, what a joy that he shall have an heir!"

"A joy indeed, Cousin Jenna," Lane said, smiling. "Please don't think that I am not also delighted. 'Twas only—" he threw an aggrieved glance at Bayard "—that it came as somewhat of a shock."

"The babe could just as easily be a daughter, so it's quite possible Bayard will still inherit," Jenna reminded them. "As the child is not due for some months, I would prefer not to make any public announcement just yet. 'Tis...'tis my last link to Garrett and I should prefer to keep it a private matter."

"We shall respect your wishes, of course," Lane said. "But you must take special care! Are you certain riding is wise? Bayard, as head of the family—" he imbued the words with a trace of sarcasm "—do you not think you should forbid Jenna to put herself at risk?"

Bayard shrugged. ''I expect she knows what's best.''

A knock sounded at the door, followed by the entrance of Cousin Bayard's personal servant. A swarthy bear of a man, he resembled less a manservant, Jenna thought with an inward smile each time she encountered him, than one of the convicts who'd chosen to join Wellington's army rather than face punishment at home.

The man bowed to the assembled company with a swagger that belied the deferential gesture. ''Beggin' your pardon, your ladyships. Master, the supplies you ordered are being delivered. You need to show me where to stow 'em.''

''Thank you, Frankston. I'll come at once.''

''Bayard, you cannot leave now! We haven't yet settled the details of Garrett's service!'' Aunt Hetty protested.

''I'm sure you can arrange something suitable without me,'' Bayard said. ''I've more important work.'' Ignoring Hetty's wail of protest, he strode out the door.

Frowning, Lane watched his cousin leave. ''Work more important than upholding the honor of the Fairchild name? Dash it, Jenna, I hope to heaven Garrett's child *is* a son!''

''As long as the babe is healthy and safely delivered, I shall be content,'' she replied.

''So do we all hope! Finish your tea, cousin. You must keep up your strength now—and we shall have to take special care to see that she does, shall we not, Aunt?''

''Naturally. Now, about the service.'' Hetty glanced at Jenna, the frown returning to her face telling Jenna her sojourn in that lady's good graces had just ended. ''It must be something suitably solemn and impressive. Though 'tis scandalous, to be reduced to holding a *memorial* service for a viscount whose family can trace its roots back to the Conqueror! I can't imagine why you had Garrett buried in heathenish foreign land, rather than bringing his bones back to rest among his ancestors at Fairland Trace.''

Half-choking on her tea, Jenna swallowed the mouthful in one gulp. Did the woman have no discernment? Given the extent of Garrett's wounds—knee, thigh, chest, shoulder—did she not realize to what condition his poor lifeless body would have been reduced after the several-day transit in July heat from Brussels to distant Northumberland?

A flash of memory seared her—finding Garrett, after a frantic all-day search, lying among the dead on the Waterloo plain, no more than a valiant spirit stubbornly holding on in a ragged scrap of flesh. Nausea seized her stomach and her throat closed in anguish.

She couldn't bear to remember. Tea sloshed over the rim as she set her cup down. ''It—wasn't possible.''

Shooting Aunt Hetty a warning look, Cousin Lane took her hands in his and rubbed them gently. ''I'm sure it wasn't. You did everything you could, under the most ghastly of circumstances. We realize that.''

The older woman sniffed. ''All the more reason to hold the most impressive of services. St. George's, Hanover Square, I should think. Prinny and the cabinet will certainly attend, and Wellington, of course. We could have a funeral cortege from the house—''

''No!'' Jenna cried. ''No funeral. I've buried him once. I will not do it again.''

''Now that I am aware of your delicate condition, my dear,'' Hetty said with a thin smile, ''I will make some allowances, for ladies in your circumstances sometimes take the most peculiar ideas into their heads. But the decision isn't yours alone. There's the family's honor to be considered, and I would be failing in my duty if I allowed

Garrett's passing to be commemorated in less than a fashion befitting a Viscount Fairchild of Fairland Trace.''

''What was being viscount to Garrett?'' Jenna exclaimed. ''He never expected it, was shocked to learn of the accident that brought him the title. Garrett lived and died a soldier. He's buried near the field where he fell. Let him rest in peace!''

''Please, ladies, don't upset yourselves!'' Cousin Lane appealed to them. ''Surely we can arrange something which will accommodate Jenna's grief while still upholding the dignity of the family. Aunt Hetty, why do you not plan on a memorial service like the one we discussed? I believe Society would understand if Jenna does not attend, given the recentness of her bereavement. She could receive the mourner's condolences at the reception here afterward.''

He turned to Jenna. ''Do you think you could bear that, Jenna? Just a reception, to honor Garrett and let his friends mourn with you?''

Jenna took a shuddering breath. Could she force herself to nod and shake the hands of the gawking curious, most of them strangers? But at least she'd be spared the torment of a long funeral service lamenting Garrett's loss and extolling his many virtues.

She had that litany of regret by heart.

Suddenly she felt overwhelmingly weary, tired of tussling with Aunt Hetty over the running of the house, of dealing with her petty criticism of everything Jenna did—or didn't do—of carrying the crushing burden of grief. Slumping back, she said, ''Yes, I suppose I can endure it.''

''You look fatigued, my dear,'' Lane said with concern.

''I am, a little,'' she admitted.

"Why not go upstairs and rest? Aunt Hetty and I will finish here. I'll walk Jenna up," he said to his aunt.

"If you must," Aunt Hetty said, her tone implying she felt Jenna sadly lacking to shirk so important a duty.

Putting a solicitous hand under her elbow, Lane escorted her from the room. When they reached the hall, he said softly, "Please try to forgive Aunt Hetty's pettishness. She'd been living in straited circumstances after her husband's death and was thrilled when Garrett invited her to come here to look after Fairchild House while he remained away with the army. Now that you have arrived, she's terribly afraid you will supplant her and send her back to her modest lodgings in Bath."

"If she fears that, I should think she'd be making herself agreeable, rather than crossing me at every turn."

He smiled wryly. "So one would think. But of course, she adored Garrett, and feels strongly that his demise should be commemorated with all due pomp and ceremony. An aim, I must admit, with which I am entirely in sympathy. All the years I was growing up, Garrett was my hero."

Jenna felt her eyes filling. "He was mine, too. Do you not think I wish him suitably honored?"

"Of course, and you are being wonderfully brave about all this. 'Tis so difficult, even for me, to accept his loss. I cannot imagine how terrible it must be for you."

There being no answer to that, Jenna gave none.

As they ascended the stairs, Lane hailed a passing footman. "Tell Lady Fairchild's maid to bring up tea in an hour." After the man trotted off, he turned to Jenna. "I'm sorry, that was rather presumptuous. Forgive me?"

Too tired to resent a usurpation of her authority for which, in another life, she would have given him a sharp setdown, she shrugged. "It appears everyone wants to dictate my actions. At least you, cousin, seem to have my welfare at heart."

They reached the door to her chamber, but when she turned to go in, he retained her hand, halting her. "I'm sorry you must suffer through this all over again. I hope you indeed realize I will do everything within my power to make things as easy as possible for you."

His kind words brought tears once again to the surface. "Thank you, cousin. I appreciate that."

Grief and the coming child did exhaust her, for she fell asleep as soon as her head touched the pillow. She woke an hour later at Sancha's knock, feeling much refreshed. Before she could decide whether to ride yet again, choose a book from the library downstairs, or take a carriage to inspect the selection at Hatchard's, a footman knocked to inform her that she had callers below.

She wondered who it might be. Since she had no acquaintance in London beyond her husband's family, it must be someone from the army who had learned of her return.

Ah, that it might be Major Hartwell or Captain Percy, good friends and two of her late father's finest subordinates! Feeling a stir of interest for the first time since arriving in England, she instructed the footman to tell the visitors she would be down directly.

But her enthusiasm checked the moment she stepped across into the parlor. Rather than those old compatriots, smiling at her from the sofa was Mrs. Ada Anderson, wife to the colonel of the Fighting Fifth's neighboring brigade.

Before she could utter a word, the woman spied her. "Jenna, so you left Brussels at last! I had to call as soon as I learned you'd arrived and convey my deepest, sincerest sympathy!"

"Thank you, Mrs. Anderson." Jenna pasted a smile on her face while mentally kicking herself for coming down without first ascertaining the identity of her visitors. Now she would have to remain at least half an hour or be thought unpardonably rude. ''Please, do sit down. How kind of you to come with—'' she indicated the tall, angular woman in the modish bonnet and pelisse.

''Lady Fairchild, allow me to present my sister Persephone, Lady Montclare. You may remember I intended to send you back to her in London after your papa died at Badajoz. Except that you snabbled yourself a husband first! I was, you will recall, quite vexed at you for throwing away your chance at a London Season and entrusting your hand and fortune to a mere younger son. Who knew then he'd turn out to be viscount one day, eh, you clever girl?''

''Charmed to meet you at last, Lady Fairchild.'' Lady Montclare rose from her curtsy to subject Jenna to a penetrating scrutiny. ''My sincerest condolences.''

''Oh, yes—such a tragedy!'' Mrs. Anderson lamented. ''With his ability and your fortune, I expect he should have become a general. Not that he had any need of a military career, once he inherited, of course.''

''Given his responsibilities as the new viscount, after his brother was lost in that storm off Portsmouth, I am surprised Garrett did not immediately resign his commission,'' Lady Montclare said.

''After Bonaparte escaped from Elbe, Garrett would not have considered leaving the army, nor, I suspect, would the Duke have permitted it had he asked. With so many Peninsular veterans dispersed from India to the Americas, he needed every battle-tested commander.''

''Given how things turned out, I imagine you now wish Lord Fairchild had not remained with the army,'' Lady Montclare observed.

''I would not have had Garrett shirk his duty or disregard his loyalties,'' Jenna replied stiffly, ''regardless of how 'things turned out.'''

''Well, 'tis no matter,'' Mrs. Anderson said. ''You must now think to your future—which means carefully evaluating the new contenders for your hand.''

''Contenders for my—?'' Jenna gasped. ''I hardly think it necessary to concern myself about that yet!''

''I know you were sincerely attached to Garrett,'' Mrs. Anderson said. ''But a widow with a fortune as vast as yours is not likely to be left to mourn in solitude. As soon as the ton finds out you are established here in London, you can expect all manner of invitations.''

''Your husband's aunt is charming,'' Lady Montclare said, ''but I fear she doesn't move in the first circles. Since you quite rightly wish to pay proper honor to poor Garrett's memory, 'tis of the utmost importance that you know which invitations to accept, which you should refuse. Ada and I will be happy to assist you.''

''It will be our privilege! The first thing you must do—'' Mrs. Anderson cast a pained look at Jenna's three-year-old gown ''—is procure a proper wardrobe.''

Reining in the temper that urged her to demand that the visitors leave immediately, Jenna forced herself to speak politely. ''Mrs. Anderson, Lady Montclare, I appreciate your kindness in offering to help, but I haven't the least interest attracting 'contenders' for my hand.''

''Come now, Jenna, you were with the army long enough not to be missish about this,'' Mrs. Anderson countered. ''You wed Garrett before your papa had been dead a month!''

''That was...different! I couldn't remain with the army alone, and I loved Garrett.''

''Desire it or not,'' Lady Montclare said, ''your youth, beauty and wealth—added to the connection you now boast to the ancient name of Fairchild—will catch the interest of every bachelor of the ton on the look for a bride.''

''Since you cannot avoid scrutiny, 'tis only prudent to plan on it,'' Mrs. Anderson advised. ''Reconnoiter the ground and use it to your advantage, my husband would say! And as one of Lady Jersey's bosom bows, Persephone stands in perfect position to advise you on the most select entertainments—and most desirable gentlemen.''

Both ladies beamed at her, appearing supremely confident that Jenna must be thrilled at their offering to guide her in her choice of beaux. Appalled by the notion, for a moment Jenna contemplated informing the ladies of her pregnancy. Surely a widow who was increasing would be less appealing to discerning ton courtiers.

But though her condition would soon be obvious, for now she did not wish to share the news of her secret joy with these sisters whose supposed concern for her welfare barely concealed their relish for obtaining a social pawn they might manipulate.

As the mantel clock chimed, signifying the elapse of the requisite half hour, Jenna rose and offered a curtsy. ''Ladies, I am quite...overwhelmed by your offer. Please know I will carefully consider it.''

Obligated to rise as well, the sisters returned her curtsy. ''I'm staying with Persephone while Walter prepares for his next posting,'' Mrs. Anderson said. ''Call on us any day—your butler has the card with our direction.''

''Indeed,'' Lady Montclare said. ''I shall be very happy to take you under my wing, dear Lady Fairchild.''

Stifling the impulse to tell Lady Montclare just what she could do with that wing, Jenna made herself incline her head politely. ''Good day, ladies.''

Long after Manson had escorted them out, Jenna stood staring at the closed door, recalling the various ton gentlemen she'd observed during her rides—Dandies and

Bucks in skintight coats and trousers, elaborately arranged cravats, ridiculously high shirt collars. She'd found their appearance quite amusing.

The idea of such men calling on her was less amusing. Men who had remained safely at home while other men fought and bled to protect their liberty. Indolent men with nothing better to do than drink, gamble away their nights—and entice widows of large fortune into marriage.

The handsome face of one such dark-haired, gray-eyed man materialized out of memory, his lips curved in a sardonic smile that was half interest, half disdain. Heat rose in her cheeks as she forced the image away.

Cousin Lane seemed thoroughly familiar with the London ton. Perhaps she should ask him whether the sisters' prediction about the interest she would arouse among its gentlemen was likely to prove true.

For if dealing with reprobates like Lord Anthony Nelthorpe was to be her fate in London, the convention about living with Garrett's relatives be damned, she would start immediately looking for a residence elsewhere.

CHAPTER THREE

TWO WEEKS later, Jenna sat in the parlor, trying to keep a polite smile pasted on her lips while the notables of the ton paraded past to offer their condolences, their gimlet eyes and assessing glances evaluating the dress, manners and breeding of Viscount Fairchild's widow. She'd even overheard one dandy, in a whisper just loud enough to reach her ears, compare her unfavorably to the Lovely Lucinda—the fiancée who had jilted Garrett for an earl.

Nearly as annoying, Mrs. Anderson and Lady Montclare arrived early "to support dear Jenna through her first public reception." Effusing with delight at their thoughtfulness, Aunt Hetty had chairs installed for them beside Jenna's, where the two were now dispensing sotto-voce commentary on each caller who approached.

Jenna had thrown an appealing glance at Lane, seated beside Aunt Hetty on the sofa, but he'd returned nothing more helpful than a sympathetic shrug of his shoulders. While Cousin Bayard, alleging anyone who wished to convey their regrets to him had had ample opportunity during the service at St. George's, abandoned the parlor minutes after the reception began.

Not that she'd really expected to escape the function—or her two watchdogs. Apparently Lady Montclare did wield as much influence among the ton as she'd claimed, for Aunt Hetty had been both shocked and ecstatic to learn of her call, and did everything she could to promote the connection. In her listless state, Jenna had neither sufficient interest nor strength to oppose them, and had soon found herself trotted around to all the merchants Lady Montclare favored, pinned and prodded and led to purchase a vast quantity of items those ladies deemed essential for a recently bereaved viscountess.

She'd felt a twinge of conscience at expending blunt on gowns that in a matter of a few weeks she'd be unable to wear. Someday soon, when the simple business of waking, rising, and surviving each new day didn't exhaust all her meager mental and physical reserves, she'd sort out what to do about the sisters—and her life without Garrett.

Onward the crowd continued—like buzzards circling a kill, Jenna thought—an endless progression of names and titles. In vain she looked for the real comfort that might have been afforded by the friendly faces and heartfelt condolences of "Heedless" Harry or Alastair Percy or other men from Garrett's regiment. By now, she realized with resignation, her military compatriots had doubtless returned to their respective homes or rejoined the army.

Then a stir from the hallway caught her attention. As she'd hoped, a few moments later His Grace, the Duke of Wellington, walked into the salon, trailed by a crowd of well-wishers eager to shake the hand of the great general.

"Excellent! I so hoped he would appear," Mrs. Anderson said in Jenna's ear.

After exchanging a brief word with Lady Montclare and Mrs. Anderson, he took Jenna's hand.

"It's been a long and difficult road since India. England owes her safety to the selfless service of your father and husband. Take solace in that, Jenna."

"I do, your grace."

She blinked back tears as he kissed her hand, bowed and walked away, the crowd parting respectfully to allow the passage of England's Savior. Who, it was said, had wept while he wrote his dispatch after Waterloo at the loss of so many good friends and soldiers.

Napoleon's Vanquisher would be going on to other important duties. What was Jenna Montague Fairchild, soldier's daughter and soldier's wife who had lost father, husband and army, to do with herself now?

Think of the babe, she told herself, fighting back grief and despair. *Rebuild your life around the child.*

"How excellent of the Duke to show so singular a mark of favor," Lady Montclare murmured.

"We are old acquaintances," Jenna replied.

In the wake of the Duke's departure, the crowd in the drawing room began to thin. "My sister has presented you to everyone of note in London this afternoon, including most of the gentlemen who will be your potential suitors," Mrs. Anderson said, smiling her satisfaction.

"And your conduct has been excellent, my dear!" Lady Montclare reached over to press Jenna's fingers. "A grave demeanor indicative of continuing grief, with just the right touch of hauteur."

The woman obviously believed Jenna was assuming the role she'd been urged to play. She wasn't sure whether to dissolve into hysterical laughter—or tears.

"Oh no—not *him!*"

At Mrs. Anderson's gasp, Jenna's looked to the door, through which a gentleman now strode with languorous ease.

Jenna exhaled in relief. Though the half-mocking, half-amused smile on the handsome face of the man now approaching was reminiscent of the grin she'd so disliked on *another* gentleman, this man's hair gleamed guinea-gold rather than blue-black and his eyes were the turquoise of a tropic ocean's depths—not, praise heaven, gunmetal gray.

"The effrontery!" Mrs. Anderson whispered.

"We'll soon send him to the rightabout," Lady Montclare soothed. "Teagan Fitzwilliams, Jenna—a notorious rogue and gambler. 'Tis said he mended his ways since he beguiled a rich widow into marriage, but I doubt it. His aunt, Lady Charlotte Darnell, is the daughter of a duke and a Society leader, so you cannot, regrettably, cut him, but his reputation for seducing foolish women was well-earned. Take care to avoid him whenever possible."

A moment later the blond man bowed before them. "Teagan Fitzwilliams, Lady Fairchild, at your service."

As if fully conscious of the condemnation that had just been pronounced by her companions, after nodding to them, he seized Jenna's hands and gave them a long, lingering caress that sent heat rushing to her cheeks.

She had just opened her lips to deliver a sharp set down when he gave her a quick, conspiratorial wink, so fleeting she wasn't sure whether she'd seen or imagined it. Then he tugged on her hands and pulled her to her feet.

"By the saints, dear Lady Fairchild, your grief has rendered you pale as the shades of my Irish kin! Let me assist you to stroll down the hall, that exercise might return a little color to your lovely face." Before she could think what to reply, over the sputtering protest of her chaperones, he nudged her into motion.

Not until they reached the hallway did she realize how great a relief it was to escape the confines of the parlor. Nonetheless, torn between amusement and irritation, she felt moved to protest.

"Gracious, Mr. Fitzwilliams, you are a rogue indeed!"

"That, Lady Fairchild, is for you to decide." Turning to her with an unexpectedly sympathetic look, he continued, "Nonetheless, your expression so clearly called out 'rescue me!' that I could not help but respond."

That reading of what she'd thought to be her impassive countenance belied the carelessness of the grin with which he had, she suspected, deliberately taunted her chaperones. Though she heard again Lady Montclare's warning to avoid him, she found herself curious to know why he'd called.

Besides, over her years with the army she'd encountered men who truly *were* seducers and reprobates. The instincts that had protected her on more than one occasion were now telling her this man was neither.

"You are right, Mr. Fitzwilliams. I *did* long for rescue."

He rewarded her honesty with a smile of genuine warmth that lit his handsome face and set mesmerizing lights dancing in those intensely turquoise eyes.

Heavens! she thought, shaken by the force of his charm. If he *were* a rake, small wonder women succumbed!

"If what I'd heard of your adventures with the army had not already convinced me of your stalwart character, I knew Garrett would marry none but an enterprising lady."

"You were...acquainted with Garrett?"

His eyes dimmed and she read real sorrow on his face. "I had that honor and so offer you my deepest condolences. I cannot boast to have been one of his intimates, but at Eton he stood my friend, and when I became the focus of some...unpleasantness at Oxford, he continued to recognize me when few others, including my own family, did. He was one of the finest men I've ever known."

His heartfelt testament moved her more than all the grand tributes glibly offered by the influential of the ton. "He was indeed," she replied, her voice trembling.

"Respecting Garrett as I did, I felt I must call today, even though my aunt, Lady Charlotte, is out of town and unable to lend me countenance—or protect you from the censorious who will take you to task for having strolled with me. For which injury, I do apologize. Despite the appeal in your eyes, by whisking you off, I fear I have doomed you to almost certain criticism. I really should not have kidnapped you with you unaware of that danger."

"I'm still most grateful that you did! I have no fear of idly wagging tongues." Indeed, if a walk with Teagan Fitzwilliams rendered her less attractive to the potential suitors they were pressing on her, so much the better.

"When she returns, Aunt Charlotte will call upon you and set all to rights, so I may soothe my conscience by believing that I've caused you no permanent harm. Now, let me return you to the parlor."

"Wait!" Jenna cried, halting him. "'Tis a privilege to talk with one of Garrett's true friends. And I...I'm not ready to go back in. Not just yet."

He raised an eyebrow. "Already trying to pull and twist you into their mold, are they?"

"I shall have to fight them tooth and claw," she said with a sigh. "Once I manage to summon the energy."

He nodded. "It's walking the hallway for us, then." Tucking her hand back on his arm, he continued, "Did you really escape a bandit ambush in India?"

"It wasn't so extraordinary as it might sound. Papa's batman and I both had our Baker rifles—and faster horses."

He laughed. "It's a crack shot you are, I'll wager!"

She grinned, warmed by his sympathetic understanding. "Naturally. I've spent all my life with the army."

"I hear you fended off an attack in Spain as well."

"So she did."

At the sound of that deep, uncannily familiar voice, a chill of alarm raced up Jenna's spine. She whipped her gaze toward the entry where, before her astounded eyes, the rogue she'd hoped never to meet again began climbing the stairs, limping slightly. "As I can personally attest."

Jenna blinked, still not believing his audacity. "You!" she said in a strangled voice.

Viscount Anthony Nelthorpe reached the landing and swept Jenna a bow. "Lady Fairchild, how good it is to see you again."

No doubt divining from the sudden stiffness of her body—and the low fury of her voice—that she did not welcome the newcomer, Fitzwilliams stepped forward to block the viscount's approach. "Nelthorpe, I didn't know you'd returned to England."

"Just back from Brussels, Fitzwilliams."

Though Fitzwilliams nodded pleasantly, his eyes stayed watchful as he remained between her and Lord Nelthorpe. "Lady Fairchild, may I take you back to the parlor?"

"Allow me," Nelthorpe said, holding out an arm. "I served in the same command as Lady Fairchild's late husband and can express my regrets as I walk her back."

Fitzwilliams glanced from Jenna's face to Nelthorpe's extended arm and back. "Lady Fairchild, would you prefer that Nelthorpe escort you in—or that I escort him out?"

Jenna tried to shake her mind free of anger and outrage to determine what would be best. She'd already failed to deliver the cut direct she'd previously decided would be the most appropriate response, should her erstwhile ravisher ever approach her again. She might still have the satisfaction of turning her back on him.

But he had just demonstrated that, despite what had passed between them, he possessed the gall to confront her. Perhaps she ought to do the same and establish right now that though Garrett was no longer here to watch over her, she intended to have no dealings with Anthony Nelthorpe.

"Thank you, Mr. Fitzwilliams, but for this occasion only, I shall accept Lord Nelthorpe's escort."

"You are sure that is your wish?" Fitzwilliams asked.

"It is."

''Very well, ma'am.'' He made her a bow. ''Returning to an unfamiliar land, even the land of your birth, can be unsettling, as I have reason to know. Call on me if I may help in any way. My aunt will visit you soon. Nelthorpe.''

The two men exchanged stiff nods. After one last, quizzical look, Mr. Fitzwilliams walked away.

''You miserable cur!'' Jenna hissed as soon as Fitzwilliams was out of earshot. ''With Garrett barely cold in his grave, how dare you approach me? Not even you could be arrogant enough to think you might still recoup your fortunes by trying once again to force me into wedlock!''

For an instant he stood utterly still, surprise—or was it chagrin?—on his face, giving her the satisfaction of knowing her attack had rendered him speechless.

''Excellent as that idea might be,'' he replied, ''I must confess 'twas not my intention—for the moment. I wished only to offer my condolences and my sincerest thanks for the mercy that saved my sorry skin.''

Though she watched closely, she could find no undercurrent of mockery, no hint of arrogance in the tone of his self-deprecating words. Even the sardonic smile she'd come to associate with him had been replaced by an expression at once wry—and charming. Her face heating, she wondered if her harsh words had been overhasty.

After all, she had not spoken to Nelthorpe—when he wasn't out of his head with pain and fever—in three years.

Three years with the army could bring about a lifetime of changes in a man, for good or ill.

Before she could decide how to respond, he swayed slightly and had to take a half step to catch himself. Sweat glistened on his forehead and she noted shadowed, red-rimmed eyes that hinted of nights with little sleep.

Had he come here still half-disguised from last night's carousing? Perhaps her verbal assault had not been premature, if he'd lost no time after returning to London in resuming his habits of dissipation.

"You wish to return to the parlor?" he asked, offering his arm.

"Yes," she said, ignoring it, "as soon as I have delivered this message. Though I appreciate your...courtesy in coming to convey your regrets, in future you will not be received in this house—or in any other in which I reside. Nor do I intend to recognize you, should we meet by chance elsewhere. Have I made myself sufficiently clear?"

His lips curved in a smile that looked—regretful? "Perfectly. And, I grant, you have a perfect right to feel that way. But if I'm not to be permitted to speak again, I beg a few minutes more now. Please, Lady Fairchild?"

She opened her lips to reply that she had no interest in anything further he could say, but something about his appearance made her hesitate. Though she would never have believed it possible, the wretch looked...penitent?

A ruse, no doubt, but perhaps she could permit him one last speech. "I suppose I can spare another moment."

"Thank you," he said with what must be false humility. "When you found me on the field below Mont St. Jean, I thought you an angel. Though—" he broke into a grin "—before you feel moved to point it out, I hasten to add that I realize, were I to make my final crossing of the river Styx, it's unlikely *angels* would be dispatched to greet me. Given what you know of my character, I'm surprised you didn't leave me to finish the job of bleeding to death. Had you not stopped, I most certainly would have. And though at times during my recovery I wasn't sure surviving was truly preferable, I still want to thank you."

She could read only sincerity in his expression, which made him so unlike the Nelthorpe she'd known that she was uncertain what to respond. At last she said, "I would hope I would offer assistance to any wounded, friend—or foe."

"Which just shows my initial impression was correct. You are indeed an angel."

Baffled, she shot her gaze to his face, but could detect in his tone neither sarcasm nor irony.

Perhaps he had changed. If his pallor and unsteady gait *were* the vestiges of a drinking spree, he'd hardly be the only soldier to enjoy a liquid homecoming celebration.

Feeling guilty again, she said, "I am nothing of the sort. I…I should not have spoken to you as I did. Pray forgive me."

His smoky eyes lit and his lip quirked in a smile reminiscent—and yet unlike—the sardonic look she'd come to know when he served under her father in the Peninsula. A steady, unnervingly intense regard that had prickled her skin with a curious mix of anticipation and dread whenever she caught—or more often sensed—him watching her.

As her skin prickled now.

Disturbed by that reaction, she abandoned her attempt to determine what exactly had changed about him. *Dismiss him at once,* some instinct for self-preservation urged her.

"Best not apologize too quickly," he said. "Now that I consider it, teasing you into marrying me might be too tempting a prospect to resist."

"I should think nearly getting your throat slit would have cured you of ever risking that folly again."

He tapped his fingers below the knot of his cravat. "Ah, but I bear your mark still. How could I resist you?"

Though she'd fully intended to send him away, the intensity of his gaze held her motionless. A little thrill shocked through her, like when she'd run into warm ocean shallows off the Portuguese coast, only to find the water deeper, the current more dangerous than anticipated.

Except for the morning she discovered him more dead than alive on the battlefield after Waterloo, they had not spoken since that afternoon after the battle of Badajoz when she'd foiled his attempt to compromise her into wedding him, sending him away instead, humbled and bleeding. Yet how many times over the intervening years had she felt resting on her that steady, unnerving gaze?

Riding on the march, across the tent-filled enclosure of an encampment, from the other side of a dining room or ballroom… Though she knew after her marriage, Garrett must have warned Nelthorpe away, from Salamanca to Vittoria to Toulouse, even in Paris after the victory, she had sensed his gaze and looked about her—to find him watching.

With Garrett no longer standing guard, what was she to do about it?

While she hesitated, unsure whether to deliver a final dismissal or simply walk away from the unsettling force that seemed to emanate from him, she heard the slam of the entry door, followed by Manson's urgent murmur. A moment later, a thin woman dressed in mourning black rushed up the stairs, spotted them, and stopped abruptly.

Her eyes widening, she raised her arm and pointed at Nelthorpe. "That reprobate lives still? Then I am doubly glad you lost your husband, Lady Fairchild!"

While Jenna recoiled in shock, the stranger advanced on her.

CHAPTER FOUR

BEFORE JENNA COULD SAY A WORD, the woman continued in shrill tones, "Losing Colonel Fairchild was only what you deserved, after choosing to rescue men such as him—" the widow jerked her chin at the viscount "—whilst leaving good soldiers like my husband to die in the mud!"

'Twas no point trying to reason with this obviously grief-maddened widow, Jenna realized, trying not to let the cruel words wound her as she wondered what supposed incident had led to this outburst. Better to simply soothe and send her away. "I am so sorry—"

"Keep your regrets!" the woman cried. "Just wait until you, like I, have lost everything you hold dear!"

Before Jenna could imagine her intent, she hauled back her arm and slapped Jenna full across the face.

Reeling with the force of the blow, Jenna would have fallen but for Nelthorpe. After steadying her, he moved with surprising speed to seize the wrists of the widow, who'd drawn her hand back as if to deliver another slap.

"Madam, remember yourself!" he barked.

After a brief struggle, the woman's fury seemed spent and she burst into tears, going limp in her captor's grip.

As the butler and two footmen hurried up to assist Nelthorpe, Cousin Lane entered the hallway at a run. "Manson, what the devil is going on?"

He stopped short, taking in with a quick glance the milling servants, the weeping woman hanging in Nelthorpe's arms—and Jenna, with her palm to her stinging cheek.

"For the love of God, Jenna, are you all right?"

Fighting back a sudden faintness, Jenna nodded. "I am fine, cousin. I—I should like to retire, however."

"I'll escort you up at once. James, keep watch over this...person while Manson fetches a constable."

"No need for that," Jenna interposed. "'Twas a...a misunderstanding. Manson, have a hackney summoned. I'm sure the lady is anxious to return home."

Frowning, Fairchild seemed as if he would countermand her order before waving an impatient hand. "As you wish, Jenna. But, madam," he said, turning to the woman, "if you ever approach my cousin again, I shall prosecute you."

As the weeping woman was led away, he turned a hostile gaze on Lord Nelthorpe. "Did you bring that creature?"

Apparently her cousin's opinion of Nelthorpe was no better than her own. Little as she liked the viscount, though, Jenna couldn't let this pass. "Indeed not! In fact, he acted immediately to assist me."

Lane Fairchild's frosty gaze didn't thaw. "Did he? How convenient. I suppose I must thank you for that."

Lord Nelthorpe nodded. "Any paltry assistance I may have offered Lady Fairchild was entirely my pleasure."

With some concern, Jenna noted that Nelthorpe was breathing rather heavily and looked even more unwell. Although grateful for his aid, Jenna hoped he wasn't about to end the binge that had brought on that unhealthy pallor by casting up his accounts on the carpet.

Before she could intervene to speed him on his way, to her intense irritation, the parlor door opened and Lady Montclare stepped into the hallway, followed by her sister.

"Dear Jenna, whatever could be keeping—oh!" Lady

Montclare ended on a gasp, her widening eyes taking in Jenna's red cheek, Cousin Lane's grim face and Nelthorpe, once again swaying unsteadily on his feet.

"Nothing to concern yourselves about, ladies," Fairchild said. Ignoring the viscount in unmistakable insult, he took Jenna's arm. "My dear cousin is rather fatigued. As soon as I've seen Jenna to her room, I'll return to thank you more properly for your gallant support of the Fairchild family this afternoon."

"Of course she is exhausted!" Mrs. Anderson said, her avid gaze flitting between Jenna and Nelthorpe. "But do allow us to assist. Sister, let us take dear Jenna upstairs and offer what comfort we can."

"Nonsense, ladies, I am quite capable of going up alone," Jenna objected. "I need only some solitude in which to repose myself. Please do return to the parlor with Mr. Fairchild and refresh yourselves with some tea."

Then she felt it again—the almost palpable touch of Nelthorpe's gaze on her. Without conscious volition, she looked over to him.

"I shall take my leave now, Lady Fairchild," he said quietly. "Thank you again for your time."

"A most thoughtful suggestion, ladies," Cousin Lane interposed, again ignoring Nelthorpe. "Cousin, let me give you into these kind ladies' care."

She might not like Anthony Nelthorpe, but neither did Jenna approve Fairchild's rude treatment of the man who had just rendered her timely assistance. Turning her back on the sisters, she extended her hand to the viscount.

"Thank you again, and good day, Lord Nelthorpe."

He took her fingers. Her nerves jumped at the first contact of his gloved hands, then again at the unexpectedly intense heat of his lips brushing her bare skin.

"The honor was mine, Lady Fairchild," he said, giving her fingers a brief squeeze that sent another glancing shock through her. Then he turned and, leaning heavily on the balustrade, descended the stairs.

Mrs. Anderson imprisoned Jenna's still-tingling hand in her firm grasp. "Come along, my dear. After that encounter, I can well believe you need a respite!"

Suddenly weary, Jenna gave up attempting to escape the sisters' unwanted attentions, though she suspected this sudden urge to accompany her stemmed more from a desire to determine all that had just transpired than any genuine concern for her welfare.

Confirming her suspicion, as soon as they'd distanced themselves from the servants, Lady Montclare whispered, "Whatever happened to your cheek, my dear? Surely that wretch didn't have the temerity to touch you!"

If she hadn't been so tired, Jenna might have found it amusing to be in the novel position of *defending* Anthony Nelthorpe. "Of course not! I—I stumbled and struck my cheek," she invented. "Nelthorpe came to my assistance."

Lady Montclare sniffed. "Indeed. Though he served in the army, apparently with some distinction, Nelthorpe is exactly the sort of man you must avoid! A fortune hunter who fled England to escape his debts, I'm surprised he wasn't clapped into prison the moment he landed. Though the title is ancient, he and his father, the Earl of Hunsdon, have made the name such a byword for vice that Nelthorpe's uncle, who was to have settled a sum on him, decided to disinherit him. Without a prospective fortune to offset his other failings, Nelthorpe is completely ineligible."

"Indeed?" Jenna said, wrinkling her brow in mock-confusion. "Mrs. Anderson, do I not remember you praising Nelthorpe to me as an eligible parti after Papa died at Badajoz, before I married Garrett?"

Lady Montclare threw a look at Mrs. Anderson. "Sister! Surely you did nothing of the kind!"

Mrs. Anderson's plump face colored. "'Twas before I'd learned of the gaming debts that prompted him to flee to the Peninsula, nor had I yet heard his uncle had cut him off. As a future earl, you must admit, he would otherwise have been considered an exemplary choice."

Waving away her sister's excuse, Lady Montclare continued, "In any event, suffice it to say that Nelthorpe is a man to avoid. In fact, since he's been away from England long enough that he no longer has ties with anyone of importance in the ton, I believe you can safely give him the cut direct."

From recommended suitor to ineligible in the blink of a fortune, Jenna thought cynically. Little sympathy as she had for Nelthorpe, she could only be disgusted with the shallowness of the standards by which Society measured men.

"I assure you, there is no chance of my being taken in by Lord Nelthorpe," she said dryly.

Having reached the hall outside her room, Jenna decided with an unexpected spurt of determination to rid herself of her unwanted guardians before the sisters tried to insinuate themselves into her bedchamber.

Hands on the door handle, she said, "Ladies, thank you most kindly for your help. As I dare not keep you any longer from your tea, good day." With a nod, she slipped inside and closed the door in their faces.

She leaned against it and exhaled a long breath, feeling for the first time in many days a warming sense of satisfaction. Ah, but it felt good to take charge again!

Perhaps it was time to shake off this lethargy and find a new sense of direction.

As she wandered to the window and glanced idly down, her gaze caught on the figure of Lord Nelthorpe. The viscount stood motionless halfway down the entry stairs, both hands braced on the railing, his head hanging between hunched shoulders.

He must still be feeling ill, she thought with a dismissive shake of her head. At least he'd made it out the front door before another wave of nausea overcame him.

Then Nelthorpe straightened and, arms locked above hands still gripping the railing, stepped down—*dragging* his left leg. After hauling that limb down two more steps, he halted again, as if fighting off a wave of dizziness.

Her perceptions of his appearance suddenly realigned into a drastically different conclusion. Having nursed casualties after many a battle, she wondered with shame how she could have so badly misread the clammy skin, the shadowed eyes, the nausea and vertigo—of a man in pain.

Nor, now that she thought about it, had there been about him the odor of spirits or the cloying scent some men used to cover up the stench of liquor.

If she hadn't been so self-righteously preoccupied by nursing instead a three-year-old sense of grievance, she might also have noted the fact that he'd only just arrived in London. All but the most severely injured of Wellington's troops had returned months ago. Nor had she troubled to ask whether he'd recovered from whatever injuries had left him bleeding on the field after the end of June's great battle.

When she'd literally stumbled over Nelthorpe that day, she'd been frantic with worry, knowing Garrett would have returned to her unless he were gravely wounded—or dead. She'd expended as little time as possible seeing Nelthorpe received treatment before resuming her search for him.

And after she found her husband—confirming her worst fears about his condition—she'd devoted three weeks to the ultimately losing battle to save him. Numb, devastated, denying, she'd continued on nursing other survivors until, realizing she must be with child, she'd slowed her pace. Even then, she'd not been able to make herself leave the room she'd shared with Garrett or her life as a soldier's wife and daughter, the only life she'd known.

Colonel's daughter indeed! Shame deepening, she acknowledged that not once in all her weeks in Belgium had she thought to inquire about Nelthorpe's fate after he'd been carried away that awful afternoon. This, for a man who had once been under her father's command.

Regardless of what might have transpired between them, Father would have expected better of her than that.

Gauging by the trouble it had given Nelthorpe to navigate the stairs, she knew from her nursing experience that simply remaining upright must be akin to torture. Seized by conflicting emotions, she could not seem to tear her gaze from where he remained stoically standing, evidently awaiting the return of his horse.

The nurse in her urged her to rush downstairs and check his condition. The woman and the patriot ached for the obvious pain he was suffering.

The soldier in her saluted the pride and fortitude that had prompted him to mask his injuries and come to her aid, despite what it must have cost him to restrain the widow who'd attacked her.

She would not shame that pride by revealing that she'd observed him in his weakness.

When finally a groom appeared leading a tall gelding, she exhaled with relief. Apparently he'd mastered mounting and riding, for he managed those tasks without a falter.

Nelthorpe still rode with the same effortless grace she remembered from observing him in the Peninsula. Indeed, seeing him in the saddle, she would never have suspected his injury.

Long after he guided his mount out of sight, Jenna remained at the window, staring into the afternoon brightness as she recalled their conversation and each detail of his appearance and expression.

It appeared her first assessment had been correct. Anthony Nelthorpe had done more than just exchange his swagger for a limp.

And she owed him another apology.

IN LATE AFTERNOON of the following day, Tony Nelthorpe sat tying his cravat in preparation for dining at his club.

He'd been relieved to discover upon waking that, despite the wretched condition in which he'd returned home yesterday, he was now able to walk fairly well—so his exertions at the Fairchild townhouse had not, as he'd feared, set back his recovery. Which meant, praise heaven, that his leg must be healing at last.

Heaven knows, he'd seen little evidence of it yesterday. After having secluded himself at home for several weeks while he practiced walking, he'd decided it was time to attempt his first excursion into Society—at the reception being given to honor Colonel Garrett Fairchild.

Much as he might deserve Jenna's disdain, he rather dreaded receiving it, so the Fairchild's reception provided an ideal opportunity to meet her and attempt to offer his thanks. She would, he speculated, be less likely to publicly insult a Waterloo veteran during a reception honoring her husband's military service.

Regardless of her opinion of this particular soldier.

He'd just been congratulating himself on having actually spoken with her—and on managing the stairs without limping too dreadfully—when that widow assaulted her. His whole leg flaming in agony by the time that episode concluded, he had only the haziest of memories of the ride home, his dwindling strength being invested in the battle to remain conscious and in the saddle.

Out of yesterday's agony one bit of good news had

arisen, he thought with a smile. Once he had progressed beyond simple survival, he had grown concerned that his amorous inclinations seemed to have been snuffed out by the same injuries that had shattered his knee. Having had no blunt to test the fact, even if he'd had the desire, he'd relegated that worry to the back of his mind.

But a few moments in company with Jenna Fairchild had proven that though his longer members might never fully recover, his shorter one now functioned perfectly. Jenna Montague had roused his senses from the first day they met and time, it seemed, had not dimmed that instinctive response. Indeed, her appeal was if anything stronger—for Jenna was no longer an untried girl, but a widow who had tasted passion's full measure.

And, he was certain, she'd sensed as well as he the almost tactile pull between them yesterday. Though not surprisingly, she was no more willing to recognize it than she'd been three years ago.

Having nothing better to do at the moment, he might just have to live down to her expectation that he was planning to pester her about marrying him. His grin widened as a certain part of his anatomy offered solid support to the idea of pursuing Jenna Montague.

He was making no other progress. After three weeks at home, he still didn't know the current status of the Nelthorpe finances, his father having not yet seen fit to meet him. Anger flared and he fanned it, irritated at how much hurt lurked beneath.

But then, when had the earl ever paid any attention to his only son's activities, no matter how scandalous? Perhaps because Lord Hunsdon had always been too occupied with even more scandalous activities himself.

Well, Tony was no longer a stripling waiting with pathetic eagerness for any crumb of parental attention. As heir to the Hunsdon earldom, he had a right to know how things stood with the estate he would one day inherit.

Though by all the signs, his father would bequeath him little more than a pack of debts and a soiled reputation.

Dusting off his beaver hat, he limped out. He'd return early enough to catch his father before the earl began his evening's celebrations, hopefully while Hunsdon was sober enough to converse with some intelligence.

Three years ago, Tony had associated with a group of dissolute young men with whom he'd indulged in high-stakes gaming and dissipated revelry. Though during his three weeks of recovery, he had not called on any of them, the fact that he had returned to England would have been speedily telegraphed to the ton through the infallible network of servants' gossip.

With a sense of anticipation sharpened by unease, he hailed a hackney to White's. Would the members there greet him as a lost sheep returned—or see only the black sheep who'd disgraced himself by fleeing England with his debts of honor unpaid?

Despite his soldier's service, he suspected that a bad reputation, thoroughly earned, would prove long-lived.

Certainly Lane Fairchild had shown yesterday in what little regard he held Viscount Nelthorpe.

Half an hour later, his heart pounding—and not just, he knew, from exertion of having climbed yet another infernal flight of stairs—he stood at White's, scanning the occupants. Spotting two of his former compatriots seated around a bottle, he limped toward them.

Lord St. Ives noticed his approach and raised his quizzing glass. "Can it be?" he asked. "Despite that drunken sailor's gait, the face *is* familiar. As I live and breathe, I do believe 'tis Tony Nelthorpe!"

Aldous Wexley looked over in surprise. "Why, so 'tis. Didn't I hear you'd died after that great battle over in France, Nelthorpe? Watergreen or Watermarket—"

"Waterloo," Tony inserted.

"Ah, yes. Months ago now, though." Wexley waved a dismissive hand.

"So, Tony, tell us all about it, do! Soldiering bravely to keep England safe for—" St. Ives gestured with one languid hand "—reprobates like us."

"Damme, Grantham told me that after he joined up, he was informed he might travel with only two trunks in his baggage," Wexley said. "*Two!* Under such circumstances, how could a gentleman maintain a proper appearance?"

"There is the small matter of transporting food and munitions," Tony observed dryly.

"I hear the mud was dreadful," St. Ives said. "And the blood! Worse than a cockfight, I should imagine."

Against his will, Tony's mind returned to the battlefield as he'd seen it from his resting place beneath the two Polish lancers he'd killed after a cuirassier cut him off his horse: a sodden, muddy field of fallen men, some still, some writhing, under a pall of smoke reflected in the puddle whose reddened water lapped at his chin…

A shudder ran through him as bile rose in his throat. "Much worse than a cockfight."

"Speaking of," Wexley said with a broad wink, "have you seen the new dancers at Covent Garden? There's a brown-haired chit who reminds me of my last ladybird. Such ankles! Such thighs!"

"You must present me to her tonight," St. Ives replied. "Or there's that new hell that just opened on Russell Street. Offers fine brandy and deep play, Nelthorpe, if you'd like to join me there. As I recall, you were a bit under the hatches when you left this sceptered isle."

Wexley raised his glass. "To each his own vice."

"Let's broach another bottle before we go our separate ways, gentlemen." St. Ives lifted his glass to Tony. "In honor of our dear Nelthorpe's return from the dead."

Tony silently returned the salute, the momentary

warmth he'd felt at their offering a bottle in his honor swiftly dying. *They don't really want to know what happened in Portugal or the Pyranees or on the plain at Waterloo. Nor would they understand, even if you could find words to describe it.*

As the chat continued through another bottle and then a third, talk of wagers and women punctuated by an argument between St. Ives and Wexley over the proper trimming of a waistcoat, Tony felt more and more isolated.

Once he had sat here, guzzling and chatting and thinking like these men, oblivious to anything beyond the streets of Mayfair. But the man who'd done so had died somewhere between the barren, windswept canyons of Spain and the bloody fields of Belgium.

Tony didn't know who had taken his place. But whoever that man was, he no longer fit in here.

At length, the group stood to leave. "Which shall it be, Nelthorpe?" St. Ives asked, swaying on his feet. "Gaming with me? Or wenching with this fine gentleman?"

"I'm afraid I shall have to decline both offers tonight," Tony said, not at all sorry. "My father awaits."

St. Ives nodded gravely. "Matters of finance, of course. Chouse the old gentleman out of a few extra guineas, eh? He ought to owe you a stack of yellow boys for saving his purse by absenting yourself so long."

With a final witticism from St. Ives, the men parted. Foreboding gathering in his gut, Tony hailed a hackney to return to the Nelthorpe townhouse—and confront at last his revered father, the Earl of Hunsdon.

CHAPTER FIVE

DESPITE REMINDING HIMSELF that he was a man grown, as he stood outside his father's chamber, Tony had to quell the urge to straighten his neck cloth. After forbidding himself to do so, he rapped at the door and limped in.

Sipping from a mug of ale while his valet fastened stays around his bulging waist, the Earl of Hunsdon looked up in surprise. "Nelthorpe? Blast you, cub, how dare you barge in here with me *en déshabillé,* as if I were some damned theater strumpet you wanted to ogle?"

Anger welling up, Tony remained silent, subjecting his father, whom he'd seen thus far only from a distance, to a closer inspection. In addition to the increased girth the earl was attempting to conceal beneath a corset, his years of dissipation were clearly written in his reddened face and bloodshot eyes. Little remained of the strikingly handsome, godlike figure who had awed Tony in his youth.

"It's good to see you, too, Father," he said at last. "Had you summoned me any time this past three weeks, I should not have had to disturb you in your dressing room."

The earl regarded his only son with disfavor. "I suppose you expect me to say I'm pleased you survived the war. Though why you had to go haring off on such a misadventure I never understood."

"There was a small matter of pecuniary embarrassments that rendered my immediate removal from England rather imperative,'' Tony replied through tightened lips. Apparently the earl chose not to recall—or had been too drunk that night to remember—Tony's impassioned plea for funds to stave off disaster until he could make a recover. In reply to which the earl shouted for him to take himself off and not bother Hunsdon with his problems.

''Taken himself off'' he certainly had, catapulting totally unprepared into the midst of Wellington's army. But now to concentrate on the matter at hand.

''Let us dispense with the usual courtesies and proceed to the point. I need to know how things stand with our finances—what the current income is, what funds are available for me to draw upon. You must have realized some economies by pensioning most of the servants.''

Waving away his valet Baines, who discreetly withdrew, the earl replied, ''Didn't pension 'em off, just dismissed 'em. Why should I pay to feed 'em in retirement when they could go make themselves useful elsewhere? Would have sent Carstairs, too, but the old goat wouldn't go.''

Though he immediately recognized Hunsdon's comments for the diversionary tactics they were, his father's blatant breach of an earl's duty to his retainers brought Tony's simmering rage to a boil.

''Are you implying you're no longer paying Carstairs?''

''Damme, why should I? Told the old relic to leave.''

''How could someone of his advanced age find other employ? Besides, he has worked here all his life!''

''And had the satisfaction of serving the Nelthorpes, whose forbears rode with the Conqueror while his ancestors were dirty Saxon serfs living on roots and berries.''

The satisfaction of serving the Nelthorpes. As he gazed at his father's bloated face, a succession of images flashed through Tony's mind: the gritty marble of the entryway...the faded draperies at every window...the parsimony of furniture, most of it dust-covered...Carstairs's shabby livery and careworn face.

"Well, why are you still standing there?" the earl demanded. "Take yourself off and leave me in peace."

In a rage too deep for words, Tony held his father's gaze until, flushing, the earl dropped his eyes. With hands that trembled, he seized his ale and drank deeply.

Tony continued to stare at the man he'd once so admired and feared, whose rare praise he'd previously tried so hard to earn. A man whom, perhaps subconsciously, he'd spent most of his life seeking to emulate. But this aging roué was no longer the man Tony Nelthorpe wanted to see when he gazed into his own mirror twenty-five years hence.

He might have little idea how to avoid that fate, but he could stand firm against his father today. *I fled my responsibilities once at your command,* he thought, setting his jaw. *I'll not do so again.*

"I shall leave once I know the status of our funds."

"If you're so concerned about blunt, then by all means do something!" his father retorted. "Since you managed to survive the war—though the devil knows how, as you've never been successful at anything before—make yourself useful. Indeed, I had intended to discuss this with you directly upon your return, but I couldn't abide that revolting limp. Which, I'm relieved to note, has improved."

"Thank you, Papa, for your concern about my health."

The earl threw him a dagger glance but, to Tony's surprise, did not deliver the hide-blistering reprimand he'd expected. Clearing his throat instead, his father continued, "Snabble yourself an heiress to restore the family coffers, like I did. Preferably a landed chit. You can send her back to one of her properties when she gets tiresome, while her lovely blunt stays here in London.''

As you did. For the first time, he began to understand his mother's penchant for young footmen.

''Before I begin 'snabbling,' I must know just how empty the family coffers are.''

Giving him a petulant look, his father shrugged. ''Talking pounds and pence like some damned clerk! That's what comes of your overlong association with army riffraff. Hardly a true gentleman to be found among 'em.''

True men, if not gentlemen, Tony thought. But it was useless to attempt conveying such an idea to his father. ''I'll act the clerk if I must.''

''Can't expect me to keep something as vulgar as figures in my head. Now, if you'll *excuse* me—'' he waved Tony toward the door ''—I must finish dressing.''

''I shall be happy to withdraw, as soon as you sign this document—'' Tony drew out a paper from his pocket ''—authorizing me to act on your behalf.'' Striding to the desk, Tony seized the quill and presented it to his father.

''Accosting me in my own chamber, preaching like some damned Methodist,'' the earl grumbled. But under Tony's unwavering gaze, he reluctantly took the pen and scrawled his signature. ''Don't come here again until you can tell me you've bedded an heiress.''

Pocketing the note, Tony made the earl an exaggerated leg that sent an immediate shaft of pain through his knee. ''You may be assured of that, sir,'' he said, and limped out.

Snabble an heiress, he thought as he traversed the hall. A directive, he supposed, given to sons from time immemorial by profligate fathers who'd run their estates into ruin. Was he supposed to prowl the City, searching for a Cit seeking a title for his daughter and with little discrimination about who provided it? Or travel to India to sweep some Nabob's widow off her ill-bred feet?

He had to smile wryly. Only one heiress had ever interested him—a nabob's *daughter,* who was now a widow.

Unfortunately, being the widow of that exemplary soldier and hero, Colonel Garrett Fairchild, she would never seriously consider the hand of a reprobate-turned-who-knew-what like Anthony Nelthorpe.

No matter how many sparks struck between them.

Melancholy settling over him, Tony wandered to the library. Though he'd not awakened until midafternoon, he felt unaccountably weary. For three long years of boredom and battle, through fear, privation and pain, he'd cherished the notion that once he finally returned to England, life would resume some normal, satisfying pattern.

Well, Tony old man, it appears homecoming wasn't quite the deliverance you'd anticipated.

Though he'd never really fit in with his fellow army officers, still there had been the bond that comes from shared danger and privation and the knowledge that one is doing something important. As he sat in the darkened library, Tony had never felt more lonely.

His knee ached and his grumbling stomach reminded him of the dinner he'd not eaten at his club. Neither the beauties in Covent Garden's Green Room nor the green baize tables of Pall Mall beckoned.

With a sigh, he limped to the shelves to find his favorite volume of Cicero. He could wait until morning for a meal; Betsy had doubtless already retired for the night, and he'd been hungry before.

Tomorrow he'd ride into the City to the solicitor's office and finally discover just how low the Nelthorpe fortunes had fallen.

SHORTLY AFTER DAWN the following morning, the lure of Betsy's fresh hot coffee and perhaps a bit of last night's stew lured Tony down what still seemed an endless number of stairs to the kitchen. After leaning against the door while he caught his breath, he hobbled in and called a good morning to the rotund woman standing before the stove. "Ah, that coffee smells like the elixir of the gods!"

"Master, ye be up early this morn!" the cook said.

"Army habits are hard to break, I suppose."

"No need for ye to clamber down all them stairs. If'n you was to have rung, I'da sent up your coffee."

"But then I wouldn't be able to try to charm you out of some toast to accompany it—or perhaps something from last night's supper?"

"It ain't fittin' fer ye to be eatin' here, not with ye a man grown, but no sense ye takin' that leg up two flights of stairs. Sit ye at the table and I'll have ye some kidneys, eggs and bacon ready in a trice."

Once, Tony might have thought himself too important to take his porridge in the servants' kitchen, but after reaching the Peninsula he'd eaten in much humbler venues. Gratefully he took the seat indicated. "What would I do without you to watch over me?"

"Haven't I been doing so, ever since you sneaked down here begging more of my gingerbread when you wasn't but a lad?" She sniffed, her brows creasing in disapproval. "Seein's how them what shoulda watched ye seldom did. Besides, I'll never be forgettin' what you did for my da, may he rest in peace!"

Uncomfortable, Tony opened his lips to make some light remark, but the cook cut him off with a wave. "Nay, don't go on about bein' too castaway to remember all the blunt ye gave me for his medicines. For all yer seemin' careless ways, ye're not like *him.*" Her face darkening, she jerked her chin toward the ceiling. ''Ye may tell me I oughtn't be sayin' it, but say it I will! I woudda left last winter with the others and took Carstairs with me, too, save fer knowin' sooner or later ye'd be comin' home.''

As disturbed as he was touched by her confidence, Tony searched rather desperately for some teasing remark to defuse it. *Don't be looking at me as if I were some sort of savior,* he wanted to shout.

''I...I'm afraid your confidence may be misplaced,'' he said instead.

''Stood up to *him* last night, Baines said.'' Betsy nodded approvingly. '''Tis the first step, Master Tony.''

''I shall certainly try to put things right, Betsy.''

She nodded again. ''Well, here's yer breakfast now, so tuck into it! Bye-the-bye, if'n ye is to need aught at any hour, ye just ring, and me or Sadie will see to it. Can't be healing that leg on an empty stomach.''

He should know by now, Tony thought ruefully, that there was nothing one's servants didn't learn. He might have attempted a reproving reply, but at that moment Betsy placed in front of him a plate heaped high with such a delicious-smelling assortment of bacon, eggs, sausage and kidneys that his mouth was fully occupied watering in anticipation of that first bite. To delay would be an insult to Betsy's skill.

''Good, hearty food and lots of it—that'll do the trick,'' she said as she refilled his coffee cup.

''Excellent! Ah, the times out of mind we slept on a soggy field, dreaming of waking to a meal like this!''

She smiled with gratification. ''Thank'ee, Master Tony. Meadows said to tell you your horse be ready whenever you are.''

Half an hour later, Tony guided Pax into Hyde Park and gave himself up to the sheer pleasure of a hard gallop.

Good fresh English air did do wonders to clear the

mind, and with a full belly, he could almost believe he was capable of anything. By now it was blindingly clear that at least Hunsdon's London retainers were looking to the heir, rather than the head of the family, to halt the downward slide of the family fortunes.

But by the time he guided the spent gelding to a walk, his initial euphoria began to fade.

He was near to thirty, with a face most women called handsome and a tall figure that, in the days before a limp disfigured it, had been deemed striking. He still rode well, played—despite his sire's disparagement—an excellent hand of cards or dice, could drink nearly any man under the table, and was accounted a witty conversationalist. But he had no profession, little knowledge of estate management, none of handling investments and, most likely, next to no blunt to start with.

How was he to rescue the fortunes of his family—and safeguard the retainers in his care?

Well, he might be a farce of a "hero," who'd puked his stomach dry before every engagement and barely been able to hold the reins, his hands shook so badly before the charge, but somehow he'd managed to get through years of war with most of his troopers alive. Even better, England held no adversaries wishful of putting a bullet through him.

Except perhaps, he thought with a grin, Jenna Fairchild.

As if his thoughts had conjured her, suddenly he saw in the distance a lady whose graceful carriage on horseback proclaimed her identity as loudly as a herald's trumpet. Signaling Pax to slow, he gave himself up to admiring her.

A little voice whispered that Lady Fairchild's fortune would go a long way to restoring his shattered finances. But attractive as the idea might be of wedding—and bedding—the delectable Jenna Montague, he couldn't imagine a fortune hunter in London who'd have less chance than he of getting his grubby fists on the Montague wealth.

Though he might—depending on just how dire was the news soon to be imparted to him by the family solicitor—be able to stomach cozening up to some Cit's daughter more interested in his title than his person, Jenna Montague's kindness, valor and integrity demanded more in a partner than a half-crippled man with a sordid past. She would want another Garrett, a man of substance, courage and impeccable reputation—none of which virtues Tony had any pretense of possessing.

Best to think of her as his battlefield angel and leave it at that. As he'd learned long ago, depending too much on one's paragons was a mistake.

A memory suddenly flooded back, bringing a slight smile to his lips. He hadn't thought of Miss Sweet, his much-older sister's governess, in years. Probably because the young man he'd become after leaving childhood had not been looking to angels for his model.

She'd been the only friend he could remember from his lonely childhood, scolding when he tormented his timid tutor, challenging him to prove he could learn Latin and Greek, praising his efforts, laughing with him.

Listening to him.

And then one winter night, Miss Sweet had suddenly left Hunsdon Park without a word of goodbye.

Gathering his courage, he'd inquired about her, prompting his father to a diatribe on the perfidy of females in general and Miss Sweet in particular. Giving almost no notice, the ungrateful jade had abandoned them, his father said, to accept a better-paying position.

Tony had been devastated.

Yes, admiring from afar allowed one to focus on the

inspiring illusion that perfect goodness existed. Heaven knows, he could use some inspiration.

Despite the sensible conclusion that he ought to keep his distance, as always, something about Jenna drew him irresistibly. Knowing no one would forestall his approach—her groom was grazing his horse at the opposite side of the park—he couldn't help but follow her.

She was riding a different mount this morning—surely not her own, for even now that she'd reached the open expanse of Rotten Row, the placid beast seemed disinclined to exceed a trot. Wondering how long so intrepid a rider would content herself with so stodgy a pace, he had to grin when, a moment later, she gave the mare a light tap with her riding crop.

The smile faded when the horse jerked to a halt, then reared up, lunging and bucking as she attempted to unseat her rider. Before he could even shout a warning, Jenna tumbled sideways out of her saddle and landed facedown on the rocky path.

CHAPTER SIX

SPURRING PAX TO A GALLOP, Tony reached Jenna before her groom even noticed his mistress had fallen. Quickly he secured his horse and limped as fast as he could to where she lay, still ominously unmoving.

Awkwardly he lowered himself to the ground, the familiar taste of fear bitter in his mouth. "Jenna!" he called, patting her shoulder. "Jenna, can you hear me?"

There was no response. He touched her wrist, overjoyed to feel a faint pulse against his shaking fingers. Though she lay with her face in the mud, he dare not move her until he knew the extent of her injuries.

Detachment settling in, he traced down her limbs, then up from the base of her neck. Relief flooded him when he determined that, as best he could tell, the spine appeared intact and no bones had been broken.

By this time the thunder of approaching hoofs told him the groom must have finally seen his fallen mistress. A moment later, a panic-faced lad skidded to a stop beside Tony. "Cor, m'lord, be she dead?"

"She breathes still—no thanks to your diligence," Tony said acidly. "Help me turn her—gently!"

Tony discovered, as he'd suspected, a purpling contusion on her temple. Her even breathing and steady pulse reassured him somewhat, but he knew a brain injury could be as dangerous as a fracture to the spine. She might also have suffered other, not yet apparent hurts.

Though he was tempted to wait for a carriage to convey her home more gently, his battlefield experience argued that the longer she lay on the cold ground, the greater the danger that she might never recover consciousness or that the chill might settle in her lungs.

Horseback it must be.

"You—" he gestured to the boy "—fetch my horse, over there. Once I've mounted, you must hand Lady Fairchild up to me as gently as you can and lead us back to Fairchild House. I don't want to jostle her any more than necessary, but we must get her home as quickly as possible and summon a physician. Return for her mount later."

While the lad did as he was bid, Tony thanked God he had his horse available. With his arms well-developed from wielding a saber, lifting Jenna from the groom and balancing her before him in the saddle proved easy enough a task. He knew he'd never have been able to support her weight, slight as it was, were he on foot.

For an instant Tony wondered why Jenna's seemingly docile mount had suddenly turned so fractious. Far too worried about her condition to spare more than that moment on the thought, he hugged her limp body to his chest.

The transit home seemed to take an age. By the time Upper Brook Street came into view, he was sweating, even his well-trained muscles strained by the effort of holding her as motionless as possible.

Just as they reached the townhouse, Jenna moved at last. Eyes still shut, she murmured and nestled against Tony, as if snuggling into his warmth. Or as if, slowly rousing from sleep, she were seeking her lover.

His body stirred at the thought and, despite his worry, he had to grin. Often as he'd dreamed of having Jenna Montague in his arms again, he'd never envisioned it happening quite like this.

Finally a Fairchild servant noticed them. "Someone from the house will assist us now," Tony called to the groom. "Ride with all speed for the doctor."

A moment later, a procession of servants began streaming out, among them Sancha, the Spanish maid who had accompanied Jenna all through the Peninsula.

"*Madre de Dios, mi pobre señora!*" she cried as she ran down the steps toward them. "What happened?"

"She fell from her horse," Tony answered.

As the maid's gaze lifted from her mistress to the man holding her, her eyes widened. "The Evil One!" she gasped.

So much for Sancha's good opinion. But concern for Jenna outweighing his chagrin, he continued, "Get her into a warm bed as quickly as possible. A doctor was sent for."

After carefully handing Jenna to a stout footman, he dismounted to follow. "Nay!" Sancha cried, stepping forward to block him and making the sign of the cross, as if to ward off the Evil Eye. "You may not enter!"

Before Tony could remonstrate, Lane Fairchild trotted down the stairs. He paused for a moment as the footman carrying Jenna passed him, his grim gaze scanning her pale face, then proceeded to halt before Tony.

"What outrage is this? If you have harmed my cousin, I shall call you out, even if you are a cripple!"

"Lady Fairchild fell while riding," Tony said, ignoring the jibe about his condition and trying to hold his temper in check. "I assisted in carrying her home."

Fairchild raised his eyebrows. "*Jenna* fell from her horse? Do you really expect me to believe that?"

Tony shrugged. "I don't give a damn what you believe. Question the groom about it—indeed, I'd like to ask him myself how such a thing happened. But for now,

Sancha, go to your mistress. The doctor should be here any moment.''

Fairchild looked as if he would comment further, but chose to refrain. ''I do thank you for seeing her home,'' he admitted grudgingly. ''Now I must tend to my cousin.''

With that, Fairchild ran back up the stairs. As the front door shut behind them, the rest of the servants dispersed. For a few moments Tony stood alone, debating whether or not to continue up the stairs and demand entry. But given Fairchild's plainly demonstrated animosity, it was unlikely he'd be able to inveigle his way in. Though it galled him to leave before finding out how she was, there seemed little point in remaining.

He'd return later after the physician had examined her, he decided. He'd done all he could for Jenna, save keep vigil until the doctor came. What happened now was in the hands of her maid, her physician—and Jenna herself.

''Fight like the good soldier you are,'' he murmured. And then, shoulders aching, he mounted Pax and set off.

TWO WEEKS LATER, Tony sat in one of the new hells off Pall Mall, an untasted drink at his elbow as, hand after hand, he raked in the guineas of his opponent, a lad too drunk to count the cards in his unsteady grip.

He felt a bit ashamed, relieving this castaway stripling of so much blunt. But the grim news imparted by the family solicitor when Tony had finally consulted him, after being turned away three times from the Fairchild mansion after Jenna's accident, made the necessity of finding an immediate source of income starkly clear.

The earnings from the Nelthorpe estates, financially crippled like so many farming communities after the war's end, had diminished to a trickle that would barely pay to seed this year's crops. Not attempting to hide his disapproval, the solicitor told him that his father had sold or gambled away the investments left by Tony's grandfather, mortgaged nearly every property it was possible to mortgage, and was in arrears in paying back even the interest.

Like his father, the solicitor advised him to head off the disaster by marrying an heiress. At least this man had the grace to remain silent when Tony, angry and despairing, snapped back at him to ask which fair flower of virginity had a rich Papa, still in possession of his senses, who might agree to offer Tony her hand.

Perhaps something could be worked out, the man had said weakly. On that hopeful note, they'd parted.

He'd gone back to gaming to pay off the most pressing bills he'd found stuffed in his father's desk. Thanks to a merciful Providence, thus far, he'd been winning.

But he'd gambled too long not to know that, skillfully and soberly as he was now playing, his luck wouldn't last forever. The blunt he'd accumulated after two week's play offered a small cushion against immediate ruin, but gaming could be no more than a temporary solution.

His only real chance to recoup their fortune would be, as everyone suggested, to marry one.

However, Tony's few forays into polite Society had confirmed that his soiled reputation, no doubt reinforced by the activities of his sire, remained intact. Society matrons with marriageable daughters in tow took care to avoid him. His older sister, now Lady Siddons, had distanced herself from her Hunsdon kin immediately after her marriage and could not be looked to for any assistance.

His chances of finding a suitably wealthy aristocratic bride were thus virtually nonexistent. Accepting that fact, he'd started a list of wealthy men in the City who, rumor said, had pretensions of seeing their daughters rise in Society. He still had no idea how he was to wangle introductions to those fathers, much less charm one into gifting him with his daughter and her fortune.

The question of how he'd manage to coexist afterward with a woman who was little more than the prize in this most high-staked of card games, he avoided considering.

As Tony watched his opponent struggle to extract a card, the lad's face went slack and he slumped forward onto the table. With a resigned sigh, Tony hopped up to catch him before he slid onto the floor, then plucked a coin from the stack before him to give the servant who relieved him of the lad, instructing him to transport the boy home.

Who had ever done as much for him? he asked himself, irritated by the unpleasant taste that still lingered in his mouth as the youth was carried off. He could easily have trebled the bets, come away with a stack of the greenling's vowels as well as all his blunt. A true Captain Sharp would have done just that.

As he idly gathered up the boy's coins, his mind wandered back to Jenna. Though he'd called nearly every day, finally coaxing his way into seeing Sancha, he'd never been admitted to Jenna's presence.

She was recovering, Sancha assured him. She thanked him for his flowers and the book he'd brought, one he'd laughed through and thought she would enjoy.

If only these long nights of smoke and liquor and bad company could earn him a future with a woman like that, a woman he could respect and care about and look forward to sharing his life with, maybe he wouldn't feel so…alone.

Tony my lad, you're growing maudlin, he told himself. When, after all, had he ever *not* been alone?

"Tony Nelthorpe! By heaven, I see you made it out of hospital after all!"

Recognizing the man who'd hailed him, Tony's melancholy dissolved in a surge of gladness.

"Ned Hastings!" he cried, rising to shake the hand being proffered. "You're looking well yourself. Fully recovered from that episode in Belgium, I trust?"

"Yes, thanks to your timely intervention. And you?"

"Much better than when last you saw me."

"Praise the Lord for that! But what are you doing here?" Hastings looked about them with disdain. "Thought if you wished to play, you'd take a chair at White's."

Shrugging, Tony offered him wine. "I decided to amuse myself in a setting with a more…varied clientele."

"Everyone from old aristocracy to jumped-up Cits to Johnny Raws straight from the country." Hastings's grin faded as he took a glass. "Too many of our old Oxford mates now forever missing at White's, eh?"

Leaving it to the jackals who never served.

"And the tulips who remained while the rest of us answered the call, one doesn't wish to see," Hastings concluded, giving voice to Tony's thought.

"Indeed."

After staring into the distance, Hastings shook himself, as if to break free of the ghostly fist of memory. "So, what are you doing, now that you're up and about?" Hastings asked. "Understand the earl is up to his usual tricks. Can…can I do anything to assist?"

Tony felt his face flush. Having known him since Oxford, Hastings also knew he was perpetually purse-pinched. Discovering Tony in an establishment that possessed no pretensions to being aught but a gambling den, he could surely guess how things currently stood.

"You've already helped enough," Tony replied. "Pax is a superior mount. Given my recent difficulties in navigating on my own two limbs, I should have been in bad case indeed had you not generously provided me with him.''

Hastings waved away Tony's thanks. "'Twas little enough, considering that if you hadn't ridden down the cuirassier who was about to gut me in Quatre Bras, I'd not be here drinking wine with you tonight.''

"If I hadn't gotten him, someone else would have.''

"Perhaps, but you did, and I shall never forget that.'' Hastings took a sip before saying diffidently, "My father's investments in the India trade prosper. Should you find yourself a trifle under the hatches, I'm sure he—''

"No need. I shall come about shortly. As soon as I decide which tender virgin to honor with the offer of my hand,'' he added, trying to keep bitterness from his voice.

"'Twould be a sensible solution,'' Hastings said with a nod. "Have you anyone in mind?''

"I'm still, shall we say, reconnoitering the ground.''

Hastings's eyes brightened and he set down his glass. "You remember 'Guinea' Harris, don't you?''

"That corporal in first company who could shoot the center out of a yellow boy from fifty paces?''

"Yes. I saw him just last week. His father's some sort of banker in the city, full of juice, if rumor can be believed. Perhaps you ought to call on him. Mr. Harris might be able to suggest suitable bridal candidates for a man who, like his son, survived Waterloo.''

Probably Banker Harris, like most people awed by the great and terrible victory over the French, thought "Waterloo survivor'' was synonymous with "courage.''

Tony knew he didn't qualify. But he couldn't afford to be too finicky about honor. An influential City banker would be of great help in finding him an heiress to marry.

And so, despite his discomfort, he made himself say, "If the opportunity should arise, I'd like to meet him.''

"I'd be happy to arrange it. Mayhap 'Guinea' Harris's

papa can send some golden coins rolling in your direction!"

Tony murmured his gratitude. He ought to feel encouraged—and virtuous, that he'd made himself take this first step toward the solution everyone was recommending. A solution that was both logical and commonplace. Most men of his station married to secure alliances and fortunes.

Hadn't he, once upon a time, urged Jenna to make just such a match—with him? Though, he recalled with a grin, the bargain had been rather one-sided: her fortune for his somewhat tarnished title. Ah, what a coxcomb he'd been!

But though he had certainly coveted her fortune, there had been something about Jenna, something beyond an undeniably strong physical attraction, that had drawn him and made the idea of marrying her compelling even to a man who scoffed at the notion of love and fidelity.

Her serenity, sense of honor and courage, perhaps, qualities that had resonated when tried by the adversities of war like the steel of the finest saber.

Qualities that drew him still.

Miss Sweet's final legacy, he thought with a self-mocking smile. Somehow in his youth she'd managed to instill deep within him an ironic yearning for purity and valor, qualities he himself had never possessed. A yearning unlikely to be satisfied in the match between avarice and social advantage he was now contemplating.

Though he'd lately come to believe that courage, honor and fidelity were possible, he wasn't sure he yet believed in lifelong, selfless love. Not for Anthony Nelthorpe.

So why did the notion of binding himself in a loveless marriage of convenience continue to seem so distasteful?

CHAPTER SEVEN

A WEEK LATER, JENNA REPOSED in the sitting room adjoining her chamber while Cousin Lane settled a shawl about her shoulders. "Rest a while longer, Jenna. I've business this morning, but this afternoon, if the weather holds fair, I shall try to tempt you out for a carriage ride." He stroked her cheek gently. "Promise me you'll consider it, eh? That pretty face is far too pale."

"Thank you, cousin. I will consider it," she answered politely, then sighed with relief when he exited the room.

She turned her gaze to the window. It *was* fair today, she noted, though whether it was sun or rain mattered little to her. A book lay on the table beside her, a gift, Sancha told her, from Lord Nelthorpe—of all people! And though she found the author, one Jane Austen, quite clever, Jenna hadn't read more than a page.

Her unfocused gaze caught on the play of dust motes as they rose and fell in a sunbeam. Drifting, like she was.

Sancha would push her to ride out with Cousin Lane. Probably better to go with him than be maneuvered into accompanying Lady Montclare, who was sure to press her once Aunt Hetty informed the sisters during their daily call that the doctor had pronounced her fully recovered.

"Fully recovered." How little the doctor knew!

It seemed someone was always trying to bully her into doing this or that, when all she wished to do was sit in her chair or lie in her bed with her face to the wall and remain in that blessed, blank place without thought or feeling in which she'd floated since her accident.

She remembered nothing between riding toward the park that morning and waking, like a swimmer submerged, to a flicker of shapes and a distant murmur of voices. Compelled by some urgency, despite the pain in her body, she'd made herself battle upward to the light, struggling to stay conscious and focus on the words the doctor was uttering to Sancha. A weeping Sancha, who wrung her hands and whispered "My poor lady."

Blow. Head. Recover. Lost. Son.

With a supreme effort she moved one hand to her belly, suddenly aware of pain there that nearly equaled the pounding in her head.

Sorry. Nothing. I. Could. Do.

"Here's tea," Sancha's voice startled her. The maid set the tray on the side table. Frowning, she plucked the shawl from Jenna's shoulders and tossed it aside.

"No more sitting, lazy one! Today you go out into the sun." The maid went to pull a pelisse from the wardrobe.

Jenna eyed the garment with distaste. "I don't wish to go out."

"You did not wish to stop medicine. Or see cousins, or *los señoras* with fancy gowns and scorpion tongues. Ah, much you have lost! But you must go on." Sancha poured a cup of tea. "Drink now. You are colonel's daughter, eh?"

I don't know who I am, Jenna thought. But after a moment, having neither strength nor interest enough for a battle of wills, as she had since Sancha had weaned her from the laudanum and forced her back to the world of consciousness, Jenna followed orders and took a sip.

"I bring this." Sancha held up an envelope. "From the Handsome One with the rogue's eyes who waits below."

Nelthorpe? Jenna wondered with a faint stir of interest. But that brief emotion faded once she discovered the note Sancha presented came from Mr. Fitzwilliams.

Idly she scanned his standard expression of regret, about to put it aside when the last two lines snagged her attention. "Though I hesitate to intrude upon your grief, my aunt, Lady Charlotte, begs leave to visit. She has suffered as you suffer and earnestly desires to help."

Could anyone help? Kind thoughts aside, Lady Charlotte Darnell was but a stranger, and Jenna was already surrounded by surfeit of well-meaning strangers.

How she longed for the strong, sympathetic shoulder of Harry or Alastair, the comforting arms of her dead mother! Only Sancha knew her intimately enough to appreciate the devastation of her loss—and she had never borne a child.

Suddenly a deep desire swept through her to meet this woman who, if Jenna were interpreting Fitzwilliams's note aright, had lost a child, as she had.

"Is Mr. Fitzwilliams still below?"

"Aye, mistress. A beautiful lady waits with him."

"Show them up, please. And fetch more tea."

Sancha smiled and dipped a curtsy. "*Si,* mistress!"

The moment after Sancha left, Jenna regretted the impulse to allow their visit. Had she not already sustained a steady stream of visitors, patting her hand and expressing their deepest condolences?

First had been Cousin Bayard, who'd stiffly offered his regrets on her loss while delicately avoiding any mention of the viscount's mantle which now rested securely about his own shoulders. Not that she cared for that.

Next had come a weeping Aunt Hetty. Indeed, the only blessing of this whole episode, Jenna thought, was that Hetty Thornwald, apparently having a horror of sickrooms, limited her visits to a few moments each morning.

Cousin Lane came by several times daily, seeking with kind but unwanted solicitude to cheer her, and the Two Sisters called far too often. She'd had to bite her tongue not to order Sancha to forcibly expel them the afternoon that Mrs. Anderson, in an example of insensitivity astounding even for that thickheaded individual, congratulated her on now being able to proceed directly to the important matter of settling her future.

At that moment she heard footsteps approaching, followed by a knock at the door. Too late to back down now. Seconds later, Sancha ushered in the visitors.

A "Handsome One with a rogue's eyes" Mr. Fitzwilliams was in truth, Jenna thought with a trace of humor. Equally lovely was the fashionably dressed, blond lady on his arm.

After an exchange of greetings, Jenna said, "You will join us for tea, Mr. Fitzwilliams?"

He shook his head. "I can imagine nothing more useless at such a moment than a well-meaning but ignorant male. My sincere regards, Lady Fairchild. Aunt Charlotte, the carriage will be waiting when you are ready to return."

After Mr. Fitzwilliams bowed himself out, Lady Charlotte looked at Jenna, her deep blue eyes earnest. "You must be thinking me perfectly boorish to force myself upon you like this! But when Teagan told me you had no mother or married friend to talk with, no one but your maid, I simply had to come. You will forgive me?"

Jenna could reply in polite generalities, but as Lady Charlotte had abandoned normal conventions with her personal appeal, Jenna decided to be equally forthcoming.

"You, too, have lost a child?"

"Three," she said softly. "All before birth."

Jenna felt her throat tighten and her eyes fill. "Then you do understand."

Lady Charlotte nodded. Hesitantly she reached for Jenna's hand. "I know how hard it is to bear."

"It...it is hard," Jenna said. Suddenly a sharp, pulverizing pain ripped apart the curtain of unreality behind which Jenna had hidden since awakening after the accident. From deep within her a floodtide of grief flowed up, smashing through the pitiful barriers behind which she'd tried to contain it. Before she could stammer apology or explanation, sobs she could neither prevent nor control erupted, overwhelming her ability to resist them.

After the storm of tears subsided, without knowing how she'd gotten there, Jenna found herself on the sofa beside Lady Charlotte, her head on that lady's shoulder.

"I'm so sorry! You will be thinking me the boor."

Tears in her own eyes, Lady Charlotte shook her head. "*I've felt what you feel.* But when I lost my babes, I still had my mother, all her love and years of wisdom to console me."

After rummaging in her reticule, Lady Charlotte handed Jenna a handkerchief. "My momma told me before you can gather what remains and go on, you must grieve."

"I don't know what is left to gather. With Papa and Garrett gone, I've lost my bearings. I had been girding myself to focus on—" she swallowed hard "—on raising Garrett's child. What do I do now?"

"Don't worry about tomorrow. Just get this next minute. This next hour." Lady Charlotte squeezed her hand. "It *will* get easier, I promise. Even though I see you do not believe me," she added with a smile.

Jenna managed a smile, too. "How can I thank you?"

"Don't wall yourself away, no matter how little you desire to go out. Visit me, seek the company of friends whenever they happen to London. Indeed, 'twas partly for that reason that I called today."

From her reticule, Lady Charlotte withdrew an engraved card. ''I'm having a reception for the ton Friday in honor of Waterloo veterans. Among the guests will likely be some of your army friends. Please, do try to attend.''

Without waiting for a reply, Lady Charlotte rose. ''Now, I've tired you enough. Thank you for agreeing to see me. I…I hope it helped more than distressed you.''

''It did help,'' Jenna replied, surprised to find that was true. Though the great burden of grief still weighed upon her heart, it was in small degree lighter for having been shared with a kindred soul.

Just before Lady Charlotte walked out, Jenna found herself blurting, ''Do—do you have any surviving children?''

Her visitor paused at the threshold. ''No.''

''I'm so sorry,'' Jenna whispered.

''Call on me,'' Lady Charlotte said, and walked out.

TWO NIGHTS LATER, Jenna sat alone in the carriage as it crawled toward Lady Charlotte Darnell's townhouse on Mount Street. Warmed to confirm during her return call that the deep, immediate bond formed between them on Lady's Charlotte's first visit was genuine, she'd rashly promised her new friend she would attend her Waterloo Party. Mercifully she'd been spared Aunt Hetty's company when that lady developed a head cold this afternoon and cried off, while Cousin Lane, who had a preceding engagement, had pledged to meet her at Lady Charlotte's.

But after two hours with Mrs. Anderson and Lady Montclare this afternoon, despite the pleasure of seeing Lady Charlotte again, Jenna was having serious misgivings about the wisdom of coming tonight.

Though she'd managed to avoid being saddled with their company in her carriage, she'd had no success preventing them from extolling the long list of potential suitors she'd doubtless encounter. Her repeated insistence that she was attending only to see old army friends—not to make her debut into the Marriage Mart—they cheerfully ignored.

Until now, she'd overcome a distaste for entering Society by telling herself she must take her place there in order to secure a proper future for Garrett's *babe*. Not until tonight, as she waited with increasing trepidation in her carriage, did Jenna begin to envision what she would face, stripped of the solace of her child, confronting Society alone as a widow whose wealth and lineage would draw to her the immediate attention of the ton—and, if the sisters could be believed, that of every gentleman whose fortunes or family propelled him to seek a wife.

As the carriage moved forward, agitation set her stomach churning. Behind Lady Charlotte's doors would be a cacophony of voices, most of them false and flattering. A press of people, pressing her to call on them, dine with them. Elegantly dressed men who might mask their assessing glances and avarice behind a smile.

No, she simply couldn't face it.

She rapped on the carriage wall. As the vehicle slowed, she jerked open the door, jumped down and darted into the night.

GUIDING HIS SKITTISH HORSE through the press of vehicles on Park Street, Tony contemplated once again the wisdom of accepting Lady Charlotte Darnell's invitation.

On the one hand, Tony could count on partaking of a handsome dinner. On the other, he'd probably encounter a number of old codgers who would want him to regale them about Waterloo—an engagement he'd been trying his best for nearly six months to forget.

If he was truly honest, he had to admit the strongest

reason for attending was the hope of encountering Jenna Fairchild. He'd heard she was fully recovered from her fall, though after calling once again at Fairchild House, he'd still not managed to see her.

Her decision to avoid him was not unexpected. Still, he couldn't seem to drive from his head the image of her lying motionless on the roadway. Once he saw with his own eyes that she was well, he'd be able to put her from his mind and concentrate on repairing his precarious fortunes.

The congestion increasing as he approached the corner of Mount Street, Tony decided to proceed on foot. But as he started to dismount, Pax whinnied and reared up, nearly throwing him out of the saddle.

"What ails you, old friend?" he chided as he regained his seat. "No cannon or muzzle flashes to spook you here."

Even as he spoke, a shimmer of light passed between two carriages, sending a zing of alarm through him.

'Twas surely not a specter from Waterloo come to attend the festivities, he reassured himself. So what had it been? Dismounting, he paced toward the elusive glimmer.

And saw, as he reached the spot where he had seen it, the cloaked figure of a woman, speeding away as if truly pursued by ghosts.

Even illumined by moonlight, the park toward which she was fleeing was no place for a woman alone, especially not one whose fur-trimmed cloak proclaimed her wealth.

Was she a wife running from an argument with her spouse—or sneaking off to an assignation with her lover?

Should an eager swain be awaiting her, she'd not thank him for interfering. Still, outlined by moonlight, she would surely catch the eye of any drunken lout or cutpurse who happened to be lurking down those shadowy pathways.

No help for it, he thought with a resigned sigh. Until she reached safe escort, he'd have to follow her.

Though his leg had improved, he was still no match for a female traversing the park at nearly a dead run. Thanks to the reflections off her satin cloak, Tony managed to keep the lady in sight, but she'd reached the Serpentine when at last, sweating from his efforts and the pain in his knee, he managed to close the distance between them.

She'd halted on the bridge over the stream, a silver-edged silhouette above a silver mirror of water. Not wishing to frighten her, he called out as he approached, "Madam, may I be of assistance?"

Then a gust of wind blew back her hood, revealing the lady's face.

Jenna Fairchild's face.

Shocked, he stopped short, wincing at the jolt to his knee. What could have sent her running off into the night unattended? She'd campaigned with the army long enough to know how reckless such an action was.

"Lady Fairchild!" he called, edging cautiously closer. "What are you doing out here?"

Though he was certain she must have heard him, she remained still and silent, her face so expressionless another shock of alarm rippled through him.

"Jenna, what is wrong?"

Again, she made no reply. Uncertain what to do, he'd reached out a hand when she at last looked up.

"I expect you heard I lost the child," she said matter-of-factly. "Garrett's son, as it turned out."

Surprise swept through him, followed by dismay. "No—no, I hadn't heard. I'm so sorry."

Words, meaningless words, he thought, wishing he had

something better to offer. Even one with as little experience of love as he could imagine what a double blow this must have been, coming so close after Garrett's death. He thought of their long, slow journey from the park back to Fairchild House. Might the physician have been able to save her child, had he been able to tend her sooner?

Disturbed by the thought, Tony said, "I wish I could have gotten a doctor to you more quickly."

Her eyes flickered up. "*You* brought the doctor?"

"I sent the groom once we reached Fairchild House."

"You helped Hobbs bring me home?"

"Yes. Did no one tell you?"

"No!" She wrinkled her brow. "Sancha brought up a book she said you'd left, but I had no idea you'd assisted after the…the accident. I don't remember any of it."

"You took quite a blow to the head."

"I suppose I should thank you, then." She laughed shortly, the bitter tone surprising him. "Though it might have been more merciful to have left me there."

As she spoke, her voice faded and the fire drained from her face. The comment and her blank expression were so unlike the serene, courageous Jenna Montague he'd known that Tony was at a loss what to reply.

For long moments he heard only the sigh of the wind and the lapping of the water against the bridge. Searching for something, anything to break the silence, Tony said, "You were going to the soirée at Lady Charlotte's?"

Her gaze on the water below them, she said, "Play the rich widow, on display for all the marriage merchants of the ton like another prize of war? No, I cannot bear it."

At this second, most uncharacteristic comment, Tony's alarm deepened. "I imagine such attention might be distasteful. Show them the tart edge of the tongue with which Jenna Montague deals with scoundrels, and you'll quickly send the rascals to the rightabout."

That remark failed to earn him even the exasperated look so poor a jest deserved. Something about the downward cast of her head, her expressionless face—and her rapt fixation on the water flowing beneath the bridge was making the hair at the back of his neck bristle.

More spooked than he'd been by the thought of prowling Waterloo ghosts, he cast about for something to prod her out of this unusual, disturbing lethargy. "So you've lost the child. What do you intend to do with yourself now?"

"With them gone—Papa, Garrett, our babe, there's nothing left worth doing."

"Nothing? Why, you could..." His voice trailed off. Barely knowing what to do with himself, how could he presume to advise her?

With a deep sigh, she leaned on the bridge rail, her torso extended so alarmingly far over the frigid water, he had to clench his hands to keep from pulling her back. Of course she didn't mean to throw herself in—certainly not with a potential rescuer standing right beside her.

Once she had rescued him. If a purpose was what she needed, surely he could think of some project with which to challenge her. Then a sudden inspiration occurred.

"'Tis true that far too many good men died to keep England out of the Corsican monster's grasp. Since you were the instrument of saving my carcass, why not take it upon yourself to redeem my sad character as well? Look upon it as retribution to all those better, finer men who died."

She looked over. "A man should redeem himself."

"Undoubtedly. But you should know me well enough to judge how likely I'd be to accomplish that feat."

She tilted her head at him thoughtfully. "I've always

wondered—if I had not have escaped you, would you have held me there by force, three years ago at Badajoz?''

He let his gaze rove over her figure. ''Oh, I don't think I'd have needed force.''

She stiffened. ''You conceited blackguard. As likely could the devil reform himself!''

''You have your new calling, then. Here I stand, while Garrett lies in a Belgian grave. An outrage, is it not?''

''Indeed it is!''

''Then do something to change it. Or has Jenna Montague, the colonel's daughter, turned craven?''

''Were I slime in the gutter, I would have more courage than you!''

Truer words than you could ever know. Shaking off the shame that scoured him, he said, ''Prove it! Swear you will work until my character is well and truly reformed.''

''Nay, sir, I'll not pledge that. Redeeming you would take a miracle!''

''Until Christmas, then,'' he said, desperate to wangle some sort of promise from her. '''Tis the season of miracles, after all. And while you expend your best efforts upon my character, I can shield you from other toadies and fortune hunters.''

''You being one of the most notorious?''

''Exactly. A mutually beneficial bargain.''

She shook her head. ''I don't know.''

''Why not? You claim to cherish the memory and sacrifice of the men who died, yet you refuse to stir yourself to attempt redeeming even one sorry soul in their honor? I see your vaunted love for them is only empty, pious talk.''

She gasped in indignation. ''How dare you!''

''What is it you fear, then?'' he pressed, trying to goad her beyond resistance. ''That your character isn't up to the task of reforming mine? That I might succeed in seducing you before you succeed in reforming me?"

"Never!"

"Are you so certain?" And to prove just how desperately in need of reform he was, before Jenna could realize his intent, he swept her into his arms and kissed her.

His plan of rousing her to a furious response succeeded all too well. Though a merciful heaven accorded him an instant, while shock held her immobile, to revel in the taste as her chilled lips warmed under his, a second later she shoved him back and slapped his face.

The force of the blow knocked him off balance. He came down hard on his bad knee, which buckled under his weight and pitched him forward. Blessing the strength he'd developed in his arms, he seized the wooden railing just in time to keep from toppling into the freezing water below.

Relieved as he was to have provoked the fiery Jenna he remembered so well out of her shell of grief, even better had been that doubtless never-to-be-repeated opportunity to sample her mouth. 'Od's blood, how well she fit in his arms! One brief touch of her winter-cold lips had been enough to heat his blood to a July fever.

Awkwardly he hauled himself upright. "Ah, I do so love a passionate lady."

She had reached out as if to help steady him on his feet, but at that, she snatched her hand back. "Touch me again and I'll be 'passionate' enough to send your miserable carcass straight into the pond."

"I've much warmer places I'd rather you send me."

Whirling around, she stomped off the bridge.

He limped after her. "See how dire is the need for my reform?"

"Clearly."

"Then you'll agree? To honor the fallen heroes—and demonstrate your superior character?"

"'Tis a wicked wager."

"Ah, but I'm a wicked rogue. You could change that—for all of them." *Maybe even for me,* he added silently. "Unless you want to admit yourself more flawed than I."

She gave a huff of frustration, obviously not wishing to agree to his bargain, yet unwilling to pronounce his character superior. "Very well. Only until Christmas."

"You'll not later disavow this?"

"I always honor my word," she said with icy disdain. "And you shall lose that wager!"

"We shall see, shan't we? As for now, Lady Fairchild, I believe we have a reception to attend."

He held out his arm, not daring to say more, praying that he'd pushed her hard enough to win her acceptance but not so far that he'd alienated her completely.

For a moment she hesitated, moonlight silvering her cheeks, her hair, dancing across the satin of her cloak.

Finally, with an exasperated sigh, she laid her gloved hand on his arm. "I expect I shall live to regret this."

CHAPTER EIGHT

WHAT IDIOCY HAD SHE AGREED to? Jenna wondered as they approached Lady Charlotte Darnell's townhouse. Promising Tony Nelthorpe—*Tony Nelthorpe*—that she would attempt a reform of his sadly soiled character?

It would have made more sense to follow her vague longings and throw herself into the Serpentine.

Still, as the distraught widow had accused, she had been the means of saving Nelthorpe's roguish skin. If she could manage to transform him into a more acceptable human being, it would in some measure make up for the loss of so many good and valiant men on the field at Waterloo.

She had no other worthy activity to occupy her time.

Though she was by no means sure she could accomplish that, she had little fear that Nelthorpe would succeed in seducing her. Even were her fingers too numb to feel, there would be no frisson of attraction passing between them, she told herself, glancing at her hand on his arm.

None she could not control, she amended with more honesty. She'd been an innocent when she'd first encountered him in Spain. Ignorant of why he affected her so strongly, knowing only that he made her uncomfortable.

With the benefit of age and experience, she quickly recognized the reason behind the heightened awareness that seemed to telegraph between the two of them...the prickling of her skin under his gaze...the flutter in her gut.

So Anthony Nelthorpe inspired her to lust. He was a very handsome man, perhaps more attractive than ever now that suffering had worn the edge off his once-omnipresent arrogance. But she could control her baser impulses.

Unlike Anthony Nelthorpe, she thought with a sniff.

Before she could think further on it, Nelthorpe ushered her through the door of their hostess's house.

Lady Charlotte exclaimed with delight when she spotted them, giving Jenna a hug for braving the cold night to attend the party. Not until they continued into the room and Jenna felt the speculative gaze of Lady Charlotte's friend Lord Riverton follow her and Nelthorpe, did it occur to her to wonder how members of the ton—other than the fortune-hunting wife seekers she wished to discourage—might view her association with Nelthorpe.

She raised her chin a notch. Too late to worry about that. Besides, without Garrett's child to consider, what did she care for the approval of the ton?

A deep voice in her ear, however, shattered that bravado. "Jenna, how good to see you!"

Trying not to appear too hasty, Jenna released Nelthorpe's arm and turned to the man who'd hailed her. "Harry! How wonderful to see you, too!"

"What, I'm offered a hand? What about a hug?" Captain "Heedless" Harry Hartwell, one of her father's former lieutenants and longtime friend, demanded.

Without further thought she threw herself into his embrace. Not for almost six lonely months had she felt the comfort of a strong, caring man's arms around her. Her chest tightened and tears pricked at her eyes.

Gently Harry set her back on her feet, his clear blue eyes regarding her with sympathy and affection. "I was so sorry to hear of your loss—both of them. I've been in Vienna, helping to prepare for the Duke. The delegation returns there shortly, but if there is anything I can do..."

I will not cry, she told herself, taking a deep, gasping breath. "No. But thank you for offering."

The captain turned to the viscount. "Out of uniform now, I see, Nelthorpe. 'Twas quite a beating the Royals took below Mont St. Jean. Pleased to see you're looking better than when I visited you in hospital."

Nelthorpe bowed. "Thank you, Captain. I'm pleased to be getting around better."

A little frisson of shame warmed Jenna's face. Apparently *Harry,* good officer that he was, hadn't forgotten his former company-mate after the battle.

"Confounded the sawbones who declared you'd never walk again, I see. Must have required tremendous effort."

Nelthorpe nodded, his cheeks reddening slightly. "I exist to be contrary, I suppose."

"Jenna, what did I hear about your accident?" Harry said, turning to her. "That *you* fell from your horse?"

"Supposedly, though that blow to the head knocked any memory of it clear out of mind. I had borrowed the mount, my usual horse having thrown a shoe. Aunt Hetty seldom rides the mare, who is a real plodder, but with one nasty habit—she detests riding crops. The head groom neglected to mention it to me, so once in the park, when I urged her to greater speed..."

"A gross omission by the head groom!" Harry observed with a frown. "He should certainly have warned you if you'd not ridden that horse before."

"So my cousin thought. I understand he flew into a rage and turned the man off without a character."

"As well he should have. Come, let's get some refreshments and you can tell me what you plan next. Nelthorpe, good to see you."

The two men bowed, and Harry led her off.

Not wishing to confess to Harry her ridiculous bargain with the viscount, after accepting the wine he brought her, she said, "I...I'm not sure what I intend to do."

"Should I renew the offer I made at Badajoz?"

Jenna laughed, as he'd surely intended. "When you coerced all Papa's officers to offer yourselves to your late colonel's daughter, that she might marry one of you and remain with the army after Papa died?"

But her momentary humor was snuffed out by recalling 'twas Garrett, the serious, commanding brigade major, who'd won her hand on that occasion. Who, after convincing her he'd come to reciprocate the love she'd long cherished for him, brought her the greatest happiness she'd ever known.

And the greatest sorrow.

"I'm not the regimental colors, to be caught up from one falling hand and passed to another," she whispered.

"I didn't mean it like that! How can you even think to doubt how much I admire and respect—"

"I'm sorry," she broke in. "I know what you meant."

The blue eyes he fixed on her were grave. "I may have spoken of it jestingly, but I'm entirely serious about that offer, Jenna. I *would* be honored if you'd consent to be my wife. We've been friends for years, and what could be a firmer basis for marriage than that?"

Spoken like a man who has never been in love, she thought, both touched and rueful. How could she put into words, for one who obviously had no idea of it, the depth of contentment and breadth of rapture possible in a union between a man and woman who not only liked, but loved one another? A dimension so much richer, so far beyond friendship she could not begin to describe it.

And so did not attempt to.

"You only ask because you know I will refuse," she parried. "I am honored, but...I cannot accept."

He nodded, taking the refusal with a good grace which confirmed that opinion. "Remember, though, I am yours whenever you wish, Jenna. You have but to send for me."

"What I wish is that one day you will meet a lady who will not just win your esteem, but conquer your whole heart. When you do, I doubt you'll wait to be sent for. I expect you'll sweep her up and carry her away!"

"Perhaps," he said, grinning. "Not planning on being carried off yourself, are you?" He nodded toward the corner of the room.

Where, she discovered, Nelthorpe stood—watching them.

Jenna felt her face heat. "By Nelthorpe? I hardly think so!"

"He's not such a bad fellow now," Harry said. "No Garrett, of course, but how many men are? We didn't see him much after his transfer into the Royals, but I hear he turned out to be a rather good officer. Cautious, prudent, careful of his men. His troopers respected him."

"Papa always said that was the best measure of a soldier," Jenna said, surprised and impressed. Apparently Nelthorpe *had* changed from the bored aristocrat who'd once tried to take advantage of her. Though, she thought, remembering his kiss on the bridge, there was still plenty of rogue left in him.

"If you choose to divert yourself with him, you will come to no harm. Whatever makes you happy, Jenna."

With greater difficulty this time, Jenna stemmed the tears that seemed ever-threatening. "Thank you, Harry. I appreciate that more than you could know. But now, I believe I must find the ladies' withdrawing room."

He tossed down the last of his wine and took her glass. "I'll escort you out."

After promising to write, Jenna left him—and Nelthorpe, who seemed to be shadowing her—in the hall and searched out the ladies' room.

Meeting Harry had been a comfort—but her memories of him were so irretrievably bound up with those of Papa and Garrett that she could not see Harry, could not reminisce about their shared past, without inevitably being ambushed again by her grief over the dear ones she'd loved and lost.

Marrying Harry would not be the right solution to fill the cavern of emptiness that loomed before her, she told herself as she fixed an errant curl. Though for the next several weeks, she had a task, however ludicrous. She'd given Nelthorpe her word.

Jenna was about to depart when a tall, strikingly beautiful blond woman glided into the room. "Lady Fairchild," the lady said in a soft, breathy voice. "So good to see you out again after your sad accident. You remember me, I trust? Lucinda Blaine?"

As if she would ever forget the Lovely Lucinda, the woman whose image had been branded on her brain the moment she'd first glimpsed the miniature Garrett had carried with him until practically the day he'd proposed to Jenna. The portrait of the fiancée who'd broken her engagement—and Garrett's heart—to marry the Earl of Doone.

"Yes, I remember you, Countess," she said at last.

The beauty sank gracefully into the chair beside Jenna's. "I'm sorry I was not able to pay my respects at Garrett's service last month, but my poor nerves would just not support it!" She glanced at Jenna through her impossibly long lashes. "I suppose you understand."

"Does your husband?" Jenna asked.

The countess shrugged. "Oh, Doone? He knew when he married me that I really loved Garrett. If only Papa hadn't forced the match on me!"

From what Jenna had heard around the regiment, it hadn't been Lucinda's papa who had urged her to cry off when a wealthy and aging earl became besotted with the Season's reigning Diamond. "Indeed," Jenna said at last.

The countess sighed. "So ironic, isn't it? If only I had convinced my father to let us marry, Garrett would eventually have come into the title Papa wanted for me."

A pleasant fiction, Jenna thought acidly. But having had enough of the woman's distorted recollections, she said, "Such observations do no honor to either your husband or mine, Lady Doone. Pray, refrain from any further."

The beauty's eyes flashed. "You might not wish to hear me, but I will not be silent! You stole Garrett—"

"Stole!" Jenna interrupted incredulously. "Are you forgetting the small matter of your having already married another man?"

"Do you really think," the beauty said, looking at Jenna with contempt, "that Garrett would have married *you,* had you not somehow managed to compromise him? There could be no other reason—not when we still loved each other!"

When she'd first met Garrett in Spain, he'd been still obsessed with the beautiful, spoiled girl who'd betrayed him. But over the months, she'd watched him struggle out of her grasp. By the time circumstances pressed Jenna to marry, he'd been able to offer her his whole heart.

Hadn't he?

Anger shook her that this woman who had wounded Garrett so deeply could cause her even an instant's doubt.

"I don't believe there is any further point to this conversation. Good evening, Lady Doone."

As she tried to walk past, the countess grabbed her wrist. "Garrett visited me last March when he was back in England gathering troops for the Duke, you know. We had a long, private, quite *satisfying* visit."

Once again, the acid of doubt burned into Jenna. She and Garrett *had* been in London last March. And Garrett had been absent for hours, sometimes days, occupied with the business of organizing Wellington's army.

Might he have stopped to see Lucinda Blaine?

"So, Lady Fairchild," the countess continued, triumph in her gaze, "content yourself with his name and title, but after the loss of his child, you now have even less of Garrett that I do. For *I* know he died still loving *me.*"

Whether the countess's words held any truth or not, Jenna flinched at that blow to a wound still so raw. Rage erupted, so vast it required every ounce of her soldier's training to resist the urge to call Lady Doone the bitch she was and slap a handprint into that perfect cheek.

After a moment's inner struggle, Jenna plucked the beauty's hand from her arm. "Dear Countess, you should consult a physician. I fear you suffer serious delusions."

Head held high, Jenna stalked out of the room and down the hall, agitation rendering her so oblivious, she collided with a tall object.

Which turned out to be Anthony Nelthorpe.

For an instant they were both in danger of falling. "Jenna!" he exclaimed, steadying her as he recovered his own balance. "Did a storm out of the Irish Sea blow you down the hallway?"

Jenna's eyes focused on the drawing room behind Nelthorpe, filled with far too few Harries and far too many contemporaries—and perhaps friends—of the countess.

Into how many ears had the Lovely Lucinda whispered her sly allegations? How many ladies in splendid gowns would snigger behind their fans as Jenna walked by?

The rich widow…whose husband died pining for another man's wife.

The Jenna of last spring would have faced them down. But as her fury receded, she simply didn't have the energy.

"Take me home," she said to Nelthorpe.

Eyes widening in surprise, he glanced behind himself and back, as if wondering to whom she'd addressed that order. "Me? Now?"

"Please."

Speculation colored his gaze, but he asked her none of the questions that must be crowding his mind. "I'll summon your carriage immediately."

Relieved beyond words to escape, Jenna latched on to the arm he offered and let him lead her away.

EARLY THE FOLLOWING MORNING, rather than take his usual ride to the park, Tony directed Pax toward the City. A few days ago Ned Hastings had dropped by the hell where Tony was currently plying his gambler's trade, inviting him to an informal breakfast with Banker Harris.

Reluctantly bowing to necessity, Tony had agreed. Delaying wouldn't sweeten the bitterness or humiliation of having to barter himself in marriage. Since he'd been able to envision no other way to avoid that fate and still salvage his estate, best to embrace the unpalatable solution before his luck with the pasteboards ran out.

Having forced himself to deal with duty, as he rode to meet Ned, Tony allowed his mind to linger on the much more pleasant memory of how Jenna Fairchild had felt in his arms after they collided in the hallway last night. How surprised and gratified he'd been that she'd trusted him enough to ask for his escort home.

After that tantalizing taste of closeness, however, she

retreated from him again, enveloping herself in a cocoon of aloofness that did not invite approach.

Actually, he ought to be relieved she'd been too preoccupied to converse in the carriage. With her seated close enough that her skirts brushed his boots and her hands on the seat nearly touched his own, he'd been far too aware of her to have summoned his usual banter.

Lean but a short distance and he'd felt the softness of her breath upon his face. The warmth and scent of her so close, not close enough, made his mind stutter and his senses giddy. He let himself imagine that he'd dared lean closer still, until he captured the softness of her lips…

"Tony! Over here!"

Ned's halloo jerked him from erotic imaginings back to the prosaic bustle of the early-morning street. Relegating thoughts of Jenna Fairchild to the back of his mind, he turned his attention to the task ahead.

The house to which Ned guided him dwarfed in size, splendor and elegant furnishings that of the Nelthorpe dwelling on North Audley Street. The elder Mr. Harris's banking business was apparently thriving indeed.

Harris welcomed them and invited the newcomers to fill their plates. Conversation during the meal ranged from the status of Europe now being debated by the Congress of Vienna to the current values in the investment market to the Whig versus Tory stands in Parliament. Tony ended the meal impressed with the shrewdness and depth of knowledge of the elder Mr. Harris.

Not by luck or accident had this man made his fortune.

After they finished the meal, Harris's son invited Ned to inspect the glass house they'd installed to shelter their fruit trees, leaving Tony alone with his father. As soon as the two exited, Harris said, "My son tells me you are in need of a well-dowered bride."

Surprised the banker had proceeded so bluntly to the

point, Tony swallowed a scalding mouthful of coffee. There being no point in evading the issue, once he could talk again, he said simply, "Yes."

"What have you besides your aristocratic birth to recommend you? Since, given your reputation, your family name alone is little enough."

Once Tony might have lashed out at a social inferior who dared address him thus. His father would surely have done so today. But two and a half years of living in the face of death had taught him to strip matters to their essential truths.

He couldn't argue with this one.

Even so, chagrin and anger heated his face as he rose to his feet. "Then I expect there is no further point to this interview. Thank you for your hospitality."

"Sit back down, if you please," Mr. Harris said. "I understand pride is a luxury you can no longer afford."

Tony made him a bow. "Sometimes, sir, pride is all a man has left." As ramrod straight as if passing in review on the parade field, Tony limped toward the door.

Slowed by furious despair and the still-considerable task of walking rigidly upright, Tony made it only halfway across the room before his host caught up with him.

"Nay, my lord, please stay. I didn't mean to insult you, but I did need to take your measure."

Convinced now that coming here had been a mistake, Tony tried to edge toward the door. "Indeed?"

"You came here to ask a favor of me, accepted the hospitality of my table. Do you not owe me at least remaining until I've finished saying what I wish to say?"

Lips tight, Tony nodded and limped back to his chair. Hopefully Harris would frame his lecture on propriety into a monologue—and keep it short. Tony might be obliged to listen, but for the price of a damned breakfast he had no intention of groveling.

"First, let me say that had you argued with my statement, or admitted its truth amid a profusion of promises to reform, I should have shown you the door. But a man who can face unpleasant truths and retain his dignity is a man who *does* possess something worth bargaining over. Do you still wish to leave, or shall I continue?"

Perhaps he should hear the man out. "Continue."

"As you might imagine, testimonials to the profligacy of your character before you left England were easy to obtain and, pray excuse me, but your father's deficiencies are well-known. My son tells me, however, that you were always fair and mindful of the men in your charge. What do you hope to achieve, should you manage to wed an heiress?"

"I mean to redeem my family's debt, repair my estates and restore their ability to produce income."

"And your reputation?"

Tony sighed. "Redeeming that may not be possible."

"I expect much is possible for a man of grit and determination. I also know from observing my own son how profound a change can be wrought by army service. A change—" Harris gestured to Tony's leg "—far deeper than the merely physical.

"So I made some inquiries," Harris continued. "Since your return, you've visited your club but twice and incurred neither gaming losses or further debts with tradesmen. Such funds as you've won have been used to pay down your accounts with several merchants. And though you have visited a gaming house nearly every night, you play carefully—and virtually sober. As if," he said with a penetrating glance, "you embarked upon gaming as a means of earning an income. Am I right so far?"

Having made so extensive an inquiry, Harris must have realized that Tony did in fact game to survive. Embarrassed nonetheless, he nodded stiffly.

"Am I also correct in assuming that, given your preference, you would rather not embrace matrimony as a means of solving your financial difficulties?"

Tony laughed shortly. "You may."

"Without wishing to boast, I allow that I wield a good deal of authority among the financial community—a sort of 'Wellington of the Cits,' you might say. I was able to obtain a detailed list of your family's financial holdings at all the firms which have...enjoyed your father's custom."

"Then you know how bad the situation is," Tony said.

Mr. Harris nodded. "Indeed. Bad enough that the investors involved were happy to sell me the paper they held at a handsome discount. I now own all the outstanding obligations of the Nelthorpe family."

Dread curdled the breakfast in his stomach as Tony realized the implications. With interest payments so long in arrears and the total sum of the debts so vast, Harris could easily demand an initial payment of overdue interest far greater than the modest amount Tony had amassed. And if Tony were unable to come up with the sum demanded, Harris could foreclose.

On everything.

Total ruin. Debtor's prison. For a moment Tony's vision blurred and the room began to spin.

Fighting off the dizziness, he forced himself to focus on the banker's face. "What do you intend to do about it?"

To his surprise, Harris smiled. "I didn't amass my fortune by calling in bad debts, if that is what you fear. I have instead rather a good record of profiting on investments that, to others, seemed a bit risky. So I have a proposal for you." Once again, Harris gestured to a chair. "Sit down, won't you?"

Even his good knee now going suddenly rubbery, Tony sank back into his seat.

"I assume your solicitor has told you the total amount of the debt your father accumulated. What interests me, besides that rather amazing sum, is that the earl recently signed an authorization permitting you to handle the family's finances. Quite frankly, were I dealing with your father, I should foreclose and be done with it. But you, my lord, have shown a different mettle. And so I now propose to offer you a mortgage on the remaining assets you possess that are not currently encumbered, the money obtained to be invested in a variety of funds. The return on these—which, by the way, I expect to be considerable—I shall put toward repaying the other outstanding debts, minus a small allowance for your living expenses."

"Despite the amount already owed, you would offer us—another mortgage?" Tony said, unsure he'd heard correctly.

Harris shrugged. "An audacious gamble, to be sure. But if the investments prosper as I expect, *you* will slowly earn your way back to solvency, while *I* will recoup funds on mortgages that otherwise had no hope of ever being redeemed. Of course, if the investments do poorly, I shall forfeit only a modest additional sum, whereas you would lose all you have. But," he said with a smile, "I have every expectation of growing richer. And proceeding in this manner allows you to eventually get out of debt—without having to sell your name in marriage."

For a moment, the image of Jenna Fairchild flashed into his head. "What do you wish me to do?"

Harris raised his eyebrows. "No questions?"

"Mr. Harris, we both know I am no businessman. As you trust to my military performance as a testament of my character, I trust to your son's as an evidence of yours. In any event,'' Tony said with a wry grimace, ''I haven't many options, do I? Have we a bargain, then?''

''We do,'' Mr. Harris confirmed. ''Stop by my office later and my assistant will go over the particulars. With the small living allowance you'll be granted, I suggest you abandon your gaming efforts and concentrate on learning to manage your properties. For advice on which, I refer you to your estate agent. Given what I've seen of the estate books, he's a wizard at producing much from very little.''

Tony knew he wouldn't be able to fully comprehend this unexpected shift in his circumstances until the shock had worn off—and he'd been able to review the details with Harris's assistant. But the crushing burden that had weighed on him from the moment his foot touched English soil eased, making him feel suddenly almost euphoric.

He extended his hand. ''How can I ever thank you?''

''Prove I wasn't wrong to wager on you.''

Buoyed by the first hopeful news he'd received since his return home, as he walked out Tony was suddenly struck by the contrast between the home of the banker, a man his father would dismiss as a glorified clerk far beneath an earl's notice, and his own dilapidated and dirty dwelling.

Though he appreciated his overworked staff's efforts to keep the few rooms he occupied—his chamber, the library, and the breakfast room—presentable, the rest of the house remained in desperate need of cleaning, to say nothing of painting and repairs.

A maid's salary couldn't be much. Perhaps the services of a carpenter and painter might also be obtained for a reasonable fee—surely less than it had cost to keep one of his father's hunters in feed—before he'd been forced to sell them all, of course.

He had to smile at the look of astonishment that would doubtless cross the earl's face, should he discover his son planned to spend his winnings not on women, gaming or wine, but on cleaning and repairs.

Papa, I have lived in dirt and disorder long enough. I will not do so any longer in my own home.

Perhaps, he thought with a dawning sense of hope, Anthony Nelthorpe might salvage the family honor after all.

CHAPTER NINE

SO LOST IN REFLECTION WAS Tony that it wasn't until he noticed he was now riding down a narrow, dead-end street that he realized he must have taken a wrong turn. A street, he realized, suddenly jolted back to the present, in what appeared to be a most unsavory neighborhood.

Evidently Pax didn't find the surroundings to his liking either, for the gelding's ears pricked up and he danced and pulled at the bridle.

Tony approved his mount's obvious desire to vacate the area. No street in London was safe at night, but Tony knew that in a place like this, one might have his watch lifted—or his head bashed in—at any hour of the day.

Anger at his carelessness in wandering here alone sharpened the sixth sense instilled by years of war. Feeling more than seeing the shadows of several men approaching, he tightened his grip on the reins and prepared to give Pax his head. Weaponless but for his whip and with his weak knee, he'd be in a precarious position should anyone manage to unhorse him.

Even as that thought occurred, sending a jolt of alarm through him, a rough hand grabbed at his boot.

Jerking his foot away, Tony brought his whip down hard. His mount screamed and reared up, the menace of his iron-shod hooves sending two of the shadows fleeing. Tony swiveled, about to bring the whip down again on the man who'd grabbed his boot when a feeble glint caught his eye.

A glint, Tony realized, checking the blow, from what had once been gold lace...on a sleeve that bore a sergeant's chevrons.

The soldier staggered backward, dirty hands raised to protect his head. "Lemme go! Didn't mean ye no harm!"

"Ten-hut, Sergeant!" Tony barked.

Reacting instinctively to the command, the soldier snapped upright, swaying slightly. "Aye, sir!"

Wrinkling his nose against the strong odor of gin and sweat, Tony inspected the tattered, grime-faded uniform. "Dragoon, aren't you? Which unit?"

"Sergeant Anston of the 16th, sir!"

"Captain Nelthorpe of the Royals. What are you doing, disgracing that uniform by accosting passersby like some common footpad? Wellington would have you strung up!"

"Aye, I reckon Old Hookey would, sir. But he don't need us no more. No place for us back home neither, and a man's gotta eat."

"True, but all thievery will get you is Newgate or a prison hulk." Falling back into the familiar habit of command, Tony assessed what he could do for this particular trooper. "Follow me home, Sergeant," he said after a moment. "I'll see you get a hot meal. Then we'll discuss finding work that won't end up getting you transported."

"Thank'ee, sir, but I can't leave. Got a family of sorts what depends on me. Not me own wife, ya see, but there's a clutch of soldiers' widows and their brats here, all with no place else ta go. I help 'em out, best I can."

"When you're not full of blue ruin?" Tony asked as he bent his mind to this new complication.

"Please, m'lord, let 'im go!" A thin woman clutching a babe wrapped in rags skittered from behind one of the doorways. "He didn't mean yer worship no harm!"

"Don't ye worry yerself, Peggy," the sergeant said. "The cap'n here be only speaking with me."

At his words of reassurance, an urchin darted out of the doorway. "Spare me a penny, yer worship?"

Ruefully Tony inspected the skinny child who gazed up at him with a gap-toothed smile, one hopeful hand extended. "How many more of these are there?" he asked the trooper.

"There's two widows and seven young'ins here," the sergeant said. "Near a dozen folk the next street over."

Tony looked from the tattered sergeant to the wraith-thin woman to the grimy, barefooted urchin admiring Pax from a respectful distance. To these half-starved scare-crows, he must look like a prince.

Half-starved scarecrows who had followed their men-folk across a harsh land from battle to desperate battle. Men who had fought, bled and suffered for home and country.

'Twas unconscionable that this soldier and these soldiers' kin had been reduced to accosting the unwary and begging pennies from strangers.

Rage welling up, Tony snatched some coins from his waistcoat pocket and thrust them at the sergeant. "Take these for now, Anston. I shall bring more later."

The sergeant seized the coins and pocketed them. "Lord, Cap'n, don't be flashing yer blunt on this street! There's them what would cut yer throat fer a pence!"

Suddenly an idea occurred. "Can you paint?" Tony asked the sergeant.

The man blinked at him. "Ye mean—houses?"

"Yes."

The sergeant scratched his head. "Never done none, but I reckon I could, Cap'n."

"Then come round to North Audley Street tomorrow morning. There'll be work and coins for doing it."

"Aye, sir, I will. And thank ye, sir."

"No thanks necessary. King and country, eh?"

The sergeant saluted. "King and country, sir! Now, let me lead ye out afore some cutpurse fancies yer horse!"

As he rode off, he had to smile, imagining the look of horror on Carstairs's face when the grimy sergeant appeared on their doorstep. But his humor soon faded.

'Twas an outrage that men who had answered their country's call and the families who depended on them had been cast aside and forgotten like refuse in that alley gutter. Reduced to thievery, begging—or worse, Tony thought, recalling the babe the woman held to her chest.

He would scrape together as much as he could spare to help this small group, but his meager earnings would not stretch to maintaining nearly two dozen folk. Furious about the situation and his own helplessness, he rode back to the comfortable streets of Mayfair. But as his anger cooled, a potential solution occurred.

His own resources were limited. But if he could find words eloquent enough to describe their plight, perhaps he could persuade Jenna to intervene. Having spent much of her life tending those among her father's regiments who'd been sick, wounded or destitute, surely she would be moved to compassion by their urgent need.

As soon as he cleaned off the dust of his encounter with the sergeant, he would call on her.

JUST BEFORE LUNCHEON, Jenna stared sightlessly over her book in the sitting room that adjoined her chamber, trying to shake off the lethargy into which she'd fallen since returning home last night.

Her mind kept replaying her odd encounters with Anthony Nelthorpe. Not sure whether she meant to honor the ridiculous bargain he'd forced on her in the park, she'd planned to avoid him the rest of the evening—and yet paradoxically, when she'd felt as if she'd run mad if she didn't escape Lady Charlotte's reception, she'd been enormously relieved to stumble across him again.

He'd lived up to her instinctive trust, seeing her home in merciful silence, then bidding her good-night.

It hadn't been one.

Unhappy dreams, no doubt inspired by the poisonous allegations uttered by the Blaine woman, had troubled her rest. Dropping her book with a thump, she shook her head. She simply mustn't allow the woman's claims to upset her. In her heart, she didn't truly believe them. And besides, with the only other witness to the supposed event long dead, she would never be able to determine whether the countess's assertions were true or not.

Lucinda Blaine was a vain, frustrated beauty who could not bear to believe her former love had found someone to replace her, Jenna told herself. Perhaps she was repenting her decision to choose wealth and title over youth and affection—if she had, in fact, ever loved Garrett.

Jenna ought to dismiss the incident from her mind—if only she could remove that last tiny splinter of doubt.

A rap at the door interrupted her troubling reflections. Instead of Sancha, Jenna found Lane Fairchild upon the threshold, smiling at her.

"May I come in? I feared, when I learned you'd requested a tray here rather than taking your meal below, that you might have overtired yourself last night."

"No, I'm perfectly fine." Wondering why he felt it necessary to track her down in her private sitting room, Jenna waved him to a chair.

"You did leave Lady Charlotte's party rather abruptly. I'd scarcely arrived when I saw you departing. I wish I had had time to make my presence known, that you might have requested *my* escort home."

He must have seen her with Nelthorpe. Did he also

know what had passed between them at Badajoz? Jenna felt her face coloring. "That is kind of you, cousin, but as you can see, I arrived back safely."

"For which I can only be profoundly grateful!" He hesitated, then continued, "Jenna, I hope you will not think I am presuming to try to choose your friends, but I strongly advise you to avoid Lord Nelthorpe.

"Please—" he held up a hand to forestall her protest "—hear me out. I understand that Viscount Nelthorpe apparently served with honor in the army. However, before he put on regimentals, he was known to be a womanizer and a fortune hunter. You, who have spent your life around soldiers like your father and Garrett, might not realize that a uniform can hide a badly flawed character."

Touched by his chivalry, but also a bit annoyed, Jenna said, "Cousin, I am not so naive that I do not realize the army contains rascals as well as gentlemen."

"Perhaps not," he conceded, "but your goodness leads you to expect it in others, and your recent...losses may cloud your judgment. Nelthorpe might take advantage."

Relieved that her cousin evidently *didn't* know what had happened between herself and Nelthorpe, Jenna hid a smile. Lane's warning came several years too late.

"I appreciate your concern, but I believe it groundless. After three years of wartime service, Lord Nelthorpe is most assuredly no longer the same man he was when he left England."

"One would hope his character has improved," Lane said. "Though I doubt such a man ever fully reforms."

She had doubts about that herself. "Perhaps not. Still, I do not believe Lord Nelthorpe will harm me."

Listening to the words she'd just spoken, Jenna suppressed a laugh. To be again defending Anthony Nelthorpe! Yet she realized she truly believed what she'd said—had believed it before Harry vouched for him, despite the taunt of seduction with which he'd sealed their wager.

"You may be right," Fairchild was saying. "But Nelthorpe's reputation is still tarnished enough that being seen with him cannot but reflect poorly on your own. I understand he's looking for a rich Cit's daughter to marry." Fairchild sniffed. "She'll have to be wealthy indeed to keep Nelthorpe and his father—who is even more profligate than the son—in liquor and harlots."

So Nelthorpe was hunting a wife? she thought in surprise. Though she shouldn't be. How else was an aristocrat with no profession to repair his fortune?

Obviously misreading that emotion, Lane patted her hand. "I didn't mean to distress you! I speak only from the sincerest desire to protect you. Indeed, though I realize 'tis far too soon to mention such things, I hope that at some future time, you may grant me the privilege of caring for you—permanently."

There could be no mistaking his inference. Jenna looked away, uncertain how to respond. Since arriving in London, she'd noticed subtle things—a warmth of tone, a touch here, a guiding hand at her elbow there—that indicated Fairchild might be coming to view her in a warmer light. She'd been telling herself she was reading too much into what were only gallant gestures.

Apparently her instincts had been correct.

Best to put the matter firmly to rest. "I am, of course, honored," she said, choosing her words with care. "But much as I esteem you, I do not foresee developing between us more than a...cousinly affection."

"No more talk of it now," he said with a sweep of his hand, as if brushing aside the words—and her protest? "For the immediate future, I hope you will continue to reside at Fairchild House."

"Thank you. I expect I shall stay until the holidays at least." She already knew that residing permanently with the Fairchild clan—and in the midst of the ton—was *not* what she wanted. But she'd promised Nelthorpe to remain until Christmas, and she would honor her word.

"Excellent!" Fairchild said. "Since you will be with us indefinitely, I'm afraid I must pass along another warning. Please be...careful in your dealings with Bayard."

"With Bayard?" she echoed. "Careful in what way?"

"One not well acquainted with him might think him mild-mannered, if somewhat rough-spoken. That is not always the case, regrettably. Though he is indifferent to estate matters not related to his scientific explorations," Lane's voice took on an aggrieved note, "any person he perceives to interfere with those causes him to become extremely agitated. A few months ago, one of the footmen moved some of Bayard's chemicals in order to fetch some port from the wine cellar. Bayard flew into a rage and flung the man against the wall, breaking his arm."

"Bayard hurt someone?" she gasped, unable to credit her husband's brusque cousin capable of such violence.

"It seems fantastical, but I'm afraid it's true. I was present when the doctor examined the footman. So I suggest you avoid the area near his laboratory."

Jenna smiled to counter the little shiver that skittered down her backbone. "As I don't expect to be sneaking about the cellars filching your claret, I imagine I shall be safe enough."

"So I should hope!" he replied, returning the smile. "I would caution you to beware of Bayard's valet as well. Were it up to me, I should turn the surly fellow off in an instant. I've often urged that Bayard replace him with someone who could turn him out more in the style befitting a Fairchild! But for some unfathomable reason, Bayard's quite attached to him. And by now," he concluded with a wry shake of his head, "you must be thinking you've stumbled into a household straight out of Bedlam."

"I did think upon first seeing him that Frankston seemed more like a Spanish brigand than a gentleman's gentleman," Jenna said. "Is he as dangerous?"

"I'm sure he is not! His conduct does not approach the standards *I* would require of a servant at Fairchild House, but I did not mean to imply he might threaten anything other than your patience. The man seems to have no notion of the deference he owes to his betters."

"Then I may sleep safely in my bed?" she teased.

"Of course," he replied, his smile fading. "I know you are funning, but your safety is no joking matter. Also, please know that anytime you have need of an escort, I should be honored if you will call on me."

"You are very kind," she murmured. If Nelthorpe were in fact occupied in pursuing a middle-class bride, she might not have to honor the ridiculous bargain they'd made last night. But whether or not the viscount came calling, she didn't wish to encourage Lane—who seemed not at all put off by her little speech about cousinly affection.

He bowed and walked to the door, then hesitated. "Though I have no authority over you, of course, I must admit I should feel easier if you could assure me you did not intend to see Viscount Nelthorpe again."

A knock sounded at the door, followed by Sancha's entry. "*Pardon, señora,*" she said with a curtsy. "But Lord Nelthorpe is here. Shall I tell him you come down?"

"Lady Fairchild is occupied," Lane said.

Jenna threw him a sharp glance. She might appreciate his concern for her welfare, but she wasn't about to let him dictate her actions. Besides, much as she regretted last night's hasty promise, she *had* made it, and if the viscount held her to the bargain, she would honor it.

"Tell Lord Nelthorpe I will be down directly."

After the maid withdrew, she turned to Lane Fairchild, whose lips had pressed together in a disapproving line. "Having escorted me home last night, it is only polite that Nelthorpe call. And only polite that I receive him. Besides, though I appreciate your concern, do me the credit of believing I am capable of managing my own affairs."

The glint in his blue eyes turned decidedly frosty. "If you say so, cousin. I shall not intrude upon you further, then." After a stiff bow, he walked out.

What a charming morning, she thought with a sigh. Cousin Lane was definitely displeased with her.

And Anthony Nelthorpe waited below.

CHAPTER TEN

HAVING RIDDEN HOME as quickly as the congested London streets would allow, it wasn't until he stood in her parlor, a disapproving Sancha dispatched with a message to fetch her mistress, that Tony paused to reconsider his plan.

Despite the protests of his knee, he limped about the room, doubts beginning to assail him.

He'd managed to tease, annoy and cajole a bargain out of Jenna last night, but in the saner light of day, would she choose to honor it? Or, as had happened each time he'd called during her convalescence, would Sancha return to inform him Lady Fairchild could not receive him?

Tony prayed with all the fervency he possessed that she would receive him, though he feared less for her safety now than he had last night, when he'd seen moonlight and desperation reflected in her eyes. More important than the desire, stronger than he cared to admit, to spend time with her, the plight of the displaced soldiers demanded redress.

How could he help them if she repudiated him?

Wexley, St. Ives and others of their ilk were unlikely to care enough to offer a ha'penny, and Ned Hastings had no independent income of his own. Tony could think of no other wealthy acquaintance in London—except Banker Harris. Aside from the fact that he'd be loath to return again, hat in hand and asking for money, would a self-made man like Mr. Harris have any sympathy for unfortunates many in society would judge to be worthless vagrants who should bestir themselves to find honest work?

So what *would* he do if Jenna refused to meet him? Modest as the needs of the former soldiers and their families were, he knew his limited resources wouldn't stretch to meeting them for long.

He paced faster, seared by the same agonizing sense of helplessness that had seized him at Waterloo after the Union Brigade's charge, while he watched his exuberant fellow horsemen, having decimated the French ranks before them, ride recklessly onward, deaf to the recall being sounded by their bugler. Ride on far behind the enemy lines, to the very foot of the French guns. Where, scattered and outnumbered, they were cut to pieces.

Bile rose in his throat and a shudder ran through him. Shaking his mind free of the memory, he forced himself to concentrate on the present.

No French cuirassiers stood between him and the salvation of the little band residing off Thames Street.

Should Jenna fail to appear, he supposed he could write her a letter describing the situation. He was just starting to mentally compose such a note in his head when the lady herself entered the parlor.

"You wished to see me, Lord Nelthorpe?"

For a moment he let his hungry eyes feast on her while the potent force she always exerted over his senses drew him inexorably to her side. "Jenna," he murmured, bending to kiss the fingertips she extended as he inhaled deeply of her scent, savoring the too-brief touch of her skin.

He felt the tension in her hand, as if she wished to jerk it free. Would she honor their bargain? Perhaps he ought to determine that immediately, for if she had come down only to disavow it, he wouldn't get a chance to plead the soldier's case.

Tightening his hold, he kissed her hand again.

This time she did pull away. "When you do that, I wonder at my wisdom in permitting you to call."

She was not going to repudiate him, he thought, relief flooding him. How then to introduce the matter of Sergeant Anston? Deciding he might need more than the few minutes allowed by a morning call to convince her, he said, "Allow me to take you riding. I've a matter I'd like to discuss."

"At least it's not a proposition," she muttered.

He grinned. "See? Already you're exerting a beneficial influence."

"I'd heard you intended to make yourself agreeable to some...bourgeois heiress. Would dancing attendance on me not interfere with those plans?"

Had she cared enough to check on him? Reason damped down his momentary gratification. Probably her kinsman had heard he was gathering information in the City.

"Should you be disappointed if I were?"

She raised an eyebrow. "If you pursue a lady of wealth merely for her fortune, and she chooses to accept you solely for your title, I think you would both be getting what you deserve."

He had to laugh at that. "I must agree. So I am happy to assure you that, for the moment at least, I have managed to escape that fate. Which leaves me free to escort you to routs, musicales, breakfasts and any other activities you choose to attend. During which, you will instruct me on how to behave as a gentleman. Unless," he added, unable to resist the urge to tease, "I can persuade you instead to allow me to act the rogue?"

"We'll tread the path of virtue, to be sure."

"Are you sure?" he asked softly.

She leveled a severe look. "Absolutely."

He heaved a regretful sigh, not entirely for show. "Virtue it shall be, alas. Now, hurry to change, lest we miss more of this lovely day."

"It...it wouldn't be convenient to ride now."

She *was* trying to fob him off. An urgency unconnected with the plight of the soldiers surged through him. Instead of accepting her refusal, he blurted, "Why not?"

"It...I...I'm not dressed for riding," she said, obviously taken aback at his persistence.

"I can wait while you change."

"I wouldn't want to inconvenience you."

"I don't mind waiting."

"Well, I mind making you wait." Her tone aggrieved, she sat back in her chair. Another moment, and she would be ringing for the butler to escort him out.

Abandoning caution, he seized her hand. "Please, Jenna, just this once. When you asked me to go with you last night, I came without question, didn't I?"

Though she pulled her hand free, her defensive posture softened. "Y-yes. And I do thank you for that."

"One ride is all I request. After that, if...if you prefer, I'll not force you to honor our bargain."

She straightened, a martial light gleaming in her eyes. "I wasn't trying to renege on our agreement—foolish though it was! I never break my word. I was merely..."

"Delaying?" he suggested.

A faint color warmed her face. "Perhaps a little."

"Then you'll come with me now?" he asked, trying not to let the eagerness show in his voice.

"It will take me half an hour to change."

"I'll be waiting."

Shaking her head with a wry grimace, as if she weren't

sure what to do about him, she rose. "Half an hour, then. Should you like some sherry? I'll send Manson in."

She was treating him like—a guest. "That would be most kind," Tony said, telling himself it was ridiculous to be pleased over so trivial a detail.

Less than thirty minutes later, they rode into the park, Tony keeping her laughing during their transit with anecdotes about his army life after he'd left her father's regiment. Not until they pulled up their mounts inside the park gates did it occur to him that, given her recent accident, riding neck-or-nothing might no longer appeal.

"Shall it be decorous trot? Or a full-out gallop?"

She seemed to sense his concern. "I don't intend to let that...unhappy event ruin my enjoyment of riding," she replied. "I've few enough pleasures left."

"Ah, that I might remedy that sad situation!"

She gave him a reproving glance. "Such a comment isn't suitably addressed to a lady."

"But would a *true* lady understand my meaning?"

"A lady is merely proper, not stupid," she snapped back. "Now, what was that urgent matter?"

"First, a gallop. Once around the Serpentine. Since your mare is smaller than Pax, I'll give you twenty yards."

She stiffened. "This is my own mount, not a beast borrowed from my cousin's stable. You need not offer me any advantage, sir!"

"Then, my lady, shall we ride?"

A crack of her whip answered him. Grinning, he spurred his gelding in pursuit.

Though Pax had a smooth, ground-eating gait, Jenna's mare was fleeter of foot. In truth, Tony didn't regret being obliged to concede her the lead. Although observing the rhythmic bounce of her trim posterior inevitably led his mind to dwell on another sort of ride which he'd enjoy even more observing at close range.

They rounded the last curve, Jenna several lengths ahead when they reached their starting point. Tony reined in, trying to drag his mind back from the carnal.

"Well and truly bested, were you not, my lord?" she cried, wheeling her mare toward him.

Tony meant to return a teasing reply, but when he looked over at her, his words scattered like green recruits under fire at their first battle.

Laughing, triumphant, her cheeks wind-flushed, even the harsh black hue of her habit couldn't dim the radiance of her face. This was the lighthearted, carefree Jenna who'd first caught his eye as she raced her mount across the Spanish plains, her whole being vibrant with the sheer joy of living—a vibrancy, he now realized, that had been missing when he met her again here in London.

He'd been drawn to that fearless young woman in Spain, further bewitched by the sensuality of the mature woman she'd become. But at this moment, as he watched both those Jennas combine, the force of her stole his breath.

As he gazed at her, exulting in the joy that illumined her face, a falling sensation swept through him and he knew he'd give anything to keep that glow in her eyes.

All too soon it faded. He wanted to cry out in protest at its loss. *And say what—"Let me make you happy?" Steady, Tony, old man,* he told himself.

"Now," she said, bringing her mare into step beside his gelding as they cooled the horses at a walk, "what did you wish to discuss?"

"Coming back from the City this morning, I strayed into a back alley and nearly had my purse stolen—by a former sergeant of Dragoons."

"Surely not a dragoon! Those regiments accept only

volunteers—never conscripts or petty criminals pressed into service."

"True enough, but he was indeed a cavalryman. With the fields he once worked enclosed by the local landowner, he said, he came back to the city and has ended up a sort of protector to several army widows and their children. Apparently they've been surviving by begging at street corners and petty thievery."

"That's dreadful!" she cried. "You...you didn't turn him over to a magistrate, did you?"

"Please, give me more credit than that! And besides," he said with a wry twist of his lip, "I've suffered the pangs of an empty purse myself on occasion."

"Without resorting to thievery, I hope!"

Recalling the castaway stripling of a few nights ago, he laughed shortly. "No, I call it 'gaming.'"

"So what did you do about the sergeant?"

"I gave him what coins I had and an offer of work. But the problem is graver than that, for he told me that in the neighborhood roundabout him are nearly two dozen former soldiers, widows, and orphans in the same situation."

"Two *dozen?*"

"So Sergeant Anston says. I...I haven't the funds to care for so large a group," he confessed, his face heating. Having to make that admission to Jenna, he found, was more humiliating than he anticipated. "I know your father often assisted troopers and their families. So when I cast about for some means to assist them, I thought of you. Some of these might be from the Fighting Fifth, though I don't—"

"It makes no difference which regiment they come from!" she interrupted. "Of course I'll help. 'Tis an outrage, after all they've done to have them return to England and end up starving on the streets of London!"

Hearing her affirm her intention to help eased the anxiety that had weighed him down since he left the City this morning. ''Thank you.''

She waved away his gratitude. ''What do they need? Food and clothing to start with, I should think.''

''Food for certain, warm clothes, and shoes—though I'm not sure the children will wear them.''

''Come, let us return at once. I'll get the kitchen staff started while I call at my bank for funds to purchase the clothing and supplies.'' She paused a moment, frowning. ''Though I may have to battle with Lane's fancy French chef to cook plain, wholesome food.''

''If you order the provisions, my cook will prepare them. Betsy's kind heart will need no persuading.''

''Excellent! Let's get started, then. If the neighborhood is as destitute as you describe, 'twould be best that we not venture there after dark.''

''No, 'tis barely safe in day—'' He stopped as the full meaning of her words penetrated. ''Surely you cannot mean to accompany me when I deliver the supplies?''

Her expression turned frosty. ''Of course I mean to accompany you.''

''A young woman whose dress clearly indicates she is Quality? 'Twould be much too risky! I'll have trouble enough persuading my groom to accompany me.''

She shrugged. ''All the more reason for me to go. I don't require persuasion, and if need be, I can wield a whip or a pistol better than your groom. Once I change into one of the plain gowns I wore on campaign, I will be in no more danger than the females who reside there.''

''Which is quite peril enough!''

''Come now, Captain, I've been in the stews of Bombay and the hovels of the Peninsula, outridden bandits and a contingent of pursuing French cavalry. I'm not afraid of what I might find on any London street. Besides, if I am to decide what sort of funding will be required, I must review the situation myself. A lady's eye is likely to see needs a man would never notice."

"That may be true," he admitted. "Mayhap I should bring a female servant along."

"And should the necessity arise, a female servant would be better able to protect herself than I am?"

He had to concede her that point. "Probably not."

"Most assuredly not!" she corrected. "I have more experience fighting off ambush than anyone you could enlist, save another soldier."

"That may be so, but I still cannot permit it."

She glared. "Do you want my assistance or not?"

He stared at her, torn between the desire to help the unfortunates and the need to protect her. When her implacable gaze did not waver, finally he said, "If your assistance comes at the risk of your person, then no, I no longer request it. I'd best get you home now."

Belligerence fading, she lifted pleading eyes to his. "Please, my lord! I...I've felt so useless since leaving Brussels. This is important, Tony. Please let me help."

Whether it was empathy for a fellow survivor of war now searching for some purpose in life—or the sweet sound of his name on her lips, he found himself weakening. "How could I live with myself if something happened to you?"

Her brilliant smile told him she knew she'd won. "Nothing will. And besides, you shall be right there to protect me. If you refuse to take me, being now aware of the situation, I might have to canvass the city on my own."

"Good Lord, Jenna," he cried, his stomach clenching at the thought, "promise me you will do nothing of the sort!"

"I think I shall send for Evers—Papa's batman, you'll

remember—to conduct the search. Besides,'' she said, wrinkling her brow as she set her horse in motion, ''though providing food and clothing is a beginning, these people need more than a temporary helping hand. They need homes and jobs. Should not Parliament do something about it?''

Tony set his horse to match her mare's pace. ''When the issue was brought up before Parliament, I understand, the Tories vociferously denounced the very notion of awarding pensions or provisions to veterans.''

''Could you not stand up and argue for them?''

'''Tis my father who holds a seat, not I—one I don't believe he's ever occupied.'' He laughed shortly. ''I doubt he could find his way to Parliament, unless the building also shelters either a gaming house or a brothel.''

She cast him a thoughtful glance, no doubt hearing the bitterness in his words. ''Then we must do all we can. Thank goodness it's barely noon! We should be able to get dinner cooked and delivered before dark.''

''So you are set upon going with me?''

''With you or—'' her eyes took on a wicked gleam ''—without you. The 'going' is not open to question.''

''If anything untoward happens to either of us,'' he said, torn between admiration and exasperation, ''I shall never forgive you!''

She gave him an upward look through her lashes that was almost—provocative. ''Then I suppose we shall just have to stay very close and keep each other safe, won't we?''

Staying very close—now that was a directive he'd have no trouble obeying. ''While dinner is being prepared, I'll summon the sergeant and some of his mates to provide an escort for when we return with the provisions.''

''Famous,'' she said, nodding. ''I begin to believe that we might get on well together after all.''

Spirits soaring at the idea of being able to help the soldiers—and keep Jenna near him, he couldn't help giving her a wicked grin. "Oh, I certainly hope so."

"Rogue!" she admonished without heat. His spirits rose higher. Perhaps he might earn her esteem after all.

As they neared the park gates, Tony spied two figures on horseback emerging from Rotten Row. Apparently spotting them as well, the couple halted. The gentleman leaned close to the lady, as if conferring with her—or trying to steal a kiss—and then rode off in the opposite direction, while the lady proceeded toward them.

The ton didn't ride in the park until much later. Had they stumbled upon a tryst? Tony wondered with a smile.

They reached the gate at the same time as the lady. Perhaps Jenna hadn't seen her, for it seemed as if she would continue through without acknowledging the woman.

"Why, it's Lady Fairchild, isn't it?" the rider called, guiding her horse to block Jenna's path.

Not until the lady turned in the saddle toward Tony did he recognize her: Lucinda Blaine, Countess of Doone.

CHAPTER ELEVEN

"LORD NELTHORPE! How nice to see you," the lady cooed.

"A pleasure to see you again, too, Countess." Out of the alcoholic fog of the past, Tony recalled having followed his friends in pursuing the "Lovely Lucinda" after her marriage to a very rich earl. Apparently the thrill of snaring the old man's money and title hadn't charmed the Beauty for long, for as a bride of several months, she'd already been willing to offer him kisses—and the promise of more, though he'd had to flee London before he'd been able to try his luck redeeming them.

Lady Doone waved a graceful hand. "How formal you've become! You used to call me 'Lucinda.'" She fluttered her lashes at him, an intimation of intimacy thick in the air.

Though Tony found it annoying that she'd make so blatant a gesture in front of Jenna, he also knew that Lucinda Blaine, acclaimed as one of the Diamonds of the ton since her debut season, was unable to resist trying to entice any gentleman she encountered. Probably because she'd married an old dried stick a generation her senior.

Though he had no desire to add his name to the list of cisebos she kept dangling, he didn't mind flirting with this undeniably beautiful woman—especially if it showed Jenna that *some* women still found him attractive.

"Countess, I should not dare be so familiar with a lady of such high rank, even if she were an...old friend."

She laughed, evidently pleased with the flattery. "But one never forgets one's friends. One's dearest, most *intimate* friends. Do you not agree, Lady Fairchild?"

"I'm sure you have much more experience in that than I," Jenna replied, her voice decidedly frosty.

Given that before her marriage to the earl, the countess had been engaged to Garrett Fairchild, Tony could understand Jenna's reserve. In fact, he recalled, when Tony had joined the Fighting Fifth in Spain, Garrett had still been pining over Lucinda's defection.

"Oh, Lady Fairchild, I expect we have more shared... experience than you would like to think," Lady Doone said. "Tony, I'd heard you'd finally returned from Brussels. In company with Lady Fairchild, perhaps?"

After Lady Doone's sly jab at Jenna, whatever mild inclination Tony had to bandy words with her evaporated. And since Lucinda Blaine was not only a hopeless flirt, but the worst of gossips, he'd better squelch the potential rumor of her second comment before it could begin.

"Alas, no...unfortunately for me. I didn't meet her again until the memorial service for Colonel Fairchild."

"Poor, dear Garrett!" The countess sighed. "To have lost him just one battle away from having him return to us for good! We held each other in the tenderest of regards."

"So tender, you broke your understanding with him to marry the earl," Jenna observed.

"But Garrett understood the necessity of it—my father's debts so great and the earl promising to be so generous. Besides, in the end—" she smiled at Jenna "—he forgave me *most* graciously."

Observing the grim set of Jenna's lips, Garrett decided she'd endured enough of Lucinda Blaine's baiting.

"We mustn't detain you further, my lady," he began.

"Indeed, I'm sure your husband must be wondering what has become of you," Jenna inserted.

Suppressing a grin, Tony continued, "Your devoted servant, Countess. Lady Fairchild, shall we depart?" With a brief bow to Lucinda, Tony kicked his horse into motion, Jenna immediately following.

Behind them, the Beauty sat in openmouthed astonishment that Tony had dared to ride away—before *she* dismissed *him*. He'd likely made an enemy there.

But getting Jenna away from Lucinda had seemed more important. He glanced over at her, noting that the color that had warmed her cheeks after their gallop had now vanished, leaving her looking pale and drained.

Perhaps it had been too soon after her accident to have urged her to ride. "Are you fatigued?" he asked with concern. "We could stop at Gunter's for some ices."

"No. I want to go home."

Anger and frustration swelled his chest as he realized that their interlude with Lucinda Blaine had effectively chilled the air of camaraderie that had warmed him during their ride. He cast about for some way to retrieve it.

Perhaps a frontal assault would be best. Hoping he wasn't about to make matters worse, Tony rode in front of Jenna's mount and halted, forcing her to pull up as well.

"What's wrong, Jenna? I hope you didn't let the Countess of Doone's nasty remarks upset you. She seems to need to imply every man she meets find her fascinating."

"You gave her no reason to doubt that supposition," Jenna snapped.

Had Jenna been a bit jealous? Pleased in spite of himself, he said, "A man may admire a showy bauble without coveting it for his own."

"But if it once *was* his own, does he ever stop regretting its loss?" she asked softly.

Tony threw her a sharp glance. Surely Jenna couldn't doubt that her husband had found his way free of whatever spell Lucinda Blaine had once cast over him.

"No intelligent man keeps a shiny bit of glass after he's discovered that 'pearl of great price,'" he said.

When she turned to look at him, Tony was horrified to see tears in her eyes. "What if he thinks to have both?"

She did have doubts. Incredulous at the realization and torn by the obvious distress on her face, Tony protested, "You can't truly believe Garrett had any warm feelings left for Lucinda Blaine!"

"How can you be certain?" she flashed back. "You two were never friends."

"True. But after you were wed, I was threatened with the direst retribution if I so much as approached you. He guarded you as he would his most precious possession."

"Perhaps he didn't want to share this particular bauble."

It must be her weakened physical state that made her prey to these nonsensical doubts. "Come now, Jenna, do you not think you are letting yourself make too much out of a vainglorious woman's innuendo?"

"Perhaps not this time, but—" Catching herself, she turned away, her face coloring. "'Tis no matter. Doubtless you are correct."

Had Lucinda Blaine plagued her on some other occasion? Tony wondered, his aggravation with the Beauty increasing. From what he knew of the woman, he didn't doubt her capable of such malice. "What *else* did the countess say to you?"

"You are right," Jenna mumbled, "I'm being foolish."

Tony made no move to let her pass. "If you want a

disinterested opinion about the value of whatever she said, you might as well tell me the whole.''

He held his breath, waiting for her to brush him off and ride away. But evidently the doubts preying upon her were disturbing enough that she felt compelled to air them, even with him, for after a moment she said softly, ''The other night, I encountered her at Lady Charlotte's party.''

Understanding dawned swiftly. ''So that was why you wanted to leave so abruptly. What did she say?''

''She claimed that when we were in London last spring, Garrett came to visit her. He was gone a great deal then, busy with the details of trying to mobilize an army. He might easily have stopped to see her, even...spent the night.''

''And that thought is what sent you fleeing?''

''No. Considering the possibility of it hurt, though it angered me more that she could make me doubt him. But then she said that with the death of his child, I now have even less to remember him by than she does. She sounded positively—*triumphant.* I care nothing for her gloating, but losing the babe...'' Jenna took a shuddering breath.

There should be, he thought furiously, a special ring of Hades for petty, vindictive beauties like Lucinda Blaine. Aching for the pain in Jenna's voice, he said, ''As you know better than anyone, Garrett was a man of impeccable honor. Even if he harbored a trace of affection for his former fiancée—which I doubt—he would never insult you or dishonor his vows by trifling with her.''

He had the pleasure of seeing her troubled brow lighten a bit. ''You truly believe that?''

''I truly do.''

''Thank you,'' she whispered. ''And I'm sorry to be a spiritless creature. Let us go to work now. We have dinners to prepare, clothes to procure, and all of it to deliver before sundown.''

She nudged her mare back toward the street. Tony guided Pax to follow, conversation ceasing as they picked their way through the traffic. As they reached the townhouse, Tony asked, ''Shall I see you in?''

''No, I must go purchase foodstuffs so your cook can begin work. As soon as I've done that, I shall shop for the necessary clothing, then continue on to North Audley Street. If that is agreeable?''

Gratified as he was that she trusted him enough to call at his home, Tony knew he couldn't allow it. ''I'm afraid it isn't. Didn't your cousin tell you a lady never calls at the home of a single gentleman?''

''How ridiculous! Since the food is being prepared at your kitchen, 'twould make more sense to set out from there. Your cook—and Sancha—can safeguard my virtue.'' A little smile lit her eyes. ''And I still carry that knife.''

''I stand forewarned,'' he replied. ''Still, it simply won't do. The women who call upon my esteemed sire are certainly not ladies. If you were to be seen anywhere near my doorstep—'' in his mind flashed the image of a pouting Lucinda Blaine ''—the malicious of the ton would delight in making mincemeat of your reputation.''

''For calling at your kitchen?'' she scoffed. ''Accompanied by my maid, a handcart full of clothing and bound upon a mission of mercy? If that is the stuff of scandal, then I care little if my reputation is lost.''

''Spoken like one confident of her good name,'' he replied a little grimly. ''You, who have lived an irreproachable life, can have no notion of how unpleasant it can be to be considered a byword.''

She gave him a long, searching glance. ''I suppose it

must be unpleasant, to have all the world ascribe to your every thought and action the most depraved of motives.''

Her observation striking too uncomfortably close to the mark, he made no reply.

''I flatter myself that my true friends have sufficient faith in my honor, and as for the ton—people will believe what they choose. Besides, I shall hardly come garbed like a ton lady. If you can contrive to find a pony cart to transport our supplies and dress yourself inconspicuously, I daresay even you may not be recognized outside your own kitchen. So, shall we say about three?''

She was coming—to him. A sense of gladness much more intense than he should have felt suffused him. Still, he made one last attempt to do the right thing. ''If you insist upon coming to deliver the supplies, 'twould still be more prudent for me to meet you here.''

''Oh, Nelthorpe, give over!'' she said. '''Tis nonsensical to waste time detouring here and you know it. Only recall your years in the army! Do you really want to deprive these poor unfortunates of the pleasure of having their meat and bread still warm when they receive it?''

He did indeed recall the intense delight he'd felt, after days or weeks of cold beef and stale bread, when circumstances permitted the troops to enjoy a hot, freshly cooked meal. His mouth almost watered at the memory.

She watched his face, smiling. ''I shall see you this afternoon at North Audley Street.''

''Managing baggage, aren't you?'' he asked wryly.

''Absolutely.'' She started up the stairs, then paused at the landing. ''We shall have quite an adventure!''

In that instant, she was once again the Jenna of the Spanish plains, buoyant with enthusiasm and confidence. He couldn't help but smile back when she winked at him before the door opened to admit her.

The warmth of knowing 'twas his project that had

brought the sparkle back to her eye and the purpose to her step glowed within him all the way home.

A FEW HOURS LATER, stripped to his shirtsleeves in the warmth of the kitchen, Tony was helping Betsy load fresh loaves of bread into baskets when the maid admitted Jenna, garbed in a gray cloak over a nondescript gown of gray kerseymere, and her maid Sancha.

The scowl on Sancha's face and the flashing look in her dark Spanish eyes told him she was none too happy about the latest scheme into which he'd embroiled her mistress.

Despite the modesty of Jenna's apparel, with her brown eyes glowing and wisps of hair curling about her determined face, she looked incredibly lovely. Gone was the vacant-eyed, passive wanderer whose appearance had so shaken Tony on the bridge at Hyde Park. Though he knew he shouldn't have allowed her to take part in this rescue mission and definitely should have forbidden her to meet him here, still he couldn't help a surge of gladness at seeing her.

"You look dressed for intrigue," he said.

"And you look—" She halted in midsentence, her eyes roving from his face to his partly unbuttoned shirt to the rolled-up sleeves that displayed the muscles of his arms.

A bolt of pure physical energy flashed between them, stirring him down to his toes and strengthening him in all the right places. He'd had hints since their reunion in London that she still felt the physical pull that had drawn them in Spain, but nothing as strong or as clearly telegraphed as this. For the first time since he awoke after Waterloo in the shattered, permanently disabled body he now inhabited, he felt—virile.

"Informal," she said at last. Her cheeks flushing, she

avoided his glance and went instead to offer her hand to the cook. "I'm Lady Fairchild, and this is my companion, Sancha. You must be Betsy. How kind of you, ma'am, to allow us to commandeer your assistance! Many a good soldier will be singing your praises this night."

Holding himself motionless with an effort, Tony thanked heaven that his cook and a still-glaring Sancha were present to chaperone. In his euphoria and gratitude at that renewed sense of potency, he might not otherwise have been able to resist dragging her into his arms.

Betsy dropped a curtsy. "'Tis right happy I am to meet your ladyship and help out the soldiers what fought with our Master Tony."

"Lord Nelthorpe boasted of your skill, and looking at the bounty spread here, I see he did not exaggerate."

"Thank 'ee, ma'am. We're glad our master were spared to come back and help put things right—and don't you be frowning at me, Master Tony! He tries to let on like he's a great care-for-nobody," Betsy told Jenna, "but there's a good heart there, if ye but look fer it."

"So I'm beginning to believe," Jenna said.

Embarrassed, Tony said, "We should load up and be on our way. We've few enough hours of daylight left."

"Polly 'n me will pack the provisions, if you will see 'em stowed in the cart, Master," Betsy said.

"Sancha, assist Lord Nelthorpe, please, while I help in here," Jenna instructed.

Hoping the cook wouldn't feel moved to share any further details about his life and character, Tony limped out, Sancha trailing in his wake. Neither the well-worn cart that waited outside nor the unprepossessing drab pulling it, both rented from a local livery, were likely to arouse much attention, either here or at their destination.

Once they reached the rig, Sancha held out a hand for the bread baskets. "You tend to the horse, my lord. Sancha will pack the cart.'' To his surprise, she gave him a glimmer of a smile. ''I have much experience.''

Tony handed them over. ''I did try to talk Lady Fairchild out of accompanying me.''

''There are soldiers hungry? Wives and babes also?'' Sancha asked. When he nodded, she continued, ''Then I do not blame you. My mistress has tended soldiers since she was a child. If there is need, no one keeps her away.''

For several minutes, the two of them worked in surprising harmony, readying the cart. When Tony turned to walk back in and tell Jenna all was ready, though, Sancha blocked his path.

''I hated what you tried to do in Spain, and still, I do not trust you. When my lady's *esposo* and then her babe were taken, she wanted only to sit alone in her room. But today, she hurries, she tells me there is important work. She is not healed—but she lives again. Thank you.''

Touched and humbled, Tony said, ''I, too, am glad.''

''And if ever again you try to hurt her, I, Sancha, will cut out your black heart.'' With that, Sancha preceded him into the kitchen.

So much for their détente cordiale, Tony thought with a grin, limping after her.

All their preparations complete, they had only to wait for Sergeant Anston to arrive and provide them an armed escort to their destination. Jenna and Tony settled at the kitchen table with some fresh bread while Betsy and Sancha took theirs to stools by the hearth.

''I'm hoping Evers—Papa's batman—will arrive within the week,'' Jenna said. ''If there are so many displaced soldiers gathered in just two blocks, doubtless there are countless about the city. Evers can search them out. You are certain there's no hope of redress by Parliament?''

Tony shook his head. ''I doubt it. The Tories are too

busy seeing anarchists behind every loom and hayrick to concern themselves with justice for former soldiers.''

''I wonder if that widow who accosted me at Garrett's reception is in need. I never learned her name.'' A faraway look on her face, she said, ''Given what has transpired, she should be content now.''

Out of memory, Tony saw the woman's venomous face. *I won't be happy until you too lose all you hold dear.*

The vague sense of something not quite right that had been troubling him since Jenna's accident suddenly sharpened. *Now you have even less of him than I do,* Jenna said the countess had told her.

A prickle of apprehension made him shudder.

Jenna was a superb rider who, under most circumstances, would be very difficult to unseat. No head groom worth the title should ever have neglected to emphasize the peculiarities of a mount he was about to release to someone who'd not previously ridden that horse, even if he thought someone else might have already mentioned them.

Had someone intended to make her fall?

''Jenna,'' he said abruptly, ''about your accident...you said your cousin had discharged the groom responsible?''

''Yes, I pleaded with him to reconsider. 'Twas as much my fault as the groom's. If I'd been more alert, caught the mare's hesitancy instantly, I might have avoided being thrown—and my child might be alive now.''

He'd meant to question her further, but one glance at the anguish in her eyes and he abandoned the attempt.

''Nonsense, Jenna!'' he hastened to assure her. ''No rider, however experienced, could maintain his seat when a horse reacts unexpectedly like that.''

A knock on the door signaling Sergeant Anston's arrival put an end to the discussion. Tony marshaled the group and moved them out.

As they rode toward the City, his thoughts cycled back to the puzzle of Jenna's accident. He resolved to find out more about it, and in case someone *had* meant to harm her, he'd ask for details first from one wholly devoted to her. Tomorrow he would call at Fairchild House and question Sancha.

He'd also need to consider tracking down the groom Lane Fairchild had discharged. For if someone harbored enough malice toward Jenna to set up a potentially fatal accident, she might still be in danger.

CHAPTER TWELVE

WHILE SANCHA DOZED BENEATH a blanket in the wagon bed, Jenna sat on the box of the pony trap in the gathering darkness as Nelthorpe guided it out of the city, buoyed by a sense of accomplishment.

Seeming to sense her thoughts, Nelthorpe interrupted the congenial silence to ask, "You enjoyed our mission?"

"Oh, yes—how good it was to be back among army folk again! Though they were all absurdly grateful for the food and garments we brought, so much more remains to be done. I shall set Evers to work with Sergeant Anston to locate as many former soldiers and their families as they can, that they may be offered immediate assistance while we devise a more permanent solution—since you believe Parliament will not act on this matter."

Nelthorpe shook his head. "Unless it's to clap them all in Newgate for vagrancy."

"They need more than assistance—they need occupation. Idle, feeling abandoned and threatened with destitution, even the best-intentioned of men might be tempted to misdeeds." She frowned, her mind examining various possibilities. "Many of them come from the countryside. Though I know nothing of farming, if I were to purchase a property and put Anston in charge, he could hire experienced lads to work the land."

"Purchase a property?" Nelthorpe exclaimed. "Would your trustees allow such a thing?"

"There are no trustees. Papa left his fortune for me to manage as I see fit, with the advice—but not under the control—of our solicitor." She raised an eyebrow at him. "He believed I could handle it as well or better than any would-be husband."

"So should you marry, your spouse would have no access to your funds?"

"Nothing that is not specified in the marriage contract—which, in the unlikely event that I should marry again, I would help draft."

Nelthorpe laughed. "My dear, publish that fact abroad and your worries about fortune hunters will cease!"

"Ah, does that mean you will desert me, too?"

He paused, creasing his brow as if considering the prospect. To her surprise, she found herself a bit offended that he hadn't immediately denied it. But then, what had she expected? He'd freely admitted himself from the first to be little more than a fortune hunter.

"As devastating a blow as that news is, I suppose I cannot," he said at last. "After all, we made a bargain. I must allow you an opportunity to redeem me while I—" he let his gaze roam from her face to her throat to her chest "—attempt to tempt you."

At the gleam in his eyes, her pulse leapt and the breasts he was eyeing tingled. Appalled to realize she *was* tempted, she said repressively, "That is not, my lord, a suitable comment to voice to a lady. You will direct your thoughts to the matter at hand, if you please."

He grinned and flicked a glance at his hands grasping the reins—at almost the same level as her breasts. "Ah, that I could lavish my attention on the matter at hand."

Her cheeks heated and that unwelcome but insistent tingling intensified, spreading from her chest down her torso. Ah, to feel his hands cupping her breasts, skimming down her belly, delving into the curls beneath—

Shocked at her wanton thoughts, she jerked her gaze

from him to stare over the horse's head. Awakening from the torpor of grief to find herself lusting was normal enough, she supposed—but over Nelthorpe?

Having not immediately protested it, she should probably ignore his improper remark. And repress her lamentable reaction, before her body turned the siren's song his body was crooning into a duet.

Scooting as far away from Nelthorpe as the narrow bench allowed, she brought her thoughts back to the plight of the army families. "There should be a school for the children. A little boy with a cherub's smile tried to filch one of my earrings right off my ear while his mama and I talked this afternoon. Fortunately he wasn't skilled enough to manage it without my noticing, but it indicates how imperative it is that we get the young ones off the street before they become totally steeped in vice."

"Or turned over to a magistrate by a prospective victim less compassionate than you. I hope you told the lad's mother. He should be given a good thrashing."

"Discipline is as important as constancy in the managing of a troop, and I imagine it's the same with children. While the little ones learn their letters, perhaps the mothers could be schooled as well. Most of them are excellent managers, having had to scrape by for years on very little. With proper training, they should make superior housekeepers and cooks. And of course, any farming endeavor will require grooms, smiths, carpenters, and other craftsmen as well as farm workers."

"This begins to sound like quite an undertaking."

"Papa left me quite a fortune. It would please him to know I was using it to help army families build new lives. And...it will give me something useful to do with mine."

"And what of our bargain? In all this excess of dogooding, I hope you will not forget that!"

She smiled, the idea forming even as she voiced it.

''Indeed not. You can assist me in my 'do-gooding.' After all, what better way to reform a character?''

He groaned. ''I had more in mind assisting you to attend balls, routs, musicales and Venetian breakfasts.''

''I suppose we could fit in a few...between visiting needy folk, inspecting properties and then staffing and equipping the farm once the purchase is complete.''

He shot her an aggrieved glance. ''Perhaps my character doesn't need quite that much improvement.''

He'd just, she immediately realized, provided her an avenue of escape from the unsettling temptation of his company. ''I imagine it doesn't. 'Twas a ridiculous bargain anyway. Why don't we call it off at once?''

A look almost of dismay flashed across his face, too swiftly for her to positively identify it. Then he shrugged, the picture of bored hauteur. ''If you think so little of upholding the vow you swore to honor the dead of Waterloo, I suppose we could. Or perhaps you are prepared to concede I am already their equal?''

He had her and he knew it. Casting a jaundiced eye over his deceptively bland demeanor, she snapped, ''Prepare yourself to visit the needy and inspect properties, then.''

''If I must, but I certainly shall not depress myself by thinking about it ahead of time. Have we not had enough of duty and sacrifice today? 'Tis time to contemplate a bit of pleasure to reward ourselves for such an excess of virtue. What function do you attend tonight?''

''My cousin and Lady Montclare are urging me to go to Lady Winterdale's musicale.''

''Then I shall sit beside you, whisper in your ear until you blush and make all your other swains jealous.''

''And I shall rap you with my fan if you're impertinent, keep you at arm's length and dismiss you entirely if I cannot make you mind your manners.''

"Sounds delightful," he pronounced with a grin. "When and where shall I meet you, my dear Jenna?"

"I am not your 'dear Jenna,' as I've been meaning to point out. You should address me as 'Lady Fairchild.'"

"And so I do, when we are in company. But I began calling you 'Jenna' long ago and I'm afraid it's too late for me to unlearn the usage. In fact, given our long association, why don't you call me 'Tony'?"

Ignoring the invitation, she replied, "As *I* recall, you usually referred to me as 'Miss Montague,' in a singularly odious, top-lofty tone."

"Did I?" he asked, sounding genuinely surprised. "What an arrogant ass I was, to be sure!"

"Was?"

His grin turned into a chuckle. "Still am, you mean. Ah, did I not warn you that my character needs much work?"

Recalling the courtesy he'd shown her here in London and the depth of his concern about the former soldiers, she replied, "Perhaps less than I used to think."

His grin faded. With slow deliberation, he focused on her a hot, lingering glance that sparked a thrill of feminine awareness all the way to her core. "Are you sure about that?" he drawled.

Doubtless he knew exactly the effect that look produced in her, the wretch. She mustn't forget he'd earned the rake's reputation that followed him to the army. Squelching her response, she replied, "Lord Nelthorpe, a gentleman does not fix on a lady such a gaze."

He returned an innocent look. "What gaze?"

"The gaze that says he wishes he might relieve her of her garments on the spot," she continued tartly.

"Even if he very much wishes to?"

Instead of a teasing tone, his voice now held an undercurrent of...longing. Startled, she felt her face heat.

"Certainly not. Such wishes should be directed toward more suitable objects—among the muslin company."

"Ah. True ladies never experience such wishes?"

She opened her lips to affirm that, but honesty made her hesitate. Mercifully, at this moment they reached the Fairchild House mews, saving her the necessity of a reply.

"You may let us down here, Lord Nelthorpe."

The gleam in his eyes as he brought the cart to a halt told her he knew she was evading an answer. After helping them both alight, he thanked Sancha, who nodded and headed back toward the house, and gave Jenna a deep bow. "Until tonight, my lady."

"Goodbye, my lord. And thank you for taking me with you. It...it was good to feel useful again."

The rogue's grin returned as he brought her fingers to his lips. "Putting you to good use shall always be my pleasure." Chuckling once more at the reproving look she sent him, he climbed awkwardly back into the pony cart. "Now, to return this magnificent equipage before any of my acquaintance sees me driving it."

"Is the ruin of a reputation built on so little?"

"Indeed it is," he said, his voice suddenly serious. "Keep that in mind."

"And the reforming of one?"

"Is much more difficult than the losing. Keep that in mind as well."

"I shall."

With a nod, he set the cart in motion. Jenna watched until he'd guided the vehicle out of sight.

With his recently acquired limp and his newly developed compassion, she mused as she strolled back to the house, Anthony Nelthorpe was a much more complex—and, she admitted, compelling—man than the arrogant, insensitive viscount who had repulsed and attracted her in Spain. Just when she was prepared to condemn him and his provocative remarks as being little better than the rake of old, he startled her with some display of concern—for her, for others—that prevented her from dismissing him so easily.

Betsy, his cook, had told her he hid a good heart under his casual rakehell manner, hinted that the influence of his dissipated father had prevented his developing it. Jenna was halfway inclined to believe her.

Perhaps his character didn't need work so much as the opportunity to reveal its true dimensions, she concluded as she took the stairs to her chamber. Although whenever she voiced a more hopeful opinion of his character, Nelthorpe was quick to deflect it with another innuendo-laden remark or heat-inducing glance designed to scatter her thoughts.

He succeeded only too well. Surely she shouldn't be responding to Nelthorpe's enticements! But then, she was a passionate woman whose passion had long been restrained.

Given the ease with which Anthony Nelthorpe seemed to be loosening those fetters, perhaps her own character needed more work.

She was about to open her door when she felt a touch to her shoulder. With a gasp, she whirled around.

"Jenna, excuse me," Cousin Lane exclaimed. "I didn't mean to startle you."

"No matter, cousin. I was woolgathering and did not hear you approach."

He looked her up and down, a frown wrinkling his forehead. "When Manson told me where you had gone, I couldn't believe it! But seeing you in that...apparel, it no longer seems so fantastical a notion. Please, Jenna, assure me you didn't go into the stews of east London!"

"I'm afraid I cannot. Oh, Lane, I'd heard there are soldiers there, still dressed in the bloodstained tatters of the uniforms they fought in at Waterloo! Widows and children, starving, some homeless. I had to see for myself if such a report could be true."

"If discovering this was so important, you should have sent one of the servants who has relations in those areas. Merciful heavens, Jenna, the rookeries around Seven Dials are so dangerous, even Bow Street runners hesitate to go there! You could have been robbed at the least, at worst—" He shuddered, looking so appalled she felt a pang of guilt.

Jenna took his hand and squeezed it. "I'm sorry to have worried you, but I'm not a witless female who faints at dirt or danger and must be protected from the realities of life. I've seen worse, and I'm quite competent at handling the pistol I took with me."

He raised her hand to his lips and kissed it fervently. "I know you are a remarkable woman, Jenna. Which only makes your safety even more important to me."

Though she regretted worrying him, she didn't wish to encourage the heated look now glowing in his eyes. Gently she withdrew her hand. "I do appreciate your cousinly concern. But since Nelthorpe told me—"

"Nelthorpe!" Lane cried. "I might have known that reprobate was responsible for this! Damme—dash it, could there be any more telling demonstration of how unsuitable an escort he is for you? Though I imagine he's intimately acquainted with London's stews, he ought to be shot for exposing you to such peril!"

"Actually, he was no happier about taking me there than you are that I went and refused absolutely to do so until I threatened to go alone. If their country will do nothing for them, someone else must. To determine how best to help, I had to see for myself what they need."

Lane's gaze flew to her face. "*You* intend to help them? How? I trust, in your womanly compassion, you don't plan to bring any scrawny guttersnipes here!"

The warmth his concern for her had generated began

to chill. "Those 'scrawny guttersnipes' risked their lives in battle after battle so you might be able to sit in London at your leisure and sip port!"

"I don't mean to disparage the soldiers' service. But the war is over now. 'Tis time they found some useful occupation, instead of loitering around gin shops and taverns grumbling about their fate and agitating against the government. Only think what happened to the Frogs when their lower orders were allowed to dissent."

His reactionary views stifled the last of her sympathy. "These men, who've taken the King's coin, aren't interested in revolution," she replied impatiently. "All they desire is what should be freely offered them—a chance to engage in honest labor and earn enough to house and provide for their families."

Lane manufactured a thin smile. "So, how many are we to employ?"

"One household cannot provide enough work even for those I've already met and I suspect there are many more. No, a much more comprehensive solution is needed."

Lane's frown returned. "Just what do you intend?"

"I am not yet perfectly sure. I must talk with my solicitor and make a more thorough canvass of the needs within the community. Perhaps I shall purchase a rural property where those who have farmed can lease land and establish a school to train the widows and youngsters."

Lane's frown ceded to a look of paternalistic indulgence. "A laudable aim, my dear," he said, patting her hand, "and a tribute to your feminine sensibilities, if wholly impractical! But your trustees would never approve such an expenditure."

For the second time that day, Jenna had the pleasure of shocking a gentleman by replying, "I have no trustees, dear cousin."

His expression was gratifyingly shocked. "No trustees? Surely you are mistaken! A female—even one as brave and accomplished as you, my dear—simply isn't capable of managing finances. Consult your solicitor, but I'm certain your papa, fine officer that he was, set up proper provisions for your protection."

At least Nelthorpe, Jenna thought, by now thoroughly irritated with her cousin, had not questioned her ability to manage what was her own, despite his surprise over the admittedly unusual arrangement. "If you doubt my word, cousin, then you may consult him about it."

"Well, we shall see, I suppose," he said after a short silence. "However matters stand, though, I beg you to think long and carefully before you attempt to implement so...radical a plan. Capable as you may be in other areas, you know nothing of managing agricultural property. The mere expense of purchasing a tract large enough to permit the scheme you're envisioning would be enormous!"

"By happy chance, so is my fortune."

"Even so, such an outlay might make severe inroads upon your principal. Bah, I shall not attempt to explain, but this could adversely affect current and future income."

Curbing the strong desire to frame a retort demonstrating her mastery of the intricacies of fund management, she decided to take another tack. "Oh, la, will it be as harmful as all that? Such a downturn in my fortune might make me a less attractive prize on the Marriage Mart. I must warn dear Lady Montclare of the sad fact, don't you think, before she wastes any more time on me? Perhaps tonight at the musicale you and Aunt Hetty are pressing me to attend."

Lane sighed. "You are displeased with me, I see. But in my defense, let me protest that if I interfere, it is only because I care deeply about your well-being. I cannot stand by and see you taken advantage of by miscreants too lazy to earn their own keep—or fortune hunters pursuing their own gain."

"Then do me the honor of believing I am capable of guarding myself and my fortune from such dangers without assistance. If you'll excuse me, cousin?"

"I shall see you later, then, Jenna."

Turning her back on Lane's bow, Jenna at last escaped into her room.

She supposed Cousin Lane did wish the best for her, Jenna thought as she closed the door, though perhaps it was his hope of persuading her into matrimony that drove his concern that she not squander any of her fortune. If his regard was inspired more by her purse than her person, this conversation should bring about a chill in his ardor.

Interestingly enough, the odd thought occurred, though he'd first expressed the same surprise as her cousin at the terms of her father's bequest, Anthony Nelthorpe had then accepted the arrangement without further question.

Nor, despite her cousin's insinuation, had he hinted he hoped to figure as one of the beneficiaries of her largesse. His concern for the displaced soldiers—and the shame she'd seen in his face that he could do little to assist them—showed her this reputed rogue did possess the heart Betsy had claimed. And he had seemed willing to let her follow hers without dispensing paternalistic advice.

Of course, Lane Fairchild had never seen her organize and manage an army camp on the march.

Still, he evidently preferred that she remain ignorant of the injustices within their society and leave dealing with difficult or dangerous matters to gentlemen.

Perhaps there *was* something to be said for a rogue.

CHAPTER THIRTEEN

AT MIDMORNING THE NEXT DAY, Tony paused in the front hallway before setting out. Observing the headway Sergeant Anston and the new maid were making in clearing away years of dirt and neglect made him feel buoyed and hopeful. Perhaps he could meet the challenges facing him after all.

Now, to get to the truth of Jenna's accident.

Having been informed during their conversation at the musicale last night that she planned to consult her solicitor this morning, he was confident that when he reached Fairchild House, Jenna would not be at home. Whereupon he would ask to speak with Sancha, that she might convey a message from him to her mistress, as she often had on his visits during Jenna's convalescence.

Fortunately, since Sancha was unlikely to believe that excuse, their mission yesterday seemed to have raised him in her esteem. Out of curiosity, if for no other reason, he was reasonably sure she would agree to meet him.

He arrived at Fairchild House to learn, as expected, that Jenna was out but that the maid would be down shortly. "What is it your lordship wants of Sancha?" she asked as she entered the room a few minutes later.

"You are devoted to Lady Fairchild," he began.

She looked at him through narrowed eyes. "*Si.* I make the vendetta against *any* who harm my mistress."

From the tone in which she made that pointed pronouncement, Tony gathered that though her opinion of him might have risen somewhat, his position in Sancha's good graces was by no means secure.

"I, too, am very concerned about Lady Fairchild's safety. For her own protection, I must ask that you repeat to no one what I am about to confide in you. Will you swear that, by the Blessed Virgin?"

Her eyebrows raised. "It is serious, this danger?"

"I am not sure, else I would act, but it could be deadly. I wish to take no chances. Will you swear?"

Sancha made the sign of the cross. "By the Blessed Virgin, I will tell no one. What harm threatens my lady?"

"Did it not seem strange to you that your mistress, as experienced a rider as she is, would take a fall during a ride through the park?"

"I am surprised. But when her *esposo* die, her heart die with him. Since then, she pays small attention to what happens about her."

"Did her horse truly need shoeing the day she borrowed Mrs. Thornwald's mount?"

Sancha raised her eyebrows. "This, I do not know. The horse was re-shoed, that is certain. Why ask you this?"

"Was there no talk among the servants about how odd it was that the head groom made no mention to her of the animal's unusual disposition?"

"They say they expect he thought Mrs. Thornwald or Mr. Fairchild had told her. *Madre de Dios!*" Sancha gasped. "You think someone meant to harm my lady?"

"I know two women ready to rejoice at her misfortune," he replied grimly. "After pondering the matter further," he lowered his voice to ensure no passing servant might overhear, "I realized someone else might be even more pleased if Lady Fairchild were never brought to bed of a son. The man that son would displace as viscount."

Sancha fixed her shrewd eyes on him for a long moment. "A viscount has much power and wealth, no?"

"Who can guess what heinous act a man might commit to retain his grasp on such a prize?"

"There is much wickedness in the world," Sancha agreed. "But this Bayard, cousin to my lady's husband, does not seem interested in such matters. Always he stays in the cellars, mixing his strange powders." Sancha crossed herself again. "Doing the devil's work, perhaps!"

"If Jenna had borne a healthy son, they would no longer be *his* cellars," Tony pointed out. "Nor his house, nor, probably, his funds to continue his experiments, though I don't know yet what revenue he has. Have you heard it said—even in a whisper—that her fall might have been other than an accident?"

Sancha shook her head. "Nay, I hear only sadness for my lady's loss. Much talk it caused, the groom being dismissed, but all approve Mr. Fairchild's action."

"Was the groom angry? Contrite? Guilt-striken?"

"This, I do not know. Only that he left before sunrise the day after my lady's fall."

Disappointed that Sancha could only confirm what Jenna had already told him, Tony continued, "Might you be able to find out where that groom is now?"

"One of the housemaids is cousin to him. I can ask her."

"If you can discover his direction, I'd very much like to speak with him. Let me call again—Thursday, perhaps—and see what you have learned."

Sancha nodded. "If weather is fine, I will make sure my mistress goes riding. Come and send for me, like today."

Tony felt a flicker of excitement. In just a few days, he might be on his way to uncovering whether there was in fact something sinister about Jenna's accident. ''Excellent! If my fears are groundless, we will have done no harm—but if they are not, we may be saving your lady from even graver injury. Remember, though,'' he added, ''to be very careful, for if her cousin should have been responsible for this, she would be in great danger should he discover anyone suspects him.''

''If someone hurt my lady, we must find him. And if she is in danger, we must protect her,'' Sancha agreed.

''You have ever been her loyal friend. Thank you.''

The maid nodded, then curtsied and walked him to the door. ''Perhaps I was wrong, my lord,'' she said as she paused on the threshold, a hint of a smile in her solemn eyes. ''Perhaps you are not so evil any longer.''

Pleased with the interview, Tony limped after her. While he hoped his fears *were* groundless, having spent much of his young manhood in roguish company, he could not help but suspect wrongdoing when an accident befell someone who threatened great wealth and aroused strong emotion.

Had someone paid off the groom to substitute an unfamiliar, unstable mount, intent on triggering a fall?

A fall that might insure no male child would supplant Bayard Fairchild as the next viscount.

Her family would have known of her condition—and how many others? Might Garrett's spiteful former lover have decided she could not bear watching Jenna parade before the ton the child of the man she'd spurned—but still cared for? Or would causing Jenna to truly ''lose everything'' been necessary to complete the revenge of a grief-deranged widow who held Jenna accountable for her husband's death?

Accepting his coat, gloves and walking stick from the butler, Tony descended the stairs and took the hackney the Fairchild footman summoned for him. Propping his knee on the squabs, he wondered whether he should warn Jenna.

No doubt the lady would insist she had a right to know. Certainly she'd shown she possessed a cool head and the ability to function in a dangerous situation. Still, unlike himself, Jenna was an honorable individual who would find it difficult to credit that anyone would wish her ill, especially a member of her husband's own family.

Worse yet, he realized, if circumstances *should* implicate someone within the Fairchild household, Jenna would be understandably furious at learning one of Garrett's own blood could have schemed to deprive her of their child. Honest as she was, she might well find it impossible to hide those feelings, thereby putting herself into further danger by revealing the suspicion.

Since she'd already lost the babe that threatened the succession, she should be safe for the moment, as long as whoever arranged her fall—if indeed someone had—did not learn anyone was investigating the incident. Better, he decided, to say nothing to Jenna, gather more information—and keep a closer watch over her.

That last posed no hardship, he thought with a smile. And though initially she'd roundly abused his character, of late he'd detected indications that she was growing fonder of him. A bittersweet, aching hope washed through him that she might become more than just fond.

Having already survived Waterloo, he dare not hope for a second miracle. And it would surely require an act of divine intervention for the widow of Garrett Fairchild to look with more than fondness upon the half-crippled, nearly destitute and completely unsuitable Anthony Nelthorpe.

Though involving her in the plight of the army families had turned out to be a master stroke, bringing out glimpses of the fiery Jenna of old. What a magnificent woman!

Of course, once she was fully herself again, she would have no further need of his help. With a pang of guilt, he had to admit to hoping the pace of her recovery did not quicken overmuch, that he might continue to enjoy the tantalizing delight of her company.

And tantalizing it was. Just thinking about her brought back in a rush the desire that always pulsed just beneath the surface. How wise he'd been to make tempting her, as she constantly tempted him, an intricate part of their bargain. Not only did his not-so-veiled innuendoes remind her of the need to improve his character, it saved him the surely hopeless task of trying to mask his attraction. An attraction she shared, at least in part, even if she wouldn't allow herself to acknowledge it.

As long as he could link the duration of their bargain to her promise to turn him into a man as worthy as the husband and father she'd lost, he should be guaranteed her company for a very long time.

Along with the deal offered him by Harris's father, that would be the best thing that had happened to him since surviving Waterloo.

LATER THAT EVENING, Jenna allowed Lane Fairchild to hand her into the carriage. "Do hurry, Jenna," Aunt Hetty's aggrieved voice said from behind her.

"Since the event is to honor Waterloo veterans, 'tis likely to be even more crowded than usual," Lane explained.

"I'm surprised there are enough veterans in London to justify two fetes within the same week," Jenna remarked.

Lane chuckled. "If Lady Charlotte Darnell held a very successful fete, then the Countess of Ellsmere must needs have one even more lavish. The countess has considered

Lady Charlotte 'une rivale amicale' since they debuted together in their very first Season."

"It is most unfortunate, Jenna, that you refused Lady Montclare's offer to accompany us tonight. It could be very injurious to the family if the Countess takes offense at your befriending Lady Charlotte. With her intimate knowledge of the ton, Lady Montclare could help avoid any damage," Aunt Hetty said.

Jenna had no intention of apologizing for having evaded being saddled with Lady Montclare's company for the whole of the evening—bad enough that she would doubtless suffer her presence and advice during the function itself. Nor would she express regret at having accepted Lady Charlotte's offer of friendship.

She recalled how congenial their lunch had been today. Far from expressing disapproval at Jenna's foray into east London, Lady Charlotte had been admiring and deeply sympathetic to the plight of the soldiers. She'd assured Jenna she would ask her friend Lord Riverton, who held an important government post, to see if it were possible to do something for them through official channels. She'd also recommended that Jenna establish a philanthropic trust to augment her own efforts and pledged to contribute to it.

Indeed, Lady Charlotte was the only one Jenna had met thus far within London Society who seemed to understand the grief she bore and her need to work through it her own way—one that didn't include a hasty remarriage.

Except for Nelthorpe—although he wasn't precisely a Society member in good standing. Would he attend the fete?

Though it bothered her to admit it, she regretted missing his visit this morning. She was also eager to discuss with him what she'd learned from her solicitor.

She could almost hear him advising her, with that roguish glint in his eye, not to give a rap about trying to navigate her way through whatever undercurrents of jealousy surrounded tonight's hostess and her newfound friend.

To her surprise, she was finding he shared more of her views than she would ever have credited upon meeting him again mere weeks ago. He also cared deeply about the soldiers whose welfare was now her most pressing interest. And thanks to the silly bargain she'd agreed upon, they would be allies of a sort for a few more weeks.

Could she truly hope to turn Anthony Nelthorpe into a principled gentleman in so little time?

Recalling the caress of his gaze upon her, warmth flushed her cheeks and tension spiraled in her belly.

Did she really want to?

A sharp rap from Aunt Hetty's fan recalled her. "Jenna, you are not attending, and 'tis important!"

"I'm afraid Aunt Hetty is correct, Jenna," Lane inserted with a placating smile. "I realize you may not yet be aware how such subtle intrigues can create lasting good or harm. Perhaps it would be wise to seek out Lady Montclare immediately upon our arrival, that she may advise you on how best to greet the countess."

Jenna nearly laughed at the absurdity of asking counsel on how to properly say hello, but a glance at Lane's face showed him to be quite serious. If scores were indeed kept over so trivial a matter as one's friendship with rival ton hostesses, then she'd best see about removing herself from London Society as soon as possible.

Perhaps Lord Nelthorpe could help her do so tonight.

Confining herself to a noncommittal murmur, as soon as she exited the carriage, Jenna began scanning the crowd, hoping that before her relations found the bobbing ostrich plume and shrill laughter that would mark Lady

Montclare's presence, she might spy the dark head or distinctive limping gait of Anthony Nelthorpe.

In the anteroom a few minutes later, Aunt Hetty rose up on tiptoe, waving her handkerchief to signal to someone who could only be Lady Montclare. Feeling as trapped as a picket before the approach of enemy cavalry, Jenna was on the point of inventing some urgent need to visit the ladies' withdrawing room when, across a sea of nodding heads and waving fans, she spied Anthony Nelthorpe.

She no sooner saw him then he smiled a greeting. Relieved this time that, as always, he seemed to have been watching for her, after confirming Lane and Aunt Hetty were gazing at Lady Montclare, she gestured him to approach.

A slow grin spreading across his face, he began making his way toward her through the crowd—as, from the opposite corner of the room, was Lady Montclare.

Nearly tapping her toe in impatience, she waited, hoping that despite his limp a cavalryman would prove swifter in his mission than a Society matron.

He didn't disappoint her. Before Lady Montclare had crossed half the chamber, Lord Nelthorpe reached her side. "Lady Fairchild, what a fortunate encounter," he murmured, gray eyes dancing as he gave her an elaborate bow.

She threw him a warning glance. "Fortunate indeed."

He raised her hand to his lips and proceeded to subject each height and valley of her knuckles to a slow and highly improper caress that sent a volley of little shocks ricocheting to all parts of her body.

"I can't tell you how delighted I am that you want me," he murmured for her ears alone.

Irritated by her response, but too much in need of his

help to risk scolding him at present, she pulled her hand back, resisting the urge to rub away the residual tingling.

"I was hoping I might see you, my lord. Evers, my father's old batman, arrived this afternoon, bringing with him the names of several troopers in need. He's eager to start canvassing London for more."

Evidently overhearing this exchange, Cousin Lane pulled his gaze from Lady Montclare's approach. His smile faded when he perceived to whom she was speaking.

"Nelthorpe," he said in frigid tones.

The viscount's grin widened. "Mr. Fairchild."

"You mean to continue working among the soldiers?" Lane asked her.

"Yes, cousin, with Lord Nelthorpe's assistance, as I believe I already told you. Were you, ah, able to gather the information I requested, my lord?"

"Information?"

"Yes," she replied, shooting him an urgent look.

"Ah, that information. 'Tis rather complicated. Shall we discuss it further?" Nelthorpe offered his arm.

Frowning, Lane waved it away. "Lady Fairchild has not yet greeted her hostess. And besides, 'tis not the time nor place to debate the merits of such a course. Cousin, I beg you to refrain from discussing so…inappropriate a matter in the middle of Lady Ellsmere's ball."

Jenna's ready anger stirred. "Inappropriate to talk of the plight of his Majesty's soldiers? Then perhaps I should leave—"

"Lady Fairchild," Nelthorpe interrupted, "we are distressing your cousin. Stroll with me so we may speak of this more discreetly." Before Jenna or Lane could respond, Nelthorpe appropriated her elbow and urged her away.

"Can't have you brangling with your cousin in the

middle of the anteroom. Very bad ton, you know, and certain to upset the countess,'' Nelthorpe said.

''Who, if I may believe my aunt and cousin, is already offended that I have become a friend of Lady Charlotte's.''

''Quite probably. Now, did you require of me more than a rescue? I am, of course, ever eager to service you.''

As he'd no doubt intended, her nimble mind was momentarily deflected by the naughty innuendo. She gave him a stern look. ''*Be of* service, you should say.''

He smiled, showing dimples. ''I prefer my original wording. But no more!'' He lifted a hand to forestall a protest. ''If your relations were ringing a peal over you, no wonder your gaze begged me to come to your rescue.''

''I wasn't begging!'' At his raised eyebrow, she admitted, ''Well, perhaps I was...anxious to get away. Lady Montclare was approaching, and once she latches on, she's as difficult to detach as a burr in a saddle blanket.''

''And about as pleasant.''

Jenna stifled a choke of laughter. ''Indeed! She's determined I must begin seeking to remarry to advantage, and none of my protests that I have no interest in such a project will discourage her.''

''But since she'll not wish to risk the contamination of my company, you should be safe from her as long as you remain on my arm. Let us pass through the gauntlet of the receiving line. With luck, your relations will be offended enough to leave you alone the rest of the evening.''

''Accept your escort for that and I shall be scolded all the way home. I'm not sure what would outrage Cousin Lane more—my intention to spend money on what he believes are homeless 'reprobates' or to spend time with you.''

''He probably considers them one and the same. Nay,

my lady, in for a pence, in for a pound. Having nobly dashed to your rescue, I demand the pleasure of your company, at least for a time.''

''Very well,'' she capitulated. ''I can hope the novelty of my arriving on your arm will distract the countess from remembering I am supposedly allied with her chief rival.''

''I can be quite distracting when I try,'' he murmured.

Under the guise of patting her hand, his fingers massaged hers in something closer to a caress. The skilled, hypnotic touch set off a tingling, which once again rapidly conveyed itself from her wrist up her arm to radiate through the rest of her body.

''A little less distraction, please,'' she said through gritted teeth, ''or I may have to choose Aunt Hetty.''

As his thumb completed one last stomach-fluttering circuit across her palm, he glanced down at her. The teasing light had vanished, leaving in his gaze an intensity that sent another little shock through her.

''I suppose I can let you go if I must,'' he said in a low voice, and released her hand.

By the time Jenna recovered her disordered wits, the butler was announcing them to Lady Ellsmere. A tall, elegantly dressed woman a few years Jenna's senior, the countess inspected her from forehead to slippers, as if sizing up a potential rival, Jenna thought with amusement.

Unconcerned about this stranger's opinion of her, Jenna had a hard time suppressing a giggle when the countess, having evidently decided Jenna posed her no threat, looked back up with a sniff. ''Lady Fairchild, a pleasure,'' she murmured as Jenna curtsied.

Then, expression warming, she turned to Nelthorpe. ''So the reports I'd heard of your return were true. Why remain away so long? London has been dull without you.''

''There was the small matter of the war,'' he replied dryly. ''But if my absence distressed you, I am desolated.''

Laughing, she tapped him with her fan. ''Rogue! I'm sure I must have been lonely a time or two. Perhaps, now that you *are* here, we can...renew old acquaintances.''

''I am ever at your ladyship's service.''

At that gallantry, which so closely echoed the compliment he'd offered Jenna earlier, an instinctive and totally irrational anger swept through her. Before she could utter a word, however, with a firm tug on her arm, Nelthorpe led her away.

She couldn't be—jealous! she thought, appalled by the reaction. Nelthorpe was no more to her than a congenial companion and friend. Whomever he chose to spend his more...intimate moments with was immaterial to her.

She surfaced from those reflections to note that Nelthorpe still propelled her across the room, one insistent hand at her back. ''You needn't haul me away like a beached carp,'' she objected. ''I'm not such a rustic that I would have made some inappropriate remark. Or interrupted your planning for a cozy tête-à-tête.''

Nelthorpe's eyes brightened. ''Jealous, my dear?''

''Certainly not!''

He sighed. ''I thought not. Nor have you any need to be. The Angelic Anellia's tastes run to young bucks of youth and fashion. She'd hardly deign to waste an evening with a half-crippled war relic, whatever our history.''

A half-crippled war relic. Was that how he saw himself? Jenna had never considered that his injuries diminished him—rather the opposite—but such a view was probably a very masculine one. With an unexpected pang of sympathy, she began, "You have a bit of a limp, but—"

"Please, no more on so dismal a topic," he stopped her. "Tell me what your solicitor said."

Happy to embark upon a less disquieting subject, Jenna summarized her solicitor's advice. Mr. Samuels had been admiring of her plans and enthusiastic about the investment opportunities inherent in purchasing land when property values were relatively depressed.

"He believes I should eventually make a good return on my capital, should I later decide to sell. Although I'm inclined to offer the soldiers terms that enable them to buy the plots they work, rather than sell the whole."

"I imagine the men would leap at such a chance."

"I hope so. As I mentioned, Evers arrived. I shall pair him with your Sergeant Anston to seek out soldiers and their families and be guided by their advice on the type and size of property to purchase. But the solicitor knew of two prime tracts within an easy ride of London, and I've arranged to view one tomorrow. Would you like to come?"

"I should be happy to escort you, of course."

"I mean to depart early—if that will be acceptable?"

"I shall endeavor to limit my drinking and wenching so as to stagger over at whatever hour you require, my lady."

"Good of you," she replied, not sure he was joking.

At that moment, someone called her name. She was delighted to discover Alastair Percy, a lieutenant who'd served under her father's command, flanked by two other officers in Life Guards uniforms.

After introductions all around, the group bore Jenna off to the refreshment room, Nelthorpe limping in their wake. Jenna noted that, like "Heedless" Harry, Alastair shook Nelthorpe's hand and greeted him cordially. Since a poor reputation traveled in the relatively small world of the officer corps even faster than rumors seemed to circulate among the ton, Jenna concluded that, among his army mates, the viscount had earned respect.

Which counted for far more in her opinion than the views of London's ton.

The dinner room was already crowded. Indeed, she'd not seen so many military men together at a social gathering since the Duchess of Richmond's ball on the eve of Waterloo. The countess, Jenna thought with a suppressed smile, evidently wanting to ensure attendance at her gathering to honor the soldiers surpassed that of Lady Charlotte's, must have sent runners to haul in every military man within a day's ride of the metropolis.

After the inevitable offering of condolences that still made her heart twist, her chats with various acquaintances progressed from reminiscences of campaigns past to a description of her ongoing efforts to assist the demobilized soldiers. Her work met with general approval and several generous pledges of support.

Nelthorpe, who remained at her side—which, as he predicted, did indeed serve to keep Aunt Hetty and Lady Montclare at a distance—was behaving with perfect propriety. Surrounded by soldiers and their wives who had shared many of the same experiences she'd lived through, Jenna found herself relaxing and enjoying the gathering more than she had any since coming to London.

Soon after, the musicians struck up. Humming along as the orchestra played, Jenna was upon the point of accepting a dashing junior officer's invitation to dance before she remembered her mourning status. Stung by guilt made more cutting by a lingering, ignoble regret that she must refuse him, she turned down his offer.

How could she have forgotten, even for a moment? she thought, shame and anguish twisting in her chest. Suddenly the room seemed overcrowded and airless. Breathless, almost dizzy, a desperate need to escape seized her.

Wheeling around, she took two running steps and stumbled. A pair of hands grabbed her shoulders from behind, steadying her.

Nelthorpe. Evidently once again watching out for her.

"Easy, my dear," he murmured. "'Tis a bit close in here. Shall we get a breath of air?"

She nodded, allowing him to lead her from the room, down a hallway, and onto a balcony which ran the length of the house. Light glowing at its end and the faint strains of music indicated that it must also adjoin the ballroom. For a few moments in the darkness, she leaned back and breathed deeply of the cool, crisp evening air.

"Was that young pup importunate? I'll be happy to plant him a facer for you."

"Oh, no! 'Twas my fault entirely. He...he asked me to dance, and wretch that I am, I nearly accepted."

"And what was so wretched about that? As I recall from Spain, you love to dance." He smiled wryly. "As did I, once upon a time."

She felt a pang of remorse. Her period of mourning would end, even if her grief did not, and dancing would be a possibility again. His injuries were permanent.

"Do you miss dancing?"

He shrugged, and it struck her that although he teased and encouraged her, he said very little about himself. Though she knew his financial condition to be perilous, he never complained of it. Nor, except for an occasional taunting reference, was he making any real attempt to seduce—much less coerce—her into solving his monetary difficulties by marrying him.

"I can still ride, and that's more important," his answer broke into her musing. "Would it be so scandalous for you to have accepted the young ensign's offer?"

"You know it would! I am not yet out of blacks."

"Do you think Garrett would find that reason enough for you to refrain?"

"I...well, no, I expect he would tell me to do what I enjoy, and Society be damned."

He made a flourish with his hand. "I rest my case."

"I know Garrett wouldn't expect it. But others do, and should I commit the folly of ignoring the conventions, Society will say I lacked affection for him. Whereas I grieve for him still," she added with a touch of defiance.

"All the more reason to allow yourself some small pleasures. You have few enough, these days."

She couldn't dispute that. Although her new task of assisting the soldiers brought her satisfaction, that emotion was tepid compared to the fiery intensity of delight and passion that had been her life with Garrett.

"Perhaps you are right," she admitted after a moment.

"Of course I'm right. And so, my lady—" he offered his arm "—may I have the honor of this dance?"

"D-dance?" she stuttered.

"I'm afraid my knee will not allow a grand sweep of a waltz, but I can manage a semblance. The music beckons, you've already admitted Garrett would never begrudge you the pleasure and no one shall see you here. So, my lady, dance with me."

Though Garrett might quibble about her choice of partner, she knew he would have encouraged her to seize whatever comfort presented itself. And the music did call to her.

No one will ever know, a little voice whispered.

At that, her resistance crumbled. Accepting his hand, she said, "I should be delighted, my lord."

CHAPTER FOURTEEN

THOUGH HE HEARD THE WORDS, Tony had to shake his head to make sure he wasn't dreaming. He never expected Jenna would agree to waltz with him.

Here, in the intimate dimness of the deserted balcony.

Given how the merest touch of her—and he'd nearly scared her off tonight, succumbing far too often to the temptation to touch her—fired to a boil the ever-simmering longing to pull her back into his arms, waltzing was probably a very bad idea. His leg, as well as other already-throbbing parts of his anatomy, was going to give him agonies when the music ended and he had to let her go.

But he also knew that nothing less than a squad of provost marshals would keep him from her. Already his hands trembled with anticipation and desire made his throat so thick he couldn't voice a reply. Instead he pulled her toward him.

She stepped into his arms, close enough that her honeysuckle scent and the warmth of her skin enveloped him in a dizzying cloud that set his pulse trip-hammering before they'd taken the first step. As his knee would not, in truth, support his spinning her away from him in the requisite circles, he was required to simply hold her near as he led her in gentle spirals.

Their slow, swaying progress across the balcony turned a dance which, he now discovered, had been justly condemned as scandalously intimate, into an even closer approximation of an embrace. The potent power of her nearness stimulated every nerve to acute sensitivity. Within moments, his whole body was sheened with perspiration, his fingers clenched in his gloves as he struggled to resist the imperative to turn this pseudoembrace into a real one.

Still, he must resist, for if he pulled her any closer, she would learn beyond doubt how much he desired her. At the thought, his knee gave a bit and he stumbled.

Instead of pushing away, she steadied him and—miracle of miracles—stepped closer. Her hands tightening on his arm, his shoulder, she laid her head against his chest.

After the first moment of shock, from somewhere deep within him tenderness welled up, a sense of awe that tempered the sharp edges of lust. Hardly daring to breathe lest he disturb her, he bent to brush his cheek against her hair and closed his eyes, wishing that the music and the magic might never end.

Of course, far too soon, the orchestra finished. Not until she lifted her head did he reluctantly loosen his grip. But the face she turned up to him, illumined by moonlight and radiant with delight, sent another wave of tenderness spiraling through him.

How could he ever let her go?

"Ah, Nelthorpe, that was wonderful!"

"No—you are wonderful," he answered.

She smiled and shook her head a little, as if denying it. And then he just couldn't resist any longer. Though he'd probably get his face slapped and his ears blistered for the lapse, he simply had to kiss her.

Once again, though, she surprised him. Instead of jerking away as she had that night on the bridge, she leaned into his kiss. Desperate to avoid frightening her into flight, he kept his touch light, just a gentle brush of his mouth against hers.

Until with a sigh, she dug her fingers into his shoulders and slid her tongue across his lips.

A shock of pleasure blasting through him, eagerly he opened his mouth. After allowing her a moment of exquisite exploration, with a cautious, tentative touch, he stroked the velvet plush of her tongue.

She moaned deep in her throat, clutched him tighter and fit her body into his, the sweetness of her belly pressing against his throbbing erection. Almost too dizzy to stand, he deepened the kiss, meeting each thrust and parry of her tongue in an ageless dance of pleasure.

Already lost to place and time and well beyond reasoning, Tony didn't know how much further they would have progressed had not a gust of warm air accompanied by a loud trill of laughter announced the arrival of other guests onto the balcony.

Jenna jerked away immediately, Tony responding a bare second later to draw Jenna back into the shadows. Heart still hammering, he turned to position himself in front of her, blocking her from view should the newcomers chance to glance their way. And not sure whether to curse or bless the interlopers who had put a premature, but probably prudent end, to their interlude.

Mercifully they remained undetected, the chatting couples returning to the ballroom once the orchestra struck up again. After he was certain the others had departed, he turned to her. "I'd best get you back."

Head lowered so he could not read her face, she nodded. Neither of them speaking, he led her down the once again deserted balcony and back inside, where he halted to permit her a moment to smooth her hair and gown. Not able to stand it any longer, at last he allowed himself to tilt up her chin.

Though he'd expected withdrawal, nonetheless a pain

much sharper than he'd anticipated lanced through him when she pulled away, refusing even to meet his gaze.

"I should get back now," she murmured, lifting her skirts as if to step around him.

He didn't want to let her go—not now, not like this. With a touch of desperation, he blocked her path. "Without first slapping my face?"

She shook her head, still evading his eyes.

"I suppose I should apologize—though I can't in good conscience say I am sorry. For upsetting you—if I did upset you, yes. But not for the kiss. At least no one saw us. I did make good on that promise. I shouldn't blame you if you did strike me, though."

Faith, now he was babbling, he realized, clamping his lips shut. But would she not say something, anything?

"How could I, in good conscience, slap you, when what...happened was more my fault than yours? But please—" she raised a hand to forestall his reply "—I do not wish to speak of it further."

Obviously, what had been a moment of pure enchantment for him she saw as regrettable and embarrassing. But what had he expected, he asked himself, suppressing a burgeoning sense of hurt and disappointment. She was no Lady Ellsmere, to whom moonlight rendezvous and serial lovers were sport.

No, this lady would not give her person without first giving her heart. And that, she had made perfectly clear three years ago, she would never offer to a man like Anthony Nelthorpe.

The distress he felt now went deeper than the chagrin he'd suffered on that occasion. This despairing sense of loss, he suddenly realized, more sharply resembled the emotion that had engulfed him all those years ago when Miss Sweet abandoned him to the tender mercies of his father.

Hadn't he learned then that no lady who was truly a lady would concern herself with him?

That Jenna had permitted him close at all was simply testament to how unsettled grief had left her. No doubt she was already chastising herself for the lapse.

Perhaps he could at least do something about that. "Had I not insisted on a dance, it wouldn't have happened. You mustn't reproach yourself for it."

At last she looked up. "You are too kind."

Her face was so bleak that a second wave of anguish skewered him. He would infinitely have preferred that she struck him or shredded his character, heaped all the blame on his shoulders. Anything but know that the crime of kissing him had left her desolate.

With a little sigh she dropped her eyes, squared her shoulders and stepped beyond him, back toward the hall.

He raised a hand to halt her, then let it fall. What else was there to say? Probably better that he not accompany her back to the ballroom, lest her eagle-eyed cousin assume them to have enjoyed a tryst.

An assumption both too close and much too far from the truth.

He followed at a discreet distance, arriving just in time to see Jenna, face once again a serene mask, being hailed by Lady Charlotte Darnell. Not sure whether he wished to leave immediately or try approaching her again after he got his chaotic thoughts in order, he halted behind a pillar some distance away, still close enough that their voices carried to him.

After a warm exchange of greetings, Lady Charlotte said, "Our arrival was so delayed, I feared you might have already departed. Lord Riverton brought a friend who's just returned to London—and whose conversation was so fascinating, we quite forgot the time."

A distinguished-looking man with dark hair graying at

the temples, Riverton bowed to Jenna. Beside him stood a colonel in the dress uniform of the Coldstream Guards, his tall form erect and his gold-burnished hair glowing almost as brightly as the braid trimming his regimentals.

The soldier was opposite Tony, giving him a clear view of the handsome face and intelligent eyes now fixed, with obvious interest, on Jenna.

An instantaneous, instinctive dislike bristled the hair at the back of Tony's neck.

"Lady Fairchild," Riverton said, "may I present Colonel Madison Vernier. He was, as you can see, formerly of the Guards before the Duke requested his services."

"Mayhap you know each other already?" Lady Charlotte interposed. "Lady Fairchild is the daughter of the late Colonel Montague of the Fighting Fifth and accompanied her father both in India and on the Peninsula."

"An honor, Colonel," Jenna said, curtsying. "Though we've never met, I've heard of Colonel Vernier, of course. Who has not thrilled to the tales of his regiment's valor at Barrosa, Salamanca and Vittoria? Not to mention their glorious efforts in holding Hougoumont and saving the Duke's right flank at Waterloo."

A flush rising in his cheeks, the colonel waved a deprecating hand. "My lady, the honor is mine. Though the regiment fully deserves those accolades, I must protest that I did no more than my duty, like any other soldier."

Tony clenched his jaw. He'd heard of Vernier, too—the man was a gazetted hero, frequently mentioned in Wellington's dispatches. And modest as well, it appeared.

"Would that every soldier had performed so excellently," Jenna replied.

"I met your father several times, though we never served together. And I'd been told my old Oxford mate Garrett married a beauty. I see rumor was correct."

Tony frowned. Not only was the man a golden-haired hero, he was silver-tongued as well.

Damme him.

"Now it is you who are too kind," Jenna said coolly, relieving Tony a trifle. Not his Jenna, to be reduced to simpering gratification by a handsome man's compliment.

"My sincerest condolences upon your loss, Lady Fairchild," Vernier said. "I knew Garrett from Eton onward and often enjoyed working with him. His competence, courage and character will be sorely missed."

Did Jenna blush as she nodded in acknowledgment? Mortified, perhaps, to remember how much less exemplary was the man she'd just kissed in the moonlight?

Glaring at the colonel, as if it was Vernier's fault he'd made such mice-feet of the situation on the balcony, Tony missed entirely the man's next words.

Which was just as well. Now that Lady Charlotte had presented Jenna to a military man who was even more a paragon of virtue and valor than her late husband, he might as well go home. Jenna Fairchild was unlikely to spare another thought tonight for the likes of Tony Nelthorpe.

Who had taunted rather than praised her for her virtue and tempted her into succumbing to the pull between them, a connection her senses relished but her mind refused to admit. Thus inducing a lapse in behavior which would likely cause her to keep him at a chilly distance, if she did not terminate their agreement altogether.

Yes, Tony, quite an evening's work you've accomplished, he told himself bitterly.

But like a castaway gamester who had lost his last sovereign and yet stayed at the table, compounding the damage by scrawling vowel after vowel, he could not seem to make himself leave. After Lady Charlotte's party departed for the supper room, he trailed them.

Contrary to her declared disinterest in potential suitors, Jenna did not seem adverse to the colonel's attentions.

And after observing them for some minutes, teeth clenched, Tony's masculine intuition told him that despite his courteous demeanor and impeccable manners, Colonel Vernier was definitely interested in Jenna Montague as well.

Vernier might not let his hands or eyes linger, but he certainly took every opportunity chance afforded him to stay close, taking her elbow to assist her through the crowd, clasping her hand when she placed it on his arm, leaning over to murmur in her ear as they walked.

Finally having enough of observing this subtle courtship-in-the-making, Tony was debating whether to interrupt the group and bid Jenna good-night when Lady Charlotte's party, with Jenna still on Colonel Vernier's arm, exited the supper room.

By the time Tony managed to reach the hallway, Vernier had already handed Jenna into her evening cloak and was leading her in the wake of Lady Charlotte and Lord Riverton, whose carriage it appeared they would be sharing.

Was the colonel conveying her home? Or would he persuade her to remain for an intimate tête-à-tête at the house of Lady Charlotte?

Whatever enjoyment he'd once had in the evening now completely dissipated, Tony limped out into the cold night to summon a hackney.

It seemed only fitting that the moon that had kissed her before he did had now vanished behind a veil of clouds that spit a chill drizzle into his face.

He still had tomorrow's excursion, he told himself. Regardless of how taken she might be with her Perfect Hero, Tony knew Jenna would not abandon her work for the soldiers. Though after tonight, would she still allow him to escort her?

Suddenly the chill seemed to creep into his bones, as it had on more nights than he'd care to remember as he lay shivering in sodden blankets under a Peninsular downpour. His knee, strained by the dance and several hours of walking about, had commenced a familiar, resonant aching.

Grimacing as he climbed out of the hackney, he limped in to the faint glow of the single light Carstairs had left burning in the front hallway. He'd take Cicero and a brandy up to bed, the book to wean his thoughts from this evening's events and the brandy to take the edge off his throbbing knee.

Tomorrow would be soon enough to discover whether that enchanted episode in the moonlight was a memory to cherish—or a curse, for having robbed him of Jenna's company forever.

LATE THAT NIGHT, Jenna sat at her bedside, sipping a sherry to ward off the chill. Lady Charlotte's offer of a ride home had spared her the scold she knew Cousin Lane would have given her for having spent so much of the evening in Anthony Nelthorpe's company.

She could only shudder to think what more he'd have to say should he know how much she truly had to regret. Thank heavens a merciful Providence had spared her discovery!

Having long ago learned 'twas useless to repine over events already transpired, she wasted no further time chastising herself for tonight's appalling indiscretion.

The more important question was what did she mean to do about Anthony Nelthorpe?

She frowned and took another sip of the sherry. She could hardly blame that sorry episode of bad judgment on him. She and only she had furthered their intimacy by laying her head on his chest—and turning his gentle kiss into something quite different.

But how good it had felt to sway with the music, to feel strong, caring arms around her! To be held close and kissed as if she were cherished and desired. Though she'd been appalled, in the stark light of reason afterward, at how fierce was the desire he'd aroused in her.

She'd known for some time he provoked her lust. Hadn't he predicted from the outset that he would tempt her to succumb to it before she managed to reform him? It appeared he had more reason for that boastful claim than she'd initially credited.

For a few moments she toyed with the notion of refusing to see him again, but that smacked of cowardice—and a lack of control. Now that she was fully cognizant of the strength of her desire, she would not allow herself to stray into a situation where the intensity of that need could overcome good sense.

Still, diligence was only a short-term solution. Her marriage had shown her to be a passionate woman, and it seemed that passion survived even after love died. Though she was by no means ready to look for another lover to fill her husband's place in her heart, it appeared her body was fully ready to find one for her bed. Perhaps she ought to admit the fact and look for a suitable gentleman with whom, after a proper interval, to allow that passion free reign.

Perhaps even consider the possibility of remarriage.

Could he speak to her now, she knew Garrett would tell her that as soon as she could, she should put away grief and search for something—or someone—to make her happy. He would probably even agree that reforming Anthony Nelthorpe was an admirable goal, although she was considering it less and less likely she would accomplish that feat.

But in no way could she convince herself Garrett would approve Tony Nelthorpe for his replacement, as either husband or lover.

It seemed, then, that she had better begin considering other candidates. Ones who did not make her, as she had tonight, cringe with shame at her weakness.

Someone like…Colonel Madison Vernier, perhaps?

Colonel Vernier was a man about whom not even the discriminating critic could find anything to complain. His reputation was spotless, his family, Lady Charlotte had later confided to her, the junior branch of a clan that boasted an earldom and he was reputed to possess a tidy fortune. Neither Garrett's family nor Lady Montclare could justify pushing her at other candidates, should it seem she had caught the eye of the colonel.

As for her own preferences, he was appealingly handsome in the uniform she'd grown up admiring, still toiling in the cause for which her husband and father had given their lives. He seemed attracted to her, though it was too soon to tell for sure.

And even if her heart never warmed to another, should he be amenable to becoming her lover, he would doubtless prove congenial, thorough and discreet.

Very well, she decided, sipping the last of the sherry. If Colonel Madison Vernier did show an inclination to pursue her acquaintance, she would encourage it. At least, he might become a congenial friend with whom she could relax and be herself. At most, he might be a friend who turned into a lover, perhaps even a husband.

While keeping Lord Nelthorpe relegated where he belonged, as a casual and occasionally seen acquaintance.

The decision settled smooth and satisfying as the taste of the sherry on her tongue. And when that rogue called for her in the morning as he doubtless would, despite what had transpired between them, it would allow her to face Anthony Nelthorpe with self-confidence and serenity restored.

CHAPTER FIFTEEN

ALTHOUGH SHE'D TOLD NELTHORPE she wished to set out early, Jenna was surprised the next morning when Sancha came in before she'd even left her chamber to inform her that the viscount awaited her in the front parlor.

"Shall I tell him stay or come back, mistress?"

Jenna walked over to peer out her window, a hazy plan forming in her mind. A glance at the sky told her old campaigner's eye that the day would prove fair.

"Help me into the new carriage dress, then go down and ask him to wait. Lady Charlotte told me last night that on the way to the property we will pass Richmond Hill, which has a lovely vista over the city. If I have the kitchen prepare us a basket, we can breakfast on the way."

Thereby avoiding Lane—and a possible scold—in the breakfast parlor downstairs, she thought.

Shaking off the vague disquiet engendered by the thought of spending a day with Nelthorpe, she let Sancha fasten her into the gown. "Pray tell Lord Nelthorpe we'll join him shortly. I'll meet you in the kitchen."

With a nod, Sancha left her. Jenna finished her preparations, grabbed her warmest pelisse and hurried into the hall.

Where she almost stumbled over Cousin Lane, who was slipping from his chamber, a dressing robe belted about him and his golden hair sleep-tousled. Looking as surprised to see her as she was to see him, he halted.

"Heavens, Jenna, where are you off to so early?" he asked. "'Tis barely dawn!"

"'Tis somewhat later than that, cousin," she replied with a smile. "Having lived most of my life with the army, I'm accustomed to rising early. I hope I didn't wake you."

"No, no," he muttered, waving a hand vaguely. "But you look dressed for traveling. Whither are you bound?"

A part of her resented his inquiries, for he had no real authority over her—and she knew he would likely disapprove this trip. But despite Bayard's official claim to be head of the household—and understandably enough, given the titular viscount's disposition—Lane seemed to feel it incumbent upon him to act the responsible male of the family. One of which duties would be to watch over the welfare of its female members.

Rather than waste further time, better to forestall him with a brief explanation.

"I've an appointment to inspect some property outside the city. Sancha as well as John Coachman and two footmen will accompany me, under Lord Nelthorpe's escort. Now, you must excuse me, for the others are waiting."

As she expected, at the mention of the viscount's name, her cousin's face darkened. "Nelthorpe again? I wouldn't have thought that reprobate capable of dragging himself out so—"

A soft noise caught her attention. Lane must have heard it, too, for he broke off and turned to peer down the dim hall. "Don't stand there eavesdropping on your betters, man," he commanded. "Get about your business!"

Emerging from the shadows cast by a large armoire, Bayard's valet Frankston shuffled into view. "Begging your pardon, my lord, Lady Fairchild," he said, eyes lowered as he bowed and hurried past toward the servants' stairs.

Taking advantage of the interruption, Jenna said, "I really must go. I shall see you tonight."

Lane muttered a protest as Jenna dipped a curtsy and walked past him. To her relief, Lane did not attempt to call her back. With any luck, he would be occupied this evening and she'd be spared his lecture until tomorrow.

As she descended the stairs, her spirits rose at the prospect of spending a day out of the noisy, grimy confines of the city. Perhaps this tour into the countryside might give her a glimpse of some place in which she could eventually settle.

But even that vague reference to a future without Garrett caused a painful contraction in her chest. Not wishing to spoil her outing by letting herself be dragged once more into the abyss of mourning, she forced the thought out of mind.

Half an hour later, picnic preparations well under way, she entered the parlor to find Lord Nelthorpe by the window, tapping one booted foot on the floor.

"Good morning, my lord," Jenna said, feeling a bit guilty for having kept him waiting. "I'm sorry to be so tardy. I hope you haven't been too much inconvenienced."

After giving her a bow, he said a bit pettishly, "I was beginning to believe you were not coming at all."

Having not seen him other than charming, Jenna raised an eyebrow. She couldn't recall him indulging in truculent behavior when he'd been one of her father's subordinates in Spain. Perhaps his injuries made him testy in the morning, when his knee was likely to be at its balkiest.

Deciding to overlook it rather than take him to task for his tone, she said pleasantly, "When I explain the reasons for delay, I am sure you will be once more in charity with me. Shall we leave, then?''

''Indeed,'' he replied, his voice still aggrieved. ''Are you sure you will not be too *preoccupied* to go with me?''

Perplexed, Jenna knit her brow. ''I thought we'd agreed last night to view property today.''

''While I tapped my heels in this cursed parlor, I thought—though at this unholy hour I could scarcely credit it—that perhaps you'd decided to allow your new friend to accompany you instead.''

''My new friend?'' she echoed, wondering what maggot had got into his head until, in a flash, an explanation—however improbable—for his churlishness occurred. ''You are referring to Colonel Vernier?''

''You've met some other rich, well-spoken war hero between last night and this morning?''

She *had* noted Nelthorpe observing her from the crowd last night after she was introduced to Colonel Vernier, but as he often watched her when they attended the same entertainment, she'd not given it much thought.

However, combined with his mulish stance and still-irritated expression, incredible as it seemed… ''You are jealous of the colonel?'' she blurted out.

His stance grew even stiffer. ''Now, why should I be jealous? Since I promised to turn away only undeserving suitors, why should I be concerned if a gallant guardsman who still has full use of his faculties, a soldier Wellington himself pronounced 'the bravest man at Waterloo,' should dangle after you?''

''Colonel Vernier wasn't 'dangling,''' she objected, not sure whether to be annoyed or amused by his attitude. ''He was merely being polite.''

''Being 'polite,' was he?'' Nelthorpe retorted hotly. ''Hanging you on his arm, monopolizing your company from the moment you were introduced until your departure?''

''You *are* jealous,'' she repeated wonderingly. Though she knew it should not, a quiver of entirely feminine satisfaction ran through her. ''Have you breakfasted yet?''

''What has breakfast to do with this?'' he retorted.

''I thought not. I've never known a gentleman who wasn't cranky until he'd been fed. Stop this nonsensical brangling and let's depart. I've had a picnic breakfast assembled. We shall stop at Richmond Hill on our way out of town. Lady Charlotte highly recommended the view.''

''I am not jealous,'' he pronounced, his tone still belligerent. ''But I am hungry.''

''Get along, then.'' Jenna gestured to the doorway. Looking a bit mollified, Nelthorpe walked toward it.

As he passed, Jenna had the oddest desire to smooth his dark hair, which stood up a bit in the back, as if he'd been too hurried to comb it thoroughly. For some reason, this flaw in his normally impeccable appearance, combined with the fact that, deny it or not, he *was* jealous of Colonel Vernier, created a warm glow within her.

Heavens, she must be as addled as he, if she were developing an affection for Nelthorpe!

Shaking her head at such folly, she followed him out.

RIDING BESIDE JENNA'S carriage, Tony could only shake his head at his idiotic performance in her parlor. After reminding himself he must be on his most charming—and proper—behavior, should he be lucky enough after last night's stupidity to have Jenna still receive him, he'd acted like a bacon-brained moonling.

'Twas true that he'd slept poorly and awakened shorter of temper than usual. Worried that Jenna might leave London without giving him a chance to apologize, he had thrown on his clothes and rushed to Fairchild House without pausing even for a cup of Betsy's coffee.

Tired, famished and plagued by anxiety, he'd then waited nearly an hour, increasingly convinced that she must indeed have left without him—doubtless in the Perfect Hero's company. So that when she finally did appear, irritation had run away with him, freeing the jealousy he had no right to feel from reason's control.

He could only thank his guardian angel Jenna had not ejected him on his ear.

It not being prudent to count on that angel to intervene should he commit any further idiocies, he promised himself that for the remainder of the day, he would be the soul of wit, courtesy and consideration.

During the limited chat they'd had since Jenna embarked in the carriage, Jenna had not once referred to their interlude on the balcony. Grateful to have a semblance of camaraderie restored, Tony was content to let the distressing matter rest.

The early winter day being unusually mild and sunny, when they reached Richmond Hill, Jenna decided to have the picnic set out on a blanket in front of a copse of trees on the far side of a meadow that bordered the road.

The earth of the meadow being too soft for the carriage to cross, Tony helped the footmen carry over the repast. Jenna had also thoughtfully provided several camp stools, sparing him the humiliation of struggling to lower and raise his stiff leg off the ground.

Sancha and the footmen settled on the blanket, assuring their mistress the thick wool protected them from the ground's chill. Though he'd intended to eat sparingly and concentrate on drawing Jenna out about her plans for the property, the cheerful warmth of the sunshine and Jenna's insistence that he sample a good portion of the repast

Cook had packed soon had him neglecting conversation to devote his attention to the fine assortment of victuals.

Though loath to break the companionable mood, Tony was about to recommend that they pack up the remains and be on their way when the calm of the morning was shattered by the crack of a rifle shot, followed immediately by a menacing and all-too-familiar whine.

Sancha's scream echoing in his ears, Tony instinctively launched himself at Jenna, dragging her down onto the blanket and shielding her body with his own.

"Lord Nelthorpe!" Jenna protested, while Sancha exclaimed in a volley of Spanish and the footmen traded exclamations.

"Silence, all of you!" Tony barked, keeping Jenna flat beneath him while his ears strained for the sounds of crackling underbrush, stealthy footsteps, the metallic click of a rifle being loaded or cocked. After a few long moments, during which he heard nothing but a distant birdsong and his own ragged breathing, he straightened.

What he saw made the breath catch again in his throat. A bare inch above where Jenna's head had been a moment before, embedded in the tree truck behind them glittered the metal casing of a rifle bullet.

It took two attempts before he could get his voice to function. "Are you unhurt?" he was finally able to demand.

"I'm fine!" Jenna said, trying to wriggle out from under him. "But how careless of the hunter to discharge his weapon so close to the main highway. 'Tis a wonder—"

"'Twas no hunter," Tony said, instantly convinced in the wake of Jenna's fall that this had not been a random shot. When Jenna tried to rise, he pushed her back down. "Please, Jenna, not yet." A hand on her shoulder to keep her from moving, he rapidly surveyed the area.

"Pack up everything and return to the coach," he directed Sancha and the footmen, "then have the coachman drive you and my horse back down the hill to that small inn we passed. I'll conceal Lady Fairchild in the copse and make sure whoever fired that bullet is no longer in the vicinity. Once I'm sure it's safe, we'll make our way to the inn under the cover of the trees."

"Should you not take her in the coach?" Sancha asked in a low, urgent voice.

"Too much open ground between here and there." He gestured to where the vehicle was drawn up some two hundred yards away. "I'll not give whoever might be watching a clear field of fire while she crosses this meadow."

"Aye, my lord. Keep her safe. We do as you say."

"Oh, really, Sancha, there's no need..." Jenna's words trailed off as, swiftly following Tony's instructions, the maid piled dishes in one of the baskets and set off with it at a trot. Her eyes widening, Jenna's gaze followed the girl, obviously surprised by her instant compliance.

She looked back at Tony, eyebrows raised. "You certainly succeeded in spooking Sancha," she said, amusement mingled with aggravation in her tone. "But at the risk of stating the obvious, my lord, this isn't Spain, nor are there likely to be French sharpshooters trying to use us for target practice."

"That bullet was entirely too close, Jenna. I'll not risk allowing whoever fired it another shot. Now, while I remain in front of you, back quickly into the trees."

"Nelthorpe, this is ridiculous!"

"Just do it, Jenna! I'll explain later." Uttering a quick prayer of thanks that the thick blanket on which they'd been picnicking was a dull brown, he gathered it up. "James," he called to the footman who was completing the packing of the crockery, "a hand up, if you please."

Jenna looked for a moment as if she would protest

further, but by the time the footman had hauled Tony back to his feet, she evidently had decided to cooperate—at least for the moment. Cautiously, as he'd instructed her, she began to back toward the thick stand of evergreens.

"Thank you," he said as he covered her movements, a trace of humor in his voice. "I was afraid for a moment you were going to make me carry you."

As soon as they'd penetrated within the thick cloak of greenery, Tony came to her side and seized her hand, half-dragging her across a small clearing to a large fir tree. Pulling her beneath its sheltering branches, he threw the blanket over her, leaving only her face free.

With a soft exclamation of annoyance, she whispered, "Now I'm to be swaddled like a bandit? This delusion has gone far enough! Why would anyone shoot at us?"

"Trust me a bit longer, Jenna," he whispered back. "I'm not hallucinating that I'm back on some Peninsular battlefield. Stay here and don't move, speak, or do more than breathe until I get back."

"There'd better be a good explanation for all this when you do," she muttered.

"There will be. Do you still carry that knife?" When she nodded, he continued, "Take it out. And if anyone but me comes near, use it."

CHAPTER SIXTEEN

HOPING HE'D CONVINCED JENNA to remain under cover, Tony limped back to the edge of the copse. Was he making too much of the incident?

But after peering out over the meadow in the direction from which the bullet had been fired, his soldier's instinct, which had saved his neck on several occasions, still warned him the shot had been deliberate.

For one, except for the dense grove in which he'd hidden Jenna, the area was relatively open, not prime territory for hunting game of any sort, particularly not with its position adjacent to a major thoroughfare. Across the road beyond the meadow, the ground rose under a scattering of trees, barren now of leaves but numerous enough to offer cover and a vantage point to an attacker.

The same open ground that had led him to conceal Jenna rather than send her back to the carriage would now prove useful. Knowing that no one could cross the meadow to hunt for her without Tony seeing him, he would be able to search the hillock from which the shot had been fired.

Of course, to do so, he would first have to cross that same field, leaving himself open to a second shot, should an attacker still be lurking. But given how relatively useless his war injuries had left him, he couldn't see why anyone would go to the bother of putting a bullet in him. 'Twas far more likely that Jenna had been the target. To protect her, he needed to find out as much as possible about this attack.

A slow, deadly rage coiling in his gut, he limped from behind the sheltering evergreens. Bad knee or no, he'd welcome the opportunity to confront anyone who would target a defenseless, unarmed woman.

Pausing first by the tree in which the bullet had lodged, Tony estimated its approximate trajectory, then loped awkwardly across the meadow and into the trees.

After a bit of searching, he found a wide oak with a clear view over the meadow, behind which the greenery had been matted down. From the spot, boot prints in the soft earth led to fresh horse droppings and a set of arriving and departing hoof prints. Concluding from those that whoever had ambushed them had already departed, Tony retraced his steps to the copse.

That it had been an ambush, he was now virtually certain.

Which meant, like it or not, he would have to share his suspicions with Jenna.

Shouldering his way back into the thicket, Tony was pleased to note that not only had Jenna stayed hidden, so well was she concealed that, even knowing she was somewhere under the fir tree, he could not locate her. At his call, she pulled back the branches, gesturing for him to follow her through a narrow tunnel of greenery to a spot beneath another fir where she'd spread the blanket over a cushion of pine straw. "Sit," she said, pointing to the makeshift couch, "and tell me what this is all about."

Grateful he wouldn't have to try to haul himself up from flat ground, Tony lowered himself to the wool-cushioned surface.

"Quite a bower you've created," he said.

"I've had a bit of practice over the years. But tell me,

what did you find, and why did you think someone would fire on us?"

Briefly he described the scene on the hillock and then reluctantly related the questions that troubled him about her accident.

He saw on her expressive face the moment incredulity progressed to doubt. "You—you actually think," she cried, interrupting his narrative, "that someone deliberately set out to rob me of my child?"

"All I have are suspicions. Before I can draw any intelligent conclusions, I'll need to question the groom involved."

"Who was conveniently turned off," she muttered. Then she straightened, her eyes widening as the full implications of his doubts penetrated. "B-but that would mean," she gasped, "that Garrett's own *cousin* conspired to injure me? The man under whose roof I've been living for nearly two months? No, I cannot believe it!"

"If the accident was deliberate—and mind, I'm not claiming that yet—'twas not necessarily Bayard who arranged it. Can you think of others who might wish you ill?"

Understanding flashed in her eyes. "The widow at Garrett's reception who accosted me— And...and Lucinda Blaine, too, I suppose. Perhaps even Aunt Hetty, who seems to resent my presence so fiercely. Though I don't know how any but my husband's aunt could have known I was with child."

"If your relations knew, their servants did. Such news travels."

"But how could any woman be vicious, monstrous enough to plan and execute such a thing?"

He sighed. "Despite living with an army, you're still such an innocent. Venality exists in the world, Jenna."

Pushing away memories he had no desire to examine, he said, ''I've seen its face.''

She studied him. ''While you were earning your tarnished reputation?''

All his life, he thought, but he didn't want to talk about his father. Besides, they needed to concentrate on the problem at hand. ''Grief could, I suspect, be as effective as a lust for power in driving someone beyond the restraint of reason. As could jealousy.''

''But if making me lose the child were the goal, why would someone be firing on me now?''

That was the question that troubled him. ''I don't know. Without the child, you are no longer a threat to Bayard and the succession. Perhaps the widow's grief-maddened rage would not be satisfied unless you too are dead, like her husband? Or did Lucinda Blaine find having you in the midst of the ton, still carrying Garrett's name and recognized as his wife, too much to tolerate?'' He sighed. ''I admit, it all seems rather far-fetched.''

Her face troubled, she nodded agreement. ''Perhaps the fall and the shot are just coincidence.''

''Perhaps,'' he conceded. ''But that bullet in the tree out there is real. We can't afford to underestimate the gravity of the incident until I've had time to investigate more thoroughly.''

He frowned, the implications of this new attack, if it had been planned as an attack on her, suddenly crystallizing. ''However, if this is not some odd coincidence, you are still in danger. You really should leave Fairchild House.''

She laughed shortly. ''And go where?''

''Could you not arrange to stay with Lady Charlotte for a time?''

She shook her head. ''If I am in danger, I would not wish to put someone else at risk. Besides, I'm my father's daughter, and cannot stomach running from a threat. If someone deliberately caused the accident that cost me my child, I want to find out. I want to deal with the person or persons responsible. And if there is a plot to discover, I am more likely to find it if I remain at Fairchild House, going on as normal."

"Do you really think you can go back to Fairchild House with the doubts you now harbor and 'go on as normal'? You've never been one to dissemble. For your own safety, as well as to further the investigation, you should leave. Inform the Fairchilds you wish to visit old friends, or—"

She held up a hand. "Don't try to tell me I should stay away while you search for the truth. This is my life, my child who was lost, and I cannot sit by idly doing nothing!"

"Even if remaining might place your life in greater danger? That's not a risk I'm prepared to accept."

"'Tis not *your* risk to accept. Besides, of what great value is my life? Oh, I go through the motions of doing something useful. But beneath the surface..."

She paused and took a deep breath, her eyes filling with tears and on her face that expression of numb anguish he'd seen that night on the bridge over the Serpentine.

"Beneath the surface," she continued, her voice hardly above a whisper, "there is...nothing."

"Nonsense," he countered, alarm prickling his nerves. "You have your work, your friends—"

"I have nothing, nothing that truly matters!" she cried. "Don't you see that? The only life I've ever known, everyone I've ever loved—my mother and father, Garrett, and now his child—all of it is gone."

She looked up, accusation in her face and raw agony in her eyes. "Why? Why did he have to die, and you lived?"

No sooner had the words left her lips than she gasped and clapped a hand to her mouth, shaking her head as if to deny what she'd just uttered. "I'm sorry! I didn't mean—"

"Don't you think I ask myself that every day?" he interrupted, her outrage touching some deep answering chord within him. "Why I was spared when so many other men—worthier men, braver men, were taken?"

Perhaps it was delayed reaction to the shock of being shot at, or perhaps her grief, too rigidly restrained for too long, just overcame her. Whatever the reason, she put her head in her hands and began to weep.

The deep, wrenching sobs shook her slim body and clawed at his heart. Unable to bear watching, he leaned over and pulled her into his arms.

"Please, *querida*, don't cry," he whispered into her hair while she clung, weeping, to his chest. "Don't you know I would have died in his place, to make you happy?"

Rocking her in his arms, stroking her hair and muttering endearments, he held her until the gasping sobs slowed and her breathing quieted. Finally she lifted her head from his chest.

"I'm so sorry," she whispered again. "For—for saying that. For—"

"It doesn't matter," he whispered back fiercely. Tipping up her chin, he kissed her.

'Twas a gentle caress, meant to comfort and reassure—at least, he thought he'd meant to begin thus. But as he kissed her, the pressure of her lips—or was it his?—grew more intense, his grip on her—or was it hers on him?—tightened. And at some point, his lips parted at the urging of her tongue.

He had no time to puzzle it out, for almost before he realized what was happening, her hands were stroking his shoulders, her mouth urgent, her tongue aggressively exploring his, and tenderness had dissolved into a fire that seared him to the marrow.

Before prudence melted completely and all the blood in his brain rushed to his nether regions, he made himself break the kiss and pull away. "Jenna, don't! I want this—Lord knows how much I want it—but you will hate yourself for it. You know that!"

She looked up at him, her eyes dark with desire and anguish. "Please, Tony, don't push me away. Don't leave me all alone!"

Please, Tony... When she seemed to need him so badly and called him by name, how could he not heed her plea?

Were he a better man, he might have summoned the wit to find a safer way. As it was, when she reached up and pulled his head down, captured his lips and delved into his mouth, his rioting senses rejoiced. Only the last, tiny functioning bit of his brain wondered despairingly whether, after this voyage to heaven was done, she would ever forgive him.

His final conscious thought before he gave himself up to the long-anticipated pleasure of her arms was if he must face hell's wrath later, he would savor every taste of paradise now.

He tried, he really did try, to hold himself back, slow the pace, but Jenna was having none of it. Her tongue scouring his, she nibbled and sucked at his mouth while her impatient fingers pulled at his garments. Swiftly dispensing with the fastenings of his greatcoat, she tugged aside his coat and waistcoat, yanked at his shirt. He heard the protesting rent of fabric and then, in an electrifying slide that made him gasp, felt the soft warmth of her hands against the bare skin of his chest.

He tried to pull her closer, but she fended him off, mimicking with her fingers on his nipples the glancing caresses of her tongue against his. Groaning, he stilled, allowing her this pas de deux of tongue and fingertip, pleasure coursing through him and bringing him very close to the limits of his control.

He would like to have returned the favor, but her pelisse and gown were protected by an army of tiny fastenings his lust-clumsy fingers could not conquer. While he fumbled at her neckline, she caught his hands, moved them down to her skirts.

Comprehending the request, he began pulling the fabric upwards, hungry for the feel of her bare skin under his hands. At last he worked the material up high enough to be able to stroke the glorious roundness of her calves.

Intent on his goal, he'd just blessed his woolen trousers, whose muffling thickness might allow him to stave off completion long enough to bare and caress and taste her essence, when her clever fingers suddenly transferred themselves to his trouser flap. His hands, any remaining thought and all movement stilled as she plucked open the first straining button.

With a fumbling, disjointed movement he tried to resume his own quest, but she caught his hand. Still nibbling and teasing his tongue, she popped open two more buttons.

Much as he wanted to taste her, knowing instinctively what she intended, he could not bring himself to stop her, even though her touch there might well catapult him beyond control. Clever torturess that she was, she seemed to sense he would not try to prevent what her swift, deliberate actions promised.

He sucked in a breath at the feel of chill air against his overheated member, then stopped breathing altogether when she grasped him and took his measure in one firm stroke of his shaft. Her tongue still working his, she feathered her fingers up and down his length, caressed with her thumbs the taut throbbing skin at his tip.

Well beyond words or caution, immobilized by her touch, he didn't think the sensations could get more intense without driving him over the edge—until in one swift motion, she bent and tasted him. After laving the head of his erection with quick, glancing strokes, she paused to suckle, sending scorching waves of pleasure radiating throughout his body and wrenching a cry from his throat.

Seeming to sense just how close to the precipice she'd driven him, she released him and moved away. Before the guttural exclamation of protest left his lips, she'd guided him back against the pinestraw cushioning, pulled up her skirts, and straddled him.

For a moment the sheer wonder of finding himself enclosed within her warm flesh paralyzed him, swelled his chest with a sweetness as piercingly intense as his desire. But before he had a chance to savor it, to pull her face to his and cover it with kisses, she began to rock her hips, driving him deeper.

Wanting desperately for the loving to be as rapturous for her as it was for him, he bit his lip, knowing he wouldn't be able to last much longer under that exquisite onslaught. But suddenly she tensed, her fingers biting into his shoulders as she uttered a fierce cry.

Caught off guard by the swiftness of her climax, he exterminated the protest of his thwarted body and simply held her, drinking in the sound of her gasping breaths as they eased and steadied. Relieved to have pleased her, loath as he was to have passion ended, he was about to make himself pull gently away when, hugging him close, she once again rocked her hips.

His rigid shaft, still sheathed deep within her, leapt in response. Murmuring in what sounded like approval, she quickened the pace, pulled his head down to lick his lips with greedy impatience. His member tightening at each stroke of her tongue, though he craved the satisfaction of hearing and feeling her dissolve into climax around him again, he wasn't sure he could hold off long enough the explosion building within.

But as before, her desire spiraled quickly, and within a few moments her even breathing had deteriorated to ragged gasps. He reached down to cradle her buttocks and bring her closer, increasing the force and depth of each thrust. And seconds later, her fingers once again clenched on his shoulders and her body convulsed.

Like the most exquisite starburst, the tension within him exploded, firing every nerve with sensations that lingered, scintillating and shimmering, in long slow aftershocks. As rapture cooled to simmering hum, he fought the urge to sink into blissful unconsciousness.

Knowing how little time he had left to savor the incredible gift she'd just given him, he cradled her against him, tangling his fingers in the damp tendrils that had escaped the pins of her coiffure. Until he realized that the small, slight tremors now shaking her body were not the aftermath of passion—but stifled sobs.

Anguish skewered his chest. He wanted to comfort her, offer words of affection, but the syllables clogged in his throat. He could only hug her more tightly while moisture filled his own eyes and dripped down into her hair.

He wasn't sure how long they stayed thus, but some time later, with a shuddering sigh, Jenna gently pushed herself upright. With quaint dignity, on hands and knees she backed away, removing herself from him—and him from her—until beyond the sheltering branches, she stood and smoothed down her skirts, turning away while she tidied herself to give him privacy to straighten his own garments.

He wished rather desperately to say something, but could not decide what. She'd likely dismiss as too facile or calculated the endearments on the edge of his tongue, however genuine and honestly he felt them. She might even resent them, believing he had no right to offer, nor she to hear, any words of affection.

As she remained silent, in the end he said nothing, either.

His humiliation deepened at knowing he was going to have to half-crawl from under the branches until he could reach a handhold far enough from the tree's base to be able to lever himself upright.

But before he could initiate that procedure, Jenna leaned closer and offered her hand. With his other arm braced against the tree and her pulling, he was able to stand up.

Touched by that kindness, an ember of hope stirred. Maybe she wasn't going to despise him after all.

But she did nothing further to encourage that optimism, turning her back on him again once he was upright and walking with quick steps back toward the meadow.

He limped after, stopping her with a touch before she could exit the curtain of greenery. Though she flinched, at least she did not pull away.

"I believe our assailant rode off immediately after he fired the shot, but let's be prudent." *As they had just been most imprudent.* "I'd prefer that we avoid the road and make our way downhill under the cover of these woods."

"Will that not be more...difficult for you?" she asked without looking at him.

She meant his leg, of course. "I can manage," he replied shortly. "Also, though the coachman and footmen seemed as startled by the shot as we, just in case someone at Fairchild House is involved, I shall tell them I've concluded it was a hunter's stray bullet."

"As you wish," she said, and stood aside to let him lead the way.

As you wish... So many things he wished for. That he could have been as strong and upright of character and frame as the man she'd loved. That she might have looked at him after their coupling with joy, or at least satisfaction, in her eyes. That she would look at him at all, now.

That she might not banish him forever.

The silence in which they made their slow descent over the often steep, rock-strewn ground did not give Tony much reason to believe any of his wishes would be granted. Not until they reached the inn yard did Jenna turn to him and say softly, "Thank you...for keeping me safe."

Before he could reply—even if he'd known what to reply—Sancha spotted them and came running, throwing her arms about her mistress with a welcoming cry. And then the footmen appeared, babbling questions, and the coachman approached, wishing to know whether they intended to continue their journey.

Deciding that until they solved the mystery of the attack, it would not be wise to take her into unfamiliar territory, after answering the inquiries with the story they'd agreed upon, Tony told the coachman to ready the carriage for a return to the metropolis. Then Sancha, her thanks ringing in his ears, shooed him away to partake of some ale and hot meat pies, telling him she had bespoken a private parlor where she could assist her mistress to bathe her face and repair the ravages crawling under pine trees had wrought in her gown and hair.

How differently might Sancha treat him, he wondered with a grim twist to his lips, if she knew what else had transpired beneath that shelter of trees?

From the moment Sancha spotted them in the inn yard,

they had no opportunity to exchange a private word. Once the ladies descended from their private room, Jenna announcing she felt quite fit for the return journey, Tony could do little but summon his horse and content himself with riding alongside the carriage, still wondering how Jenna would deal with him now.

Don't think about it, he told himself. As he had on the eve of a battle, he reminded himself that what was going to transpire would happen when and whither it would, and could not be changed by any amount of worry.

That rationale gave him no more comfort now than it had in his army days.

He struggled as well to beat out of his brain the searing images of Jenna making love to him. Faith, though he'd known in his bones since practically the moment he met her that she would prove a passionate, inventive lover, reality far exceeded his fondest imaginings. He would indeed be the luckiest bastard in Christendom were this morning to mark the start of a long-term liaison.

He might even dream, could he bedazzle her as much as she'd bedazzled him, of coaxing her to marry him, permanently solving with one blow both his monetary difficulties and the deep need that seemed to have rooted itself in him to keep Jenna Montague close.

Ah, to think of knowing she'd be waiting every night in his bed! He had to grin. 'Twould be enough to inspire a man to frequent naps in broad daylight.

But, he thought, his grin fading, her rigid silence and the silent weeping after their joining more likely signaled that, as he feared, Jenna had regretted their impulsive coupling from the moment the heat of passion cooled. The fact that he'd, however feebly, sought to prevent it probably wasn't going to help him salvage something of their relationship.

Much as he'd love to keep her as his lover, he'd settle

for trying to recapture the teasing, semiadversarial relationship they'd had before this journey.

He would, he realized, agree to virtually anything, as long as she continued to see him.

Just when, he thought bleakly, had Jenna Montague become so essential to his well-being that the thought of living the rest of his days without gazing on her face or hearing her voice had come to seem intolerable?

Idiot, he castigated himself, to have stumbled so far down that road, when he'd known from the beginning that, given their history, he was lucky she even tolerated him.

But he'd have to coerce her into doing at least that. Though he might not yet be able to prove it, all his instincts told him Jenna Montague was still in danger. He intended to protect her whether she wanted his protection or not, until he'd removed whatever threatened her.

His eyes narrowed as he recalled the chilling image of the rifle bullet buried in the tree trunk just over her head. She might not be so lucky next time.

Their midmorning return journey took much longer than the passage out, now that the streets were filled with their usual complement of merchants, urchins, vehicles and pedestrians. It was nearly luncheon when Jenna's coach finally halted before the entry to Fairchild House.

"I urge you to reconsider staying here," he said in a murmur as he waited to hand her down.

"Nothing and no one will drive me away," she replied. After hesitating, as if not wishing his assistance but unable to manufacture a plausible public reason why she would suddenly refuse it, she took the arm he offered.

Silence strolled with them up the stairs.

Somehow he was going to have to get her alone, make her talk to him and try to repair the ragged breach their lovemaking, born of her desperation and his desire, had ripped in the fragile fabric of their relationship.

But as they entered the hallway, they were met by the butler—followed by Colonel Madison Vernier.

CHAPTER SEVENTEEN

"MY LADY, YOU ARE HOME much earlier than expected!" Manson exclaimed. "I'd just been telling the colonel you were to be out of London for the day."

"We had an unforeseen…change in plan," Jenna said.

"How fortunate for me," the colonel said, bowing to her. "'Tis a delight to see you again, Lady Fairchild—and Mr.…" he let the sentence trail off.

"Viscount Nelthorpe, formerly Captain Lord Nelthorpe of the First Dragoons," Jenna said.

The colonel's assessing glance turned to approval. "The Royals, eh? A pleasure to meet you, my lord. A good show your troopers made of it at Mont St. Jean."

Dispensing with the lie that he was pleased to meet Vernier—especially not lying in wait for Jenna in her front hallway—Tony replied, "Not nearly as impressive as your stand at Chateau Hougoumont."

Vernier waved away the praise. "Am I interrupting your plans?" he asked, giving them a speculative look.

"Lord Nelthorpe was just leaving," Jenna replied. "I'm a bit…fatigued after my journey this morning, and was about to rest."

Perhaps it would be better if he did not attempt to talk with her now, Tony thought, damping down the hurt spiraling through him at her dismissal. She probably needed time to sort out her thoughts.

Some distance wouldn't hurt his perspective either.

"I am disappointed, for Lady Charlotte sent me to see

if you would join her, Lord Riverton and I for nuncheon,'' Vernier was saying. ''Actually,'' he added with a far too attractive grin, ''I asked if I might include you, and she readily agreed. We shall be devastated at your absence.''

Jenna paused, obviously considering the offer despite her alleged fatigue. ''I should hate to disappoint my dear friend.''

''We must treat with tender care those we allow close to us,'' Vernier agreed.

Color crept into Jenna's face. *So she cannot dismiss me so easily,* Tony thought, somewhat mollified.

''Indeed,'' Jenna said, not looking at Tony. ''If you do not mind waiting, after I change my gown and refresh myself from the...rigors of road, I should be happy to join you.''

''I don't mind at all,'' Vernier replied. ''Lord Nelthorpe, I hope to see you again. Thank you, Manson, I can find my way back to the parlor.'' With a bow to them both, he walked away.

Tony ought to be equally polite and take his leave, but the imperative to get some sense of how relations now stood between them made him plant his boots in the center of the hallway and stay there.

Finally she was forced to glance at him, though she still wouldn't meet his eyes. ''Lord Nelthorpe, thank you again for your care of me today.''

''For all of it?'' he asked, knowing it probably wasn't wise to force matters but compelled to ask.

Her face colored. ''I shall have to...consider matters carefully. We shall talk later. For now, I bid you good day.''

His pulse leapt and he released a shaky breath. So she wasn't going to repudiate him completely—not yet.

''Until later, then, Lady Fairchild,'' he agreed, and bowed himself out.

TAKING A COVERT GLANCE over her shoulder from her vantage on the first floor landing, Jenna watched Lord Nelthorpe limp out the door Manson held open for him.

God in heaven, what had she done?

With a sigh, she continued down the hallway. She'd thought once she reached the sanctuary of her chamber she'd be able to pawn off everyone with a plea for the solitude in which to compose herself after the shocking events of the morning—avoiding even a solicitous Sancha. Nor was she sure she was ready for company yet.

But she'd had plenty of solitude during the long carriage ride back. And Colonel Vernier's unexpected arrival would allow her to implement the tentative conclusions she'd reached during that journey.

She'd spent the first hour with her face still burning in shame at her brazen boldness. There could be little doubt what Anthony Nelthorpe thought of her now. A woman whose words proclaimed virtue but whose acts proved wantonness. She'd virtually confirmed his swaggering claim that, given the attraction between them, she wouldn't have resisted him for long, had he persisted in trying to compromise her all those years ago at Badajoz.

No, her actions today made her face what she'd been denying since that morning. Having lured her to that deserted location to, he claimed, nurse injured women being brought there from the city, Nelthorpe proceeded to ask for her hand—and the fortune she'd just inherited from her father. Having long been attracted to each other, they would deal well together, he promised. And added, lest she prove reluctant to accept his offer, that he didn't intend to let her depart until she granted him her hand—and her favors.

Under the guise of acquiescing, she'd been able to wrench free and impress him with the finality of her refusal by drawing a knife blade across his throat. But in her heart, she'd known that had he really meant to hold her there against her will, with his superior size and strength he could have wrestled the knife from her and overpowered her resistance. He hadn't, even in that instance, been quite as black a villain as she had always tried to paint him.

Afterward, Garrett had intervened to insure Nelthorpe was not able to approach her, sparing her the necessity of confronting him and her contradictory feelings.

But oh, how priggishly certain she'd remained of her own moral superiority, looking down on Nelthorpe for his reputed lapses into dissipation! So proud of her own vaunted self-control. Despite the clear warnings she'd received in their last few meetings, she'd persisted in feeling arrogantly confident of her ability to resist the attraction between them.

This morning's incident had given her a more penetrating insight into the flaws of her own character than she'd really wanted, showing her to be just as capable of such lapses and just as lacking in self-control, as Nelthorpe himself.

True, her thinking had been clouded by a sudden paroxysm of grief, Nelthorpe's suspicions forcing her to confront again all that had been taken from her. Just when it seemed that she was beginning to pull free from the morass in which she'd been dragged after the double blows of losing Garrett and his child, anguish struck her unawares, sucked her back into the vortex of pain and despair in which she'd spent most of the hellish first months after Waterloo.

Sometimes she wondered whether she would ever be completely free of it. Only to feel in the next moment a stronger guilt that she would ever wish to lose sight of the enormity of what she had lost in losing Garrett.

Pushing that thought aside, she made herself focus on the implications of her lapse in behavior. But more troubling than the lack of self-discipline that had led her into his arms was the stark realization that, even in anguish, she would not have lain with a man for whom she cared nothing.

She couldn't, for instance, imagine having reached out to Lane Fairchild, despite his consideration for her.

So she had to admit there was something about Nelthorpe that attracted her on a level deeper, more fundamental, than mere lust. A conclusion that alarmed her far more than having to admit her other faults.

Much as he'd pleasured her—and she wasn't hypocrite enough to deny the pleasure he'd given her—in his embrace she'd also found comfort. And not just the simple comfort, after eight months of desolate loneliness, of being enfolded within strong masculine arms.

She'd wept afterward on Nelthorpe's chest at the tenderness of it, with guilt that she was alive and Garrett was not, with shame at replacing him in her arms with this man of whom he would never approve. For much as Garrett might—*might*—forgive an act committed in the fog of grief and passion, she was certain he would neither understand nor forgive the...affection she was beginning to harbor for Anthony Nelthorpe.

She wasn't sure what to do about it herself, she concluded as she entered her chamber. She knew her battered spirit was still too fragile, her feelings too entangled in grief and regret, to allow her to become emotionally tied to any man.

She should put some distance between herself and Nelthorpe, let this confusing boil of emotions cool.

Besides, she concluded as she rang for Sancha and threw open the door of her wardrobe, Nelthorpe had won their wager this morning. She could dispense with the pathetic illusion of trying to reform him.

Colonel Vernier's timely appearance offered her a chance to replace Nelthorpe's escort with a man to whom not even Nelthorpe himself could fault her for turning. Who would question her forming a preference for the company of this well-respected soldier of unimpeachable character, a member of the dearly familiar army world in which she'd spent her whole life?

Should the colonel reciprocate her interest, she would have the opportunity to see, as she'd previously decided would be wise, if she could not forge a connection with this man of whom Garrett would certainly approve.

She also needed the lucidness of mind—a state she had difficulty maintaining when the viscount came near—to consider what to do about the attack on her life, if such the events of this morning proved to be. Not for Jenna Montague Fairchild to run away while some man tried to solve her problems for her.

Upon that resolve, Sancha walked in. Stopping short at the sight of Jenna at her wardrobe, she said, "Mistress, you go out? I thought you would rest."

"Lady Charlotte bids me to nuncheon," Jenna answered, not wishing to bring up with the too-perceptive Sancha the part Colonel Vernier had played in the invitation. "Getting out will clear my head, help me to think what should be done about the...incident this morning." *Thank heaven Sancha knew about only one of them.* "You did warn John Coachman and the grooms to say nothing, did you not?"

"Yes, my lady. Like you ask, I go with the carriage to the mews and beg all the men to stay silent. I tell them we do not wish your cousin or aunt to be alarmed, since Lord Nelthorpe decided the shot was accident."

"Good. By the way, what made you so amenable to doing Nelthorpe's bidding? I felt sure you would protest being hurried back to the carriage."

"One day when you were out, my lord sent for me. He told me he feared your fall was not accident."

"The devil! How dare he do such a thing behind my back, as if I were a child incapable of defending myself!"

"He said he did not wish to worry you when you have so much grief already."

Her irritation softened. It was hardly fair to hold such consideration against him.

"He knows you, my lady," Sancha said. "He knows you cannot hide your anger, if you think someone harmed you or the babe."

"It appears I shall have to develop the ability to dissemble, then."

Sancha considered that. "So what mean you to do now?"

"Try to discover if someone did cause that fall. Manson summoned a hackney for the widow who confronted me the day of our reception. I mean to discover her direction and call on her."

Sancha raised her eyebrows. "It is wise to go to her, when she wished you ill?"

"I want to watch her face and read her reaction when I mention my loss. That will tell me whether she was involved or not."

"She might also strike again, if she believes you suspect her."

"She's not that large or strong. I can defend myself if I must, Sancha."

"Aye, my lady, I know you are strong and swift. But I do not like this. Why not work with his lordship on this?"

"Work with him!" Jenna echoed in surprise. "I thought you considered him the Evil One!"

"People change, mistress. He is not so bad a man now, I think."

Nor am I as good a woman as I once thought. "I know," Jenna admitted with a sigh. "Therein lies the problem."

Sancha stared at her for a long moment. "We do what we must when it is time," Sancha said gently. "Colonel Garrett would not wish you to grieve forever."

Jenna wasn't ready to discuss that, not even with her sympathetic longtime friend. "Perhaps not. But he would disapprove if I kept Colonel Vernier waiting, so you must help me into a fresh gown and get the last of the tangles out of my hair."

Tacitly accepting Jenna's change of subject, Sancha went to fetch the hairbrush. "I will keep watch, but you must be careful, my lady. Not just with the widow, but also here. We do not truly know these people, Colonel Garrett's family. Can we not stay elsewhere?"

"'Twould look most peculiar if we were to leave my husband's home for no pressing reason. English ladies do not live alone, Sancha."

"Then I think you must let Lord Nelthorpe help you find the truth of this."

Torn between resentment and admiration at how Nelthorpe seemed to have won over the previously disapproving Sancha, Jenna replied a bit sharply, "When did you develop such an admiration for Lord Nelthorpe?"

Sancha shrugged. "He kept you safe, my lady."

That being the truth, she dare not protest further, lest Sancha become more suspicious than she already was about the nature of Jenna's involvement with Nelthorpe.

He'd kept her safe from her assailant, she thought as Sancha helped her into the gown. *But not from herself.*

Sobered by that fact, Jenna decided that when she returned from nuncheon at Lady Charlotte's, she would pen Nelthorpe a letter conveying her gratitude for his previous service, but asking him not to call again—a feat she wasn't sure she could accomplish while in his physical presence.

The coward's way out, she admitted with chagrin. But this newly self-aware Jenna Montague would no longer be arrogant enough to underestimate Anthony Nelthorpe's power over her will, her emotions or her senses.

EARLY THAT EVENING, Tony sat in the hackney Carstairs had summoned for him, headed in defiance of all his good resolutions toward Fairchild House.

He'd gone home determined to put the matter from his mind and study a portfolio of papers that had just arrived from the estate manager at Hunsdon Park. Time he began, as his benefactor Mr. Harris had advised, to learn the business of managing his own lands.

He'd bathed and changed, then lunched in the library with the papers spread across the wide desk.

All to no avail. That well-honed soldier's instinct sat heavy as a stone in his gut, the sense of unease distracting him, making the figures dance before his eyes. Neither coffee to keep him alert, nor wine to relax him, were of any use in shaking that strong foreboding.

Then in the late afternoon a package arrived, barren of card or note. Inside was a new linen shirt—doubtless to replace the one, buttons ripped off in Jenna's quest to reach bare skin, that he'd reverently folded and placed in the back of his wardrobe.

Was this her way of making restitution for damage done? Or an attempt to try to nullify what had happened?

Giving up on the papers in disgust, he'd stumped upstairs to get himself into his evening rig and set off for

Fairchild House. Though he'd not allowed Jenna much time to sort out her feelings, he couldn't stand the uncertainty any longer.

After he'd asked to see Jenna, the butler escorted him to a small parlor, his well-trained servant's impassive face telling Tony nothing. So his pulses leapt when a quarter of an hour later, the door opened.

To admit Sancha. "I am sorry, my lord, but my lady is preparing to go out. Colonel Vernier comes for her soon. But she bid me give you this." Regret in her eyes, Sancha held out a note.

Tony looked at his name written in an elegant sloping hand and the dread in the pit of his stomach intensified. With great reluctance, he took it from Sancha's hand.

"There is no chance of persuading her to grant me a few minutes?"

"I tried to persuade her. I am sorry, my lord." After giving him a compassionate look that only deepened his dismay, Sancha curtsied and walked out.

Willing his fingers not to shake, Tony unfolded the note. The message was predictable and brief.

My lord, I can never convey to you the extent of my gratitude for your many kindnesses. However, as events have made it obvious that my character has even more need of improvement than yours, I feel it best that we do not see each other again.

Evers will continue to work with Sergeant Anston regarding the welfare of the soldiers, so you may direct any inquiries on this matter to him. I remain cordially yours...

He wasn't sure how long he stood there, paralyzed by a sense of loss deeper than anything he'd ever known. Yet, what had he expected? That he, reforming rogue that he was, might ever win the affection of someone like Jenna? Especially now that a handsome, courageous career army officer so like the man she'd married had walked without a limp into her life?

Though he'd had little enough experience with the emotion, he supposed he might as well admit that, idiotic as it was, he had fallen in love with Jenna Fairchild.

What a magnificent piece of stupidity, he congratulated himself, cobbling together the remnants of the childhood heart once held by Miss Sweet and casting it at the feet of Jenna Montague.

Who, after their disastrous tryst in the glen this morning, could no longer stand the sight of him.

Some time later, Tony found himself on the dark street outside Fairchild House without any memory of how he'd gotten there. But as he limped away, too restless to be confined in a hackney, the inescapable conclusion returned.

Jenna Montague was still in danger. He would have time later to worry about gathering up the shattered pieces of the heart he'd not known he possessed, but first, he must see this campaign through. He must discover the truth behind her accident and the shot fired on Richmond Hill.

Only then could he force himself to devote his efforts to bringing his estate and finances back from the brink of ruin—while trying to salvage his equally devastated heart.

He imagined he'd not do a much better job of the latter than the surgeons had in repairing his knee.

CHAPTER EIGHTEEN

ASHAMED OF HER COWARDICE, Jenna watched from behind the curtain at her window as Anthony Nelthorpe limped down the darkened street. She should have had the decency to deliver her dismissal face-to-face, rather than by letter.

But the unwelcome swell of emotion in her chest as she watched him walk away should be evidence enough of how unwise it would have been to have risked seeing Nelthorpe. She dare not allow him the opportunity to spin once again the spell he seemed to cast over her.

She'd not been writing mere courtesies, however, when she thanked him for his kindnesses. As she composed her missive, she'd been struck by how many there were—from his forgiving her ill-tempered attack on his character that first day to the unquestioning support he'd offered her that night on the bridge and at Lady Charlotte's reception. The perceptiveness with which he'd sought to pull her from her grief by involving her with the plight of the soldiers. His understanding words on the moonlit balcony.

The tenderness with which he'd kissed her.

Still, she mustn't try to invest that regrettable interlude in the woods with too much emotion. To one as experienced in dalliance as Nelthorpe, their tryst had probably meant nothing more than an unexpected opportunity to enjoy a willing female. 'Twas unlikely physical intimacy would propel such a man to develop for her the sort of warm affection she seemed to be conceiving for him.

Enough, she told herself as he disappeared out of sight. Colonel Vernier would arrive any moment, she had a dinner to attend, people to converse with, a worthy cause to promote.

And Anthony Nelthorpe to put firmly out of mind.

As if the thought had conjured him, Sancha came in to announce that the colonel awaited her below. If he did like her, Jenna mused as she descended to meet him, it would prove useful, both in distracting her from Nelthorpe and in offering her a more suitable gentleman toward whom to direct her attention.

First, though, she needed to know him better. So she set out during the carriage ride to encourage the colonel to talk about himself and his interests.

Like most men, he was quite willing to do so, though when they arrived at their destination, he seemed surprised and a bit chagrined. ''Forgive me, Lady Fairchild! I've barely given you the chance to utter a syllable. You should know better than to get an old soldier talking.''

''Not a bit,'' she replied. ''Although you never served with my father, you were in many of the same campaigns, and I find it interesting to hear another intelligent observer's perspective on the events. I hope we shall be seated near enough at dinner to continue the conversation.''

''Since our host, Lord Mulhollan, is involved as I am in preparations for the next round in Vienna, I imagine most of the talk will center on that. Not, I'm afraid, a topic of scintillating interest to ladies. However, I've been promised there will be music and cards after dinner.''

''Now, why do gentlemen automatically assume that because they cannot hold cabinet positions or ambassadorships, females have no interest in politics? Lady Charlotte tells me that Lady Mulhollan is just as engaged in the preparations as her husband—and, in fact, offers him excellent counsel.''

''So she does, and I beg your pardon. You, too, are interested in the ongoing diplomacy?''

''If all the sacrifice at Waterloo is to have any meaning, then the diplomats must cement the peace for which so many gave their lives.''

''Capital!'' he exclaimed, appearing impressed. ''I must admit, my desire to have you present this evening was entirely selfish, that I might accomplish some necessary consultations without depriving myself of the pleasure of your company entirely. I dared not hope that you might actually enjoy the dinner conversation.''

''My father often invited officers to dinner, and they would discuss current political and army matters. So I grew up more familiar with such talk than chat about fashion or the latest ton gossip. Which perhaps makes me an unnatural female in your view,'' she added wryly.

''Rather a most intelligent and knowledgeable one.''

The carriage halted, sparing her a need to reply to that gallantry. He handed her down, then took her arm to assist her up the entry steps.

The colonel was a handsome, well-made man and Jenna found the familiar scent of shaving soap and virile male quite attractive. But, she noted dispassionately, there was no prickling at the back of her neck, no spark that radiated through her fingers when he touched her.

Which did not mean, should matters progress in that direction, that she might not at a later time find the prospect of intimacy alluring. As best she could recall, she had not had an instinctive physical response to Garrett, either, yet their lovemaking had been deeply satisfying.

She'd been drawn to Garrett for his handsome face, but even more by an unfailing courtesy made more intriguing by the melancholy that colored his face and voice. Naturally, once rumor had whispered the reason for this reserve, she had felt compelled to try to draw him into cheerful conversation whenever they had occasion to meet. As they grew to know each other, she'd naturally fallen in love with his sweetness and excellence of character.

If more time together showed she and the colonel to be equally compatible, they might eventually develop a mutual fondness. And desire would take care of itself.

With a little smile, she recalled the early days of her marriage, when she'd shocked Garrett by trying to seduce him one night under the stars. Since soldiers in an army on the march spent long stretches bivouacked under canvass or the open sky, she'd decided within a few weeks of wedding him that she did not intend to forgo the pleasure of her husband's touch unless they had the luxury of four stout walls and a conventional bed. She'd swiftly persuaded Garrett to adopt that opinion.

"Amusing thoughts?" The colonel's voice startled her.

Fortunately, the flickering light from the flambeaux flanking the entry hid her blush at having been caught entertaining carnal remembrances. "Merely woolgathering, I fear. Pray forgive me."

Heavens, she was little better than Nelthorpe! Who, the odd thought struck her, had not seemed at all shocked by the idea of trysting under the trees.

Then they were in the foyer, any chance for private chat at an end as they were conveyed to the parlor where the rest of the dinner party awaited them. Lady Charlotte, looking lovely in the deep blue shade she favored, sat with Lord Riverton, in earnest conversation with their host. On the sofa opposite, two other couples were equally engrossed. After greetings all round, the party proceeded to dinner.

During the meal, Jenna listened with interest to the discussion of the upcoming Congress, as Mulhollan and Colonel Vernier engaged Lord Riverton and the two gentlemen in a debate over which goals the British contingent should pursue and how the Duke should go about promoting them. Lady Charlotte spoke in low tones to their hostess and the wives, who provided a commentary on the personalities to be attending the Congress that formed an interesting counterpoint to the policies being talked over by the men.

Having spent the last eight months first in hospitals, then in the overheated drawing rooms of the ton, Jenna found herself reveling in this lively debate of real issues and meaningful ideas. Moreover, Vernier's comments showed him to be a keen observer who crafted his opinions carefully and was ready to listen to opposing views. An admirable trait, Jenna thought, and rather rare, military men generally having a tendency to forcefully assert the superiority of whatever action they promoted.

The men electing not to remain at table to take their port, the group retired to the parlor, Lady Mulhollan entertaining them upon the pianoforte while Lady Charlotte sang. A small group, including Colonel Vernier and their host, continued a low-voiced conversation in one corner.

As those ladies finished, Colonel Vernier broke away and came over with a smile, asking Jenna if she would like to stroll into the gallery and inspect their host's excellent collection of landscape paintings.

For a moment Jenna was taken aback. If Nelthorpe had suggested such a thing, she would immediately have suspected his reasons for wanting to get her alone. Given what she knew of the colonel's character, however, it didn't seemed creditable that he would attempt to take liberties, especially on such slight acquaintance. Curious what he did intend—and confident that she could protect herself if need be—she agreed.

They walked to the adjacent gallery, which showcased a number of fine landscapes, including several by Turner, a new artist whose diffused focus and violent colors were quite unusual. After admiring them, Jenna said, "Must you complete more consultations this evening?"

"No, we just finished the draft of the agenda the Duke requested, with which I think he shall be pleased."

"You seem to enjoy diplomatic service."

"I do. Having been a soldier throughout the Peninsula and at Waterloo, I, like you, have a great stake in securing the peace so many gave their lives to win. And now that, praise God, we've no longer a war to fight, I find the diplomatic process interesting and nearly as exciting as soldiering. If somewhat lonely."

Jenna laughed. "From what Lady Mulhollan has been telling us of the throng of visitors in Vienna for the talks, the beauty and charm of the ladies and the gaiety of the entertainments, I take leave to doubt that!"

"Oh, there are crowds of people and scores of entertainments. But in the midst of all that, one can still be lonely."

His words struck a resonant chord, and Jenna's smile faltered. "One certainly can."

"I see my observation upset you," Vernier said, studying her face. "Pray, excuse me."

Jenna forced back the smile. "'Tis not your fault. Sadness is a constant companion, but I do not intend to let it monopolize me tonight."

"I am glad of it! I did not mean to suggest my reasons for melancholy are nearly as compelling as yours. I've simply found that I sometimes wish I were back in the field, in the company of comrades with whom one could speak freely without worrying over every nuance."

''I imagine 'tis wearying to be always on display.''

''Indeed! Having had no assurance of surviving the war, until our final victory I shied away from making commitments not connected with my army duties. But now that I shall probably, praise God, never walk a battlefield again, I find that I—I long to have someone with whom I can spend time without having to watch every word. Someone who finds the work I do important, who would enjoy discussing it, perhaps even offering advice.''

So, Jenna thought, the colonel is looking for a wife—or a long-term lover. And apparently he was concluding that she might fit the requirements.

Maybe she would. And maybe he could fit hers.

''I think all of us seek that,'' she said at last.

He held her gaze. ''Do we? Then I am emboldened to speak further. Before you think, in presuming to proceed, that I am not giving due regard to your widowhood and the brevity of our acquaintance, please hear me out!''

He inhaled a shaky breath. Incredibly enough, Jenna realized, this seasoned soldier who had withstood wave after wave of attacking French infantrymen was *nervous.* About addressing *her.*

The thought was so ludicrous, she had to bite her lip to keep from giggling. Fearsome Jenna Montague, making a gazetted hero tremble.

''As you may have guessed, I shall be in London only a short time, and in any event, it is far too early for you to consider what you will do after your year of mourning ends. But as I likely will be away from London most of those months, and because you have made a most deep and striking impression on me in the few days since we were presented, I wanted to beg you to consider allowing me to call on you when I do return—once you are ready to entertain calls from gentlemen, that is.''

He cleared his throat and ran a finger along the edge of his uniform collar, as if it were suddenly too tight.

Jenna found this evidence of uncertainty in the hitherto supremely confident colonel rather endearing. "I should be honored. Now, that was not so bad, was it?"

He looked at her sharply, then grinned. "Was it so obvious? I must confess, I'd rather have undergone a barrage from Boney's artillery! I'm afraid I'm not much at expressing myself with ladies."

Jenna laughed. "That, Colonel, I refuse to believe!"

"Making fulsome compliments or conducting light flirtation is a great deal different from referring to that which deeply touches the heart. Now, I should get you back—not that you need worry that our absence might cause talk. We are among friends tonight, none of whom engage in gossip. But our host shall be very cross with me if I monopolize your company any longer."

He offered his arm, and during the transit back to the parlor, kept her amused with a story of a contretemps between one of Wellington's staff and a Prussian officer. When they reached the threshold, though, he halted and brought her fingers to his lips.

"Thank you, my lady, for warming my heart with hope."

Lady Charlotte raised a speculative eyebrow as they entered, but said nothing to Jenna until some time later, when she accompanied her to the ladies' withdrawing room.

"Did you have a pleasant chat with the colonel?"

"Yes," Jenna replied. "I found the landscapes striking, especially those by Mr. Turner."

"Vernier was not importunate, I trust," Lady Charlotte said, a trace of anxiety in her tone.

"Oh, no! Quite the gentleman. Would you have reason to suspect otherwise?"

"Not really, else I would never have allowed him to spirit you away. Though he is more Lord Riverton's friend than mine, I have never heard of him going beyond what is courteous and attentive. Which he has certainly been to you. In fact, he has been so unusually attentive I felt I must assure you that I have not been playing matchmaker!"

Jenna gave her a look. "Have you not?"

"Only so far as to introduce him and then agree to include you in several entertainments we were to attend."

"He did mention during our walk that he would like permission to call upon me, once he's completed his mission in Vienna," Jenna confessed. "When I am ready, he said. If I'm ever ready," she added in an undertone.

Lady Charlotte pressed her hand. "I did wonder, now that the war was over, if he might decide 'twas time to seek a wife. But I understand your hesitance and shall be happy to help warn him away, if you wish."

"I don't think that will be necessary, but thank you."

Lady Charlotte shook her head. "During my widowhood, I have been subjected to far too many matchmaking schemes by well-meaning friends and relations ever to indulge in such meddling myself."

Lady Charlotte's vehemence was convincing, if a bit surprising. "You have no desire to remarry?"

Lady Charlotte continued to adjust the pins in her golden hair, remaining silent for so long Jenna began to regret asking so personal a question. Finally she said softly, "I was an impetuous young girl when I married, convinced that my handsome husband and I should be eternally happy. But over the course of our marriage, I discovered that…that his desire for an heir was stronger than his affection for me."

When Jenna murmured sympathetically, she added, "Of course, every man wants an heir, so I cannot really fault him for growing bitter when we suffered disappointment after disappointment. Still, that young girl's heart never recovered. I suppose I've become a coward, unwilling to trust that any vows of affection could withstand the trials time and adversity make upon marriage.''

Even Lord Riverton's, Jenna heard the unspoken conclusion. Thanks to the loquacious Lady Montclare, she'd been told the full story of the duke's lovely daughter who'd been courted by two rival suitors, one whom she married and the other who had swallowed his disappointment to remain her lifelong friend.

How sad, Jenna thought, recalling as they walked back to the parlor how often Riverton's gaze lingered on Lady Charlotte, how he seemed ever ready to escort or assist her. Ready to be so much more.

Yet she could understand just how hard it was to risk the precarious peace one had painfully assembled out of the wreckage of one's dream by daring to embrace another.

Which recalled to her Nelthorpe's speculation that someone might have assisted in the wreckage of hers. He'd urged her to leave Fairchild House and seek refuge with Lady Charlotte.

While, for the reasons she'd given him, she had no intention of doing so at this moment, perhaps it would be wise to confide their suspicions to this lady who was highly-placed enough that, should something happen to Jenna, her demand for an inquiry into the affair would not be easily dismissed.

She *would* tell Lady Charlotte, Jenna decided—but not until after she'd called upon the Widow Owens and determined whether their conjecture about her accident had some validity or were as much a grief-stricken woman's delusion as that lady's accusations of her.

Whether by chance, or Lady Charlotte's design in the

wake of their talk, the four of them took a single carriage home. Colonel Vernier walked her into the foyer, not releasing her arm until Manson took her cloak. Then, after gazing at her a long moment, he kissed just her fingertips.

Thoughtfully Jenna watched him depart. From his expression, she guessed he'd wanted to kiss more than her hand, but had not dared. Curious how she might have reacted to that, she was a bit sorry he'd refrained.

Nelthorpe would not have hesitated.

She sighed as she mounted the stairs to her room. Surely she didn't really prefer the behavior of a presumptuous rogue like Anthony Nelthorpe to that of a true gentleman like Colonel Madison Vernier.

Near noon the next day, Tony returned to Fairchild House. Knowing Jenna would not receive him, he demanded instead to speak with Sancha.

Though Manson shook his head over Nelthorpe's request, he did send for the maid. A few moments later, Sancha met him in the smallest of the downstairs parlors—a testament, Tony thought with grim humor, to how his worth had fallen in the eyes of the butler. Still, the pose of discarded swain, which was only too close to the truth, would serve them well as a cover for his snooping.

"I am happy, my lord, that you come. I feared you would not, now that my lady..."

"Has dismissed me?" he said bluntly. "I suppose she had cause, especially after—well, enough said. Whether or not she receives me, we must still find out what happened that morning in the park. Were you able to discover the groom's direction?"

"He went to his sister's house, Minter Cottage on the Leatherhead Road near Woodcote. Southwest of the city."

Less than a day's ride. Good, he would head there tomorrow.

"Excellent work! I shall visit there directly." He paused at the door. "Thank you, Sancha. I hope your mistress appreciates you."

She looked back unsmiling, sympathy on her face. "I hope my lady appreciates you."

CHAPTER NINETEEN

IN LATE AFTERNOON THE NEXT day, Tony rode into the small village of Woodcote, praising his Maker that the former groom's sister had settled near a village off the main road and not in one down some farm track he would have had great difficulty finding in the fading dusk. From a small inn just ahead, a welcome blaze of light offered the tantalizing promise of a hot meal and a full tankard.

The modest hostelry didn't cater to the gentry traveling on the main road to Guildford, so in the nondescript dark clothes into which he'd changed for the journey, Tony looked little different from the clerks and merchants seated in the busy taproom. As an outsider, he would immediately become the focus of all eyes, so, wishing neither to attract undue attention nor excite suspicion by appearing to want to avoid it, he took a seat and waved to the landlord, who hurried over to serve him.

By the time he'd bespoken a chamber for the night and partaken of an excellent roast chicken, he'd confided to his friendly fellow-diners that Anthony Hunsdon, late of Wellington's forces, was traveling to his new position as estate agent for an Army toff under whom he'd served in Belgium. While en route, he'd promised to deliver a message to a comrade's sister who lived near Woodcote.

Accepting the offer from a clerk and a merchant to join them for a round of cards, as he proceeded to lose the first hand, Tony asked if either of them knew the whereabouts of Mrs. Staines of Minter Cottage. After a brief consultation, his opponents informed him that the former housekeeper lived with her unmarried daughter about a mile south of the village, just off the Leatherneck Road.

"Have you seen her brother about?" Tony asked casually. "I understand he was paying her a visit."

"So he was, and used to come in here to heft a pint right regular. Paid in good coin, too," the merchant said.

Working to keep his voice carefully even, Tony said, "You haven't seen him recently?"

The cardplayers exchanged a look that made Tony straighten in his chair. "Not recently," the clerk said at last. "Sorry if he be a friend of yourn, but we buried ol' Nick two weeks ago. Shot through the heart, he was."

As if a chill breeze had suddenly blown into the room, Tony felt the hair at the back of his neck prickle.

"Hunter's stray bullet, the magistrate decided," the merchant added, "though we didn't never find anyone what claimed to be shooting near there that day."

Hunting accidents were not that uncommon—even fatal ones. But the suspicion driving him could only be heightened at discovering that the principal witness to the events surrounding Jenna's accident was now conveniently dead. Killed, it appeared, by a stray bullet—just as Jenna might have been at Richmond Hill, had he not thrown her to the ground.

Anxious as Tony was to learn more, there was no point alarming Mrs. Staines by appearing on her doorstep well after dark. But first thing tomorrow, he would pay a condolence call on the groom's sister.

SOON AFTER BREAKING HIS FAST the next morning, Tony rode south on the Leatherneck Road, soon coming upon a neat thatch-roofed cottage. After tethering his mount, Tony limped to the front door, anticipation speeding his heart.

An older woman in the dark gown of a housekeeper, her graying hair topped by a white lace cap, answered his knock. "Good morning, ma'am," he said, doffing his cap. "You are Mrs. Staines?"

After she nodded, her pale blue eyes watching him warily, he continued, "Anthony Hunsdon, ma'am. So sorry to hear of your loss. My army mate's sister Maggy, cook at Fairchild House in London where your brother used to work, was concerned about him after the…trouble there. When she heard I was riding south to take up new employment, she asked if I would check about him on my way through. She'll be devastated to hear of his accident."

Was it only acute suspicion that made him think she flinched, her pale face growing paler still when he said he came from London?

"Thank you for your kind words, Mr. Hunsdon."

"A hunting accident, it seems? I don't wish to pry, but I'm sure Maggy would want to know as much about what happened to Nick as I can glean. She had a great… fondness for him," he added, shamelessly embroidering on his story.

"My Nick, he was quite a devil with the ladies," she began and then halted, a spasm of some strong emotion wiping the fondness from her face.

Grief? Or something else?

She certainly appeared nervous, though that might stem from being confronted on her doorstep by a strange man. Finally, after a long hesitation, she waved toward the interior of the cottage. "Would…would you like a glass of cider before you continue your journey?"

Tony tried to tamp down a thrill of exultation. After all, he'd learned exactly nothing yet that had not already been conveyed to him by the tavern patrons.

"That would be most kind, ma'am," he said, following her into the cottage.

"Maud," she called to a tall, thin girl tending the hearth, "pour up some cider for the gentleman and fetch some apples from the storehouse, please."

The girl dutifully brought him a brimming mug and plodded out. As soon as the door closed, Mrs. Staines looked back at him, distress evident in her face.

"Be ye a Bow Street man?"

Surprise held him speechless for a moment. "No indeed! Why would you think so?"

"Well, you said there'd been some 'trouble' in London and my Nick, he never said nothing of trouble."

"How did he explain his presence here?"

"He told me his old master had died and the new one brung in his own man. Said he'd paid Nick off right handsome, so he meant to take some time to visit here before he looked for another situation. But…but he never looked for nothing, and he acted so strangelike, keeping to himself during the day, going down to drink every night at the Ox and Cock."

"Perhaps he was despondent at losing his position."

Twisting her apron in her hands, Mrs. Staines shook her head. "Mebbe. Then after he was shot—he didn't die right off, you know—he rambled in his head some. Kept saying as how he was sorry, that he wished he'd never listened to that lady, sweet as she seemed. At first I thought he meant the squire's wife here, who told him he ought to take that job in London. But after he died, when I was going through his things to find a clean shirt to bury him in, I found—" she lowered her voice to a whisper "—a great lot of money."

Tony's pulse jumped, but he kept his voice even. "His severance pay, don't you think?"

"Seemed far too much for that. How did he come to

have such a sum? Sir, if you know that my brother committed some…crime, please tell me, and I'll turn the money over to the constable! I don't want no lord out of London coming down here, seizing my house and throwing my poor girl and me onto the street!''

A sweet lady. A great deal of money. Though his nerves hummed with excitement and alarm, Tony made himself concentrate on the harried face of the woman before him.

''Mrs. Staines, I'm sure you have nothing to fear. The Fairchilds are generous to their staff—'' Garrett would have been, anyway ''—so I'm certain the money you found represents wages honestly earned. As for his regrets about a lady, you should know that Maggy, whom your brother fancied, is about to marry. I suspect she felt guilty about causing your brother pain and was hoping I'd be able to write her that he had recovered from his disappointment.'' *Tony, you're a hopeless prevaricator.*

Mrs. Staines let out a breath. ''Be ye sure, sir?''

Offering a quick prayer that easing this woman's anxiety would mitigate the sin of all the untruths he'd spun her, Tony nodded. ''I'm certain. Keep the money your brother left without worry.'' *The brother already paid dearly for it.*

''How can I thank you?'' Mrs. Staines cried, relief lightening all her features.

Tony shrugged, possessed of enough conscience to feel ashamed at deceiving her. ''No need for thanks.''

''I've got fresh bread from this morning's baking and ham in the larder. Let me make you up some for the road.''

Tony let himself be persuaded to accept that and another mug of cider, trying not to show his impatience to be gone, now that he'd obtained the news he sought.

It appeared his instincts had been right, he thought as

Mrs. Staines prosed on. Jenna's fall had indeed been orchestrated. But by a mysterious lady, not her cousin.

The widow? The Countess of Doone? Causing the loss of Jenna's child seemed to Tony the sort of spiteful thing a female might do. But he had a harder time reconciling the shot fired at them with a woman's revenge. Still, the two must somehow be connected.

Finally able to break away, Tony directed his mount back to London. Somehow he must convince Jenna to receive him—and this time, talk her into leaving.

Knowing he'd look like a looby if he appeared at Fairchild House still covered in mud, Tony stopped briefly at North Audley Street to clean up, change and gulp down a hasty mug of ale. But he reached her house to be given the frustrating news that Lady Fairchild was out for the evening—in company with Colonel Vernier. Nearly gnashing his teeth, Tony called instead for Sancha.

After remarking delicately that gentlemen who were truly gentlemen accepted a lady's decision without hectoring her, a disapproving Manson reluctantly summoned the maid. In an urgent undertone, Tony told her what he'd learned in Woodcote and asked her to arrange an immediate audience with Jenna.

"She must leave here, Sancha, as soon as possible. 'Tis foolish to risk further danger! Surely you see that!"

Sancha sighed. "I have urged her to leave, as strong as I dare. She will not go until she learns the truth, she says—so like her father she is! Also have I advised her to work with you, my lord. She says it was her child lost and her battle, not yours. That you—endanger each other."

Tony felt himself flushing at the look Sancha leveled at him, but before he could decide what to reply, she continued, "You did not learn for certain who this lady is, or whether the groom meant for the horse to throw my mistress?''

''No,'' he admitted reluctantly.

''Then though I, too, see danger, I do not think I can make her leave—or meet you.''

Agitation and anxiety boiled in his veins. But short of tracking her to whatever entertainment Vernier had escorted her and hauling her off by force, Tony didn't see what else he could do to protect her tonight.

''Speak to her anyway, please. I'll be back tomorrow.''

''I will try again, I swear it,'' Sancha said. ''And I will sleep in her room. I, too, my lord,'' she said with a little smile, ''am good with a knife.''

With that, Tony had to be content. He hauled his saddle-weary body into the hackney Sancha summoned, trying not to think that even at this moment, Jenna might be in Vernier's arms, waltzing in secret on some balcony—letting him kiss her in the darkness. A furious hurt exploded through his fatigue at the thought of the colonel slipping with her into some deserted bedroom.

He mustn't think, he reprimanded himself, that just because *he,* rake that he was, couldn't be close to Jenna without thirsting to make love to her, that the proper colonel would be equally lost to propriety.

Idiot, a voice answered. *He's a man, isn't he?* Jenna wasn't some innocent ton virgin, beyond the touch of a gentleman of honor, but a mature woman who was mistress of her own conduct. Could any man who found her alluring—and Tony had seen lust in the gaze the colonel had rested on her—resist attempting to seduce her?

Resist, in the intimacy of some shadowed chamber, peeling down the scanty bodice of her evening gown, so much less an impediment to caresses than the traveling clothes she'd worn the morning of their tryst? Keep himself from baring her breasts, suckling the nipples Tony hungered to tease, cushioning her against the accommodating surface of a real bed while he eased up her skirts and tasted her, unleashed that rapid, fierce response?

He fought to contain the images boiling out of his brain, an amalgam of fondest memory and bitterest imagining. Until just as the hackney turned into North Audley Street, out of the agony and envy evoked by those thoughts, a more selfless realization emerged.

He, who had been banished for good cause, might not be able to get close enough to protect Jenna. But Colonel Vernier certainly could.

If he met with Vernier and convinced *him* Jenna was in danger, the colonel had just as much skill and many more resources to provide her protection.

Even if by going to the colonel, Tony was thrusting the woman he loved straight into the arms of his rival.

For the duration of the hackney ride he remained irresolute, his last hopes of solving the mystery and perhaps winning her back warring with his growing fear that, unless she were moved soon to a place where she could be better protected, she might not survive long enough for the mystery to be solved.

He might be a glib prevaricator and a rake, but when his hopes and Jenna's welfare were weighed in the balance, there was no choice about the outcome.

Swallowing the bitterest decision he'd ever had to make, Tony resolved to call upon Colonel Vernier in the morning.

CHAPTER TWENTY

AFTER DETOURING BY Upper Brook Street to obtain Vernier's direction from an obliging Fairchild footman, early the next day Tony rode across Westminster Bridge into Lambeth. With a tepid sun mitigating the chill, the ride might have been pleasant, were it not for the mission he must fulfill upon arriving.

As Tony expected of a military man, despite the early hour, the colonel was already at work, so Tony was shown directly into the study. The colonel rose as he entered.

"What can I do for you this morning, my lord? If it's collecting funds for your veteran relief effort, I have already pledged assistance to Lady Fairchild."

"I didn't come on the soldiers' behalf," Tony replied, taking the chair beside the desk the colonel indicated. "It's Lady Fairchild herself who concerns me."

The colonel raised an eyebrow, his expression growing noticeably frostier. "And what have you to do with her?"

At the innuendo, both proprietary and condescending, that he had no business having any personal dealings with Jenna, Tony's noble resolve started to crack. Instead of the diplomatic address he'd practiced during his ride over, he found himself blurting, "Just what are your intentions toward Jenna Montague?"

"Though I don't see what concern it is of yours, rather than argue the point, let me say directly that I am considering asking *Lady Fairchild* to become my wife."

'Twas what he'd feared and expected, yet still that bald declaration shook Tony to his boots. His mind gone blank, he could dredge up neither protest nor reply.

The colonel's face took on a faintly pitying look Tony resented even more than his condescension. "Since you have been something of a friend to her," Vernier conceded, "let me point out the benefits of such a connection. Her extensive experience as a campaigner and her familiarity with many of the general officers, including some of the allied commanders with whom she dealt after the fighting in Belgium, will allow her to mix easily in the elevated Society in which I move. Her person and manners are charming, and though I am not in immediate need of it, her wealth would not come amiss. Whereas I can offer her a prestigious position for which she is well suited within a military and diplomatic world she finds comfortable and familiar. I judge it an advantageous match for us both."

Position. Society. Wealth. The colonel spoke in terms of assets, as if evaluating the purchase of—of investment property. Ignoring the fact that most ton marriages were based on little more, Tony couldn't help demanding, "But how do you feel about her?"

"Feel?" the colonel repeated with a moue of distaste. "I esteem her, of course."

"A rather cold assessment."

The colonel stiffened. "Perhaps a man of your ilk can't understand the difference, but we are talking of choosing a wife, not an actress out of the Green Room."

So Vernier "esteemed" her, but passion was to be reserved for women of another sort. How dutiful and proper. Did the colonel have any idea of how very passionate and *im*proper his prospective wife could be? Damme, Jenna's fire would be wasted on this prig!

Before Tony could reply, the colonel continued,

"Now, having freely offered you any reassurances you might need of the honorableness of my intent, let me add this. Given my plans, I advise you to limit your contact with my future wife to what is strictly necessary in your consultations on the soldiers' relief. I shall urge her to eliminate even those as soon as possible. The future Mrs. Vernier must be free from any taint of scandal."

Restraining the hot replies that hovered on his tongue, Tony made himself swallow the insult and focus on his reasons for coming here. "Since you confess yourself concerned with Jenna's welfare, I must tell you I believe she is now in danger."

The colonel's eyes narrowed. "Danger? What danger?"

Briefly Tony related the facts about Jenna's accident, the shot fired at her and inquiries he had begun. "I have not yet been able to investigate all the possibilities, but since I—I am not in a position to safeguard her, I felt it necessary to bring this to your attention. I've urged her to remove from Fairchild House until the matter is resolved, but thus far she is resisting. I'm hoping you will add your entreaties to mine."

The colonel sat silently, obviously pondering what Tony had related. "You have no real evidence that her fall was other than accidental?"

"No," Tony admitted. "Not being able to talk with the groom responsible, I have no way of determining for certain whether he deliberately switched mounts and then withheld information about the borrowed horse's temperament, hoping Jenna would induce the mare to bolt."

"Although it's possible, I suppose, it doesn't seem reasonable to me that any lady of the ton—one of them a countess, no less!—would have the means or experience to arrange such an accident. To conspire with a *groom,*" Vernier exclaimed with a grimace of distaste, "much less to engage some assassin to shoot at her. And it doesn't seem unreasonable to me that a servant discharged for his negligence would have made up a story to cover his guilt—or be melancholy over a lost love."

"The latter story was my invention!" Tony protested.

"Still, your conclusions seem a bit far-fetched. Scheming relations, jealous former lovers, mysterious assassins—and you offer no proof beyond vague suspicions?"

"That shot was not fired by any wandering hunter."

"So you say. You've no proof of that, either."

"Her maid thinks the danger real as well," Tony said doggedly.

The colonel sniffed. "She, of course, being trained in intrigue?"

"She traveled all those years with the army, and developed an instinct for danger as keen as any soldier's," Tony snapped back.

"I'm sorry, Nelthorpe, but I simply don't find your so-called 'evidence' convincing, nor with all I have to do before my imminent departure do I have the time to indulge in a game of blindman's bluff with some probably imaginary villain. It would be most disconcerting as well to discover Lady Fairchild to be involved in so tawdry a scheme. However, since it *is* her welfare we are discussing, I will mention the matter to Lord Riverton. He has many contacts in and out of the government, and can investigate this properly, if he thinks it warranted."

"So you'll not urge her to leave Fairchild House?"

"On what grounds?" The colonel waved an impatient hand. "I'm to have her spurn the hospitality of her relations, insinuate that her own husband's cousin and member of a family with an impeccable reputation for honor and valor, *might* have tried to engineer the demise of her child, on the basis of no hard evidence whatsoever?"

"Then you don't really care about her," Tony said, his jaw tight.

"That is both presumptuous and preposterous, sir," Vernier retorted hotly. "I found, while investigating her fitness to become my wife—"

"You *investigated* her?" Tony said incredulously.

"—that she had been often in your company and so made some inquiries about you. Although your war record is unexceptional, your conduct prior to your military service leaves much to be desired, while your father—"

"Let's leave my father out of this."

"Given the man's character, or lack thereof, I can understand that wish. The bare truth, I'm afraid, is that your reputation remains unsavory. Though it may be easy for you to imagine rogues under every bush, I myself would not consider accusing—or suspecting—members of my own class of such villainy on the basis of nothing but wild supposition. And if you claim to actually wish the best for Lady Fairchild, then I suggest you prove it. Summon whatever nobility exists within your dubious character and distance yourself from her before her own stainless reputation is soiled by your own. Now, sir, I must ask you to leave. I have important work and little time left in which to accomplish it."

The colonel stood, indicating the interview was over. Hands curled into fists that he burned to smash into the colonel's handsome, self-righteously smug face, Tony gave him a brief nod and stalked out.

He was streets away before the fog of rage cleared enough for him to consider what he must do next. Spotting an entrance to the archbishop's gardens off Lambeth Road, he turned his mount from the busy street and rode in.

It appeared he'd held his temper and abased himself to no purpose. Tony liked neither the man's evident opinion that his diplomatic work was more important than investigating a possible danger to Jenna nor his insinuation that if the matter were true, the scandal sure to follow its disclosure would render Lady Fairchild less worthy to become Vernier's wife.

Perhaps what Jenna needed right now wasn't a scrupulously honorable man who assumed, until he had "hard evidence," that all aristocrats behaved with equal honor, but a rogue who thought like a rogue. And if the colonel could not be bothered to concern himself with taking measures to protect Jenna's safety, Tony would have to confront Jenna himself and insist on it.

A small measure of warmth kindled in his chest. To do so, he would have to see her again—soon. That resolve made, he kicked his horse to a trot. On the ride back, he'd ponder how to best accomplish that.

Just before he exited the park, he passed a woman walking, market basket over her arm. His horse was three paces beyond her before something familiar about her face and form made him pull up his mount and turn in the saddle.

A second look confirmed that first impression. Shock and incredulity warring in his mind, he wheeled his mount and rode back to dismount beside her.

"Miss Sweet?" he demanded incredulously.

The tall woman stared back at him, her expression wary. "Tony Nelthorpe," she said quietly.

"Yes! What are you doing here? How have you been all these years?" He clamped his lips shut before he could add, "Why did you leave without a word?"

"I'm quite well, thank you. I've lived here for a decade and been married nearly two to a very kind man."

If she'd lived here that long and read the journals, she would have known from the gossip in the Society columns when he'd been in residence. He gave her a twisted smile. "I was about to ask why you never contacted me, but I imagine such news as you had wouldn't have encouraged you to think it worth your while to communicate."

A flicker of a smile touched her lips. "So you are still honest with yourself, I see." That face he'd loved so dearly in childhood, still remarkably unlined, studied his for a long moment. "The only thing I regretted about quitting Hunsdon all those years ago was having to leave you in your father's care."

"I...missed you." *Dreadfully.* "But Papa said you'd found a better position, so I hoped that things went well for you, and I see they have. I am happy for that."

"So that's what he told you." For an instant, a bitter expression marred the serene face. "I always wondered what he'd said—if he said anything. Whether you hated me."

"I was confused...angry, even," he admitted. "Lonely. But I never stopped cherishing the friendship you'd offered me. 'Twas my dearest childhood memory." He laughed gruffly to cover the emotion. "Practically the only pleasant one I had."

Her eyes mirrored distress. "When you were sent down from university and the stories began to circulate, I was afraid that you'd become a younger version of your father."

"I've much to answer for in those days, but I hope I've avoided that fate," Tony retorted.

"I blamed myself. But then you left for the army, and, I heard, acquitted yourself well, so I prayed there was still hope."

He smiled. "I'm not yet a candidate for canonization, but I am trying."

"I believe you are." Once again she studied him for a long moment. "'Tis so long ago, I suppose it makes no difference, but I feel I must tell you why I left, even though you needed me so much. I had no choice, you see. I...I feared I might be with child."

He couldn't have been more shocked if she'd said she'd gone to become a courtesan or tread the boards of the Theatre Royal. "With child? Whose?"

"Whose do you think?" she asked quietly.

The knowledge hit him with the force of a punch to the gut, twisted his insides with revulsion and regret. For a moment, he thought he would be ill.

She grasped his hand. "You mustn't think I ever encouraged him—"

"No! I know you would not. Just as I know that he would have given you no choice."

"Once it...began, I knew he would not stop. I feared, until he tired of me, he would not even let me leave. So I had to sneak away in the dead of night."

"Where did you go? How did you live?"

"How did I manage not to end up on the streets, you mean?" she asked wryly. "I've been very fortunate. My old governess took pity on me, took me in. Soon after, I met a kind older man who had the goodness of heart to overlook my soiled past. We've been very happy."

"And the child?"

"Is married now to a fine young man. She believes my husband to be her father. We never told her differently."

Fury at his father, pain for all she must have suffered, engulfed him. "I'm so sorry. I—I wish there was something I could do. Something to make up for—"

"There's nothing. 'Tis long ago now. Except—I don't want him—" she spat out the word "—ever to know."

"You have my word on that."

She smiled then. "Perhaps there is something else. A life for a life? The little boy I knew had the potential to become a fine man. Be that man, Tony. Be what I hoped you could be.''

The love he'd felt for her all those years ago seemed to well up from some deeply buried, forgotten place in his soul. ''Any chance I have to do that, I owe to you.''

''Thank you. That makes me feel a bit less guilty for having failed you. Well, I should get along now. Tom will be thinking I lost my way going to market.''

''Shall I see you again?''

She paused a moment, then shook her head. ''I don't think that would be wise. Viscount Nelthorpe can have nothing in common with Mrs. Winston, the draper's wife. And remembering is...still too painful.''

He nodded, knowing he could never imagine what she had lived through, triumphed over. ''May you be happy.''

She pressed his hand again. ''May you be so also.''

Tony sat his horse and watched her walk away, the tall, elegant figure with the upright carriage and graceful stride that would always be the image of a lady for him.

A lady coerced, raped, degraded by his own father. Lord in heaven. The very thought still made him sick.

Be the man I hoped you would be.

I shall try harder, he silently promised her.

TO AVOID THE CONGESTION OF the streets, far more crowded now than when she'd left early this morning for her ride, after leaving Lady Charlotte's townhouse, Jenna directed her bay mare into Hyde Park. She'd take the path north that paralleled Park Lane, perhaps indulge in one last gallop while making her way home.

At first this morning, she'd meant only to ride as usual. But some vague, nagging sense of disquiet had disrupted the tranquility of that normally soothing activity. On impulse she'd decided to stop by Lady Charlotte's, expecting at that unfashionable hour to have the butler inform her that my lady was still abed.

Instead Lady Charlotte had invited her to breakfast. After chatting at first of inconsequential things, Lady Charlotte had then asked what was troubling Jenna enough to impel her to so early a call. After an instant's hesitation, Jenna found herself pouring out her suspicions and doubts about the events of the last few weeks.

Except for the details of her tryst with Nelthorpe, of course. She squelched an instantaneous niggle of longing by reminding herself how wise she'd been to dismiss him. She was reassuring herself that soon, this lingering ache for his company would fade, when her attention was snagged by the sound of hoofbeats approaching rapidly from behind.

A moment later, the rider reached her side.

Nelthorpe.

Her words of greeting faded on her lips. Stifling a surge of gladness at the sight of him, she tried to decide whether she should protest, reprimand his approach, or ignore him.

"Lady Fairchild," he said, his voice low and urgent. "I understand you feel it best if we do not communicate, but I have new information concerning your safety I think it imperative that you know."

A zing of alarm shocked through her. About to demand what he knew, she hesitated. 'Twould be safer to avoid him, have him convey the news via Sancha. But with him already at her side, that seemed a bit ridiculous.

While she dithered, he said quietly, "'Tis full daylight in the open park with your groom but a short distance behind us. You needn't fear I might tempt you into doing anything you'd regret."

You have no idea what you could tempt me to, the

thought flashed through her head. Nonetheless, he was right—she was well protected. For the moment.

And you don't truly want to send him away.

Squelching the little voice that whispered that insidious truth, she said, "Very well. Help me dismount and we shall talk. What information have you discovered?"

The touch of his hands as he helped her down was brief and impersonal. Still, feeling the imprint of his fingers like a brand against her, she vowed to have her groom assist her to remount.

Briefly he related his discoveries about the groom's sudden death, his unexpected windfall—and his regrets about a "sweet lady."

As he detailed his experiences in a grave manner devoid of flirtatious looks or innuendo, Jenna lost her wariness and focused on the dilemma she still faced.

"He can't have been referring to the Widow Owens—the lady who threatened me the day of the funeral reception. Unless she is the best actress I've ever seen, when I called on her, she seemed genuinely shocked to hear about my accident—"

"You called on her?" he interrupted. "Good Lord, Jenna, not alone, I hope!"

She felt her face color a little. "You needn't act as if I'm attics-to-let, stumbling heedless into danger! Sancha was waiting just outside in the hallway, and I had both my knife and my pistol at the ready. After all, I've fended off pirates in India and brigands on the Peninsular. Even had she turned out to be hostile, I believe I could—"

"You're safe, so let's not brangle over it just now. What did you discover?"

"Mrs. Owens seemed genuinely surprised about the accident. When I told her I'd lost my child as a result, she even appeared guilty, and apologized for her remarks. I believe she was telling the truth."

"So where does that leave us?"

Us. The word sent a warm feeling of comfort and security through her before she remembered there must not be any "us."

Once again, he replied before she could order her thoughts. "I know you think it wiser not to associate with me. I understand your reasons and," he admitted with a wry smile, "you are probably correct. Nonetheless, I cannot like the idea of you pursuing this on your own. I'd hoped to enlist other aide, but thus far... If I vow on the graves of the Waterloo dead to keep my distance, do you not think we could work together long enough to solve this?"

"You've been a—a stalwart friend, helping me in my grief, but you bear no responsibility for my safety, nor have you any reason to try to fight my battles. That bullet might just as easily have struck you. If there is danger—if the groom was in fact dispatched by the same assailant who fired upon us—I cannot justify involving you any further in this."

"If you call me friend, how can you expect me to stand aside and let you walk into danger alone?"

"I'm not alone any longer." As a flash of something that might have been jealousy crossed his face, she continued hastily, "Though I'm not yet prepared to break and flee, I did take your advice and confide in Lady Charlotte. She was concerned—"

"As well she should be!"

"And I admit," Jenna added with a sigh, "she too urged me to leave Fairchild House and come to her. I declined, but promised to accompany her when she departs shortly to begin Christmas preparations at her country house outside London. She also said she would ask Lord Riverton to make inquiries. But for the moment, we still know too little for me to wish to leave Fairchild House."

"We can cover more ground, faster, if we work together. Shall we cry 'pax'?" He held out his hand.

It would be more intelligent to share information. And by keeping in touch, she might more easily insure that he did not go into harm's way.

As for herself, nothing, including her personal safety, was more important now than finding—and obtaining justice against—anyone, relation or not, who might have assisted in the death of Garrett's child.

Vowing to pursue her continuing investigations as much as possible with just Sancha's assistance, she offered her hand. The brief touch of his fingers as he shook hers burned through her gloves.

"Since the groom implicated a woman and you've eliminated the widow, that leaves the countess—or, much less likely, your aunt." He frowned. "But I have difficulty believing either would go so far as to hire an assassin. That strikes more of a man's determination."

Jenna sighed. "Perhaps, though you should not underestimate the determination of a lady! Nor can I see what else Bayard could hope to gain by eliminating me now."

"What of your fortune? Were you to die without heirs, would Bayard inherit?"

Struck by that thought, Jenna considered it. "I'm not sure the terms of the settlement, but it's quite possible." A chill skittered over her skin. "I shall have to consult my lawyers."

"If it should be true, would that be enough to convince you to leave Fairchild House?"

"Probably. Still, though Bayard is…strange, I cannot see him as an assassin."

"Not all villains reveal their intentions plainly," he said with a deprecating smile. "Promise me, though, if your cousin should prove heir to your fortune, you will hesitate no longer. Damme—dash it, but I hate it that you remain there still! At least vow to be extremely careful.''

''I shall be. Sancha is staying in my room now, and both of us shall be armed. Silly as it sometimes seems in the daylight, I must admit I feel better at night with my pistol by my side.''

''In the meantime, I'm an old acquaintance of Lucinda Blaine's, and shall see what I can discover.''

''Was there no woman in London you didn't seduce before the war?'' she said, irritated at the immediate and entirely inappropriate images evoked by those innocuous words.

For an instant, the grin that was so appealing and dangerous to her self-control flashed to his lips. ''In my younger days, I but worshipped at the shrine of beauty.''

''So many shrines,'' she muttered.

''Still, you cannot deny it would be easier for me to obtain a private audience. And perhaps to persuade her into being…indiscreet.''

''I shouldn't wish you to have to do something—distasteful,'' she retorted, her tone more sarcastic than she would have wished.

''Ah, but I am ready to go to great lengths in the quest for truth,'' he replied, a naughty twinkle in his eye.

The serious note beneath his innuendo checked her irritation. ''Please, do nothing yet. I'm not sure what I mean to do if we determine that she is involved. Confronting her might arouse her suspicions—and could make her dangerous. Now, I'd better get back. Aunt Hetty is receiving and will think me very rude if I am too tardy to assist her.''

Nelthorpe nodded. ''If I discover anything, I will send word through Sancha. You will do the same?''

"Agreed. Thank you, Lord Nelthorpe, for standing my friend—in spite of everything."

He looked into her eyes, his expression so intense it sent a shock through her, made it impossible to turn away. "I will always be that. Your servant, my lady."

He waited until the groom had assisted her into the saddle, then remounted himself. Conscious of his gaze following her—always, his gaze on her—she rode away.

EARLY THAT EVENING, Jenna descended the stairs to the parlor where she was to meet Aunt Hetty. Lady Montclare was hosting a musicale, so there was no chance of avoiding the entertainment. As Lady Charlotte and her party, including Colonel Vernier, were pledged to attend another dinner and she could not hope that Nelthorpe would be invited, it promised to be a dull night.

Although she was attempting to continue with her usual activities, as Nelthorpe had predicted, now that she'd been made aware of the possibility of wrongdoing, 'twas very difficult to carry on as though nothing had happened.

She'd found herself watching Aunt Hetty closely today, looking for—what? Signs of uneasiness, guilt, a touch of menace? And finding nothing beyond the somewhat petty, querulous, complaining behavior the woman had exhibited toward her ever since her arrival, behavior that Jenna's instincts told her posed no threat.

Still, all her senses remained heightened, her eyes drawn to sudden flickers of light or movement, her ears registering small household sounds—the muffled closing of a door, the pad of a servant's footsteps in the hallway—with an acuity she hadn't experienced since leaving the battlefields of Spain. An uneasiness, not quite fear but more than caution, had seeped deep into her consciousness.

So that when, as she passed the library on her way to the parlor, Lane Fairchild's voice unexpectedly sounded from behind her, she jumped. She had just a moment to compose her startled features before the library door opened.

"Ah, cousin, I thought that was your step. And how lovely you look."

"Nearly as fine as you," she replied, noting his dark evening wear, striking against his blond good looks. "Do you accompany us to Lady Montclare's?"

"I shall escort you, but not remain. I am promised elsewhere, I fear."

"Fortunate man," Jenna muttered.

He choked off a laugh, turning it to an unconvincing cough. "Lady Montclare has been a good friend to you, Jenna. I'm sure you are delighted to accept her kind invitation. Besides, there shall doubtless be a horde of friends there to entertain you. First, I have a concern I wished to speak with you about, if you would be so good as to allow me a moment?"

Jenna's sensitized nerves whispered caution, but she saw no reason to refuse. "Of course, cousin," she said, following him into the darkened library. "What did you wish to discuss?"

CHAPTER TWENTY-ONE

LANE MOTIONED HER TO A SEAT. "Yesterday, I discovered quite by chance from one of the footmen that you paid a call upon the woman who threatened you the day of Garrett's services. Heavens, Jenna, how could you be so reckless?"

Surprised, and not sure how much she wished to divulge to her cousin, Jenna fumbled for words. "I—I am quite safe, as you can see."

"Praise God nothing untoward transpired! But I'm still most upset with you. The woman might have been deranged. If you were still troubled about the incident, why did you not say so? I should have pursued it for you. Whether or not you ever gratify my fondest hopes, you are still family, and I am committed to your protection."

After that ardent vow, a week ago she might have disclosed to him the whole. But that same cautious foreboding that had shadowed her since Nelthorpe's warning made her hold back. Perhaps, she decided, imbued with the grim sense that she could now trust no one, she ought to reveal just enough to gauge his reaction.

"I am touched by your devotion, cousin. It was just that—oh, in the wake of that visit, it seems foolish even to mention it!"

"Mention what?" he demanded.

Watching him from the corner of her eye, she rose to pace before him, as if too agitated to remain in her seat. "I'm sure 'tis naught but the fanciful imaginings of a mind still disordered by grief, but of late I've had vague dreams that perhaps my fall was not an accident. Mrs. Owens did seem to have threatened me, though after hearing her fervent apology yesterday, I no longer believe she intended me any harm. Do...do you, cousin, know of anyone else who might wish me ill?''

''I can't imagine! What would lead you to believe your fall wasn't accidental?''

He seemed neither truly shocked by her doubts nor dismissive of them. Wishing she knew him well enough to be able to read him better, she replied, ''Why would the groom mount me on a slug like Aunt Hetty's old mare and not warn me she abhorred the whip? He knew me to be an intrepid rider. He must have suspected I would urge the beast to a faster pace as soon as we reached the park.''

''Jenna, you've just admitted that you've not been thinking rationally of late. Have you discovered anything else that would lead you to believe his omission was more than mere thoughtlessness?''

''Not really,'' she admitted. ''Except this continuing feeling of unease. I—I do feel particularly uncomfortable around Bayard. Much as I shrink from even thinking such a thing, you don't suppose he might have...''

''Bayard wish you harm? No, 'tis preposterous! True, should you have been brought to bed of an heir, it would have displaced him as viscount, but you've seen how little he cares for that. All that matters to him are his cursed experiments. Why, just last week I discovered he spent an enormous sum—on rocks! Rocks shipped from locations all over the globe, some of them encrusted with shiny minerals, some that, he said, are supposed to glow in the dark. He wishes to persuade them to 'yield up their secrets.''' Lane shook his head in disgust.

''He is rather...odd,'' Jenna observed.

Lane snorted. ''When I took him to task for squandering estate funds on such a thing, he became incensed and cried that nothing could be allowed to block the advance of human knowledge, certainly nothing so trivial as—" He stopped in midphrase, as if suddenly struck. "As money," he concluded soberly.

Jenna guessed where his thoughts were likely leading. "Does Bayard have a large personal income?"

"No," Lane replied shortly. "He, like Aunt Hetty, was happy to respond to Garrett's invitation to live here, as it saved his slender purse the cost of maintaining a separate establishment. Being viscount might mean little to him, but continuing his experiments would mean the world. Not," he added hastily, "that I intend to imply I believe Bayard would ever dream of, much implement, a scheme to insure he retained the title and its wealth."

"You are sure?"

Lane hesitated a moment. "*Almost* sure. But with your safety at stake, I had better make further inquiries."

Jenna debated telling him about the shot, then decided against it. If he followed this line of argument logically, he should soon realize that if Bayard prized unlimited funds to pursue his experiments, he might well have concluded that the coffers of the estate he now controlled would be considerably enriched by the addition of the fortune that would most likely fall to the Fairchilds at her demise.

"Do you think I'm in danger?" she said instead.

"I am nearly certain you are not. But," he sighed heavily, "as far-fetched as all this seems, I suppose it would be wise to be prudent. I would keep your maid about you. And for the moment, I would recommend you avoid encountering Bayard or his valet."

A sudden memory assailed her—talking with Lane the morning she'd been fired on...with Frankston lurking in the shadows.

She shook off a chill. "I will do so, cousin."

He came over to pat her hand. "I had begun this talk hoping to allay your concerns, not create new ones! But rest assured I shall look into this matter urgently, that I might be able soon to lay all your anxieties at rest."

"You are most kind," she murmured, removing her hand.

"Any assistance I can render you, my dear Jenna, must always give me pleasure."

That subtle reference to his hopes increased her discomfort, and she blessed the fact that he would not be remaining with them at Lady Montclare's this evening. "I must leave now. Aunt Hetty will be beside herself at the possibility of arriving late."

Lane groaned. "So she shall. Tell her I will join you in a trice."

How genuine was Lane's show of concern, Jenna wondered as she continued on to the parlor. The interest in her person that he radiated was real enough to make her uncomfortable. Did that automatically mean he was ignorant of any possible wrongdoing?

She had no idea of the extent of *Lane's* personal income. If Bayard really had conspired to harm—or even remove—her, he might have promised Lane a share for turning a blind eye to his maneuvering.

Still, if Lane hoped to entice her to marry, surely he would think that an easier means of getting his hands on her fortune than by conspiring with his cousin in some risky scheme that would win him, at best, only half of it.

Damme and blast! she swore silently, almost wishing Nelthorpe had never made her privy to his suspicions. She didn't like delving into this shadowy world of evil deeds and intentions. Just thinking about it made her head ache.

All the more reason to bring pressure to bear on whoever might be involved, ending this anxiety of doubt by forcing the culprit into further action where he—or she—could be dealt with.

Perhaps later she would visit Bayard himself.

HER HEAD POUNDING IN TRUTH, shortly after midnight Jenna bid Aunt Hetty good-night and headed to her chamber.

Lady Montclare's musicale had been as insipid as she'd feared. In addition, she'd endured Aunt Hetty's sotto voce grumbling between each musical selection that Jenna and Lane's tardy appearance had made them miss the food and conversation of the preperformance reception.

Afterward she'd had to turn aside Lady Montclare's questions, naked curiosity cloaked in irritatingly playful tones, about Colonel Vernier's intentions and whether his potential courtship had caused Jenna to dismiss Nelthorpe—who, she'd heard, had taken his rejection badly and was still haunting Fairchild House, bothering the servants.

As Jenna climbed the stairs, annoyance faded and a sense of anxiety returned, stronger than any that had thus far gripped her.

Was she being reckless, insisting on remaining at Fairchild House? Was Bayard really a danger to her?

Had he been present tonight, she might have asked Nelthorpe's opinion, but not surprisingly, he had not been among the crowd of guests.

As she hesitated with her hand on the door latch, her stomach fluttering, she realized that by now, Lady Charlotte should have returned from her dinner engagement.

For a moment, she was consumed by the temptation to wheel around, march past a doubtless astounded Manson and take a hackney straight to Mount Street. But she'd look ridiculous, fleeing to her friend in the middle of the night over nothing more threatening than a bad case of jitters. Setting her jaw, she made herself enter the room.

What would Garrett have done if *he'd* suspected someone had conspired to kill their child?

The question calmed and steadied her. For she knew without doubt that her husband would have searched to the ends of the earth and faced any risk to find the truth.

How could she do any less?

Perhaps it was good that she'd given that display of nervousness before Lane. If he were involved in some way, he'd have notified his accomplices that she was suspicious, making it more likely they might move against her.

Her adversaries in London had never known her as the colonel's daughter. If this led to a confrontation, they would anticipate her being frightened and helpless. They would not expect armed resistance.

They'd not expect *her*.

Taking a deep breath, she rang for Sancha and took out her pistol.

SOMETIME AFTER SHE'D FALLEN into a restless sleep, a weapon at her side and Sancha dozing at the foot of her bed, she awoke with a start. Trying to still the sudden racing of her heart, she sat up slowly and strained her ears to listen.

She heard it again, the slow, stealthy pad of footsteps in the corridor. Forcing down a momentary sense of panic, in the moonlight from the window Sancha had purposely left uncurtained, she slid to the floor and took up her pistol, motioning the maid to silence.

If she were to be attacked, she would meet the danger straight on, not cowering in her bed, she thought as she noiselessly crept to the door.

Easing it open, she spied Bayard's valet a few paces away, his hands laden with a heavy tray that bore a single candlestick and several covered dishes.

"Frankston!" she hissed.

The valet started, nearly knocking over the candlestick as he whirled to see who'd hailed him. "L-Lady Fairchild!" he exclaimed.

"What are you doing skulking about in the middle of the night?"

"Was so sharp-set I couldn't sleep, m'lady, so's I went to get some victuals from the kitchen. Sorry I disturbed ye." He gave her a quick nod and stepped away.

And then halted again, his eyes widening, as she pulled the pistol from behind her skirts and leveled it at him. "Were you hungry, you would have eaten in the servants' kitchen—not brought food up here on a silver tray. Would you care to try your explanation again?"

"Lord, ma'am, put down that popper 'for it goes off and ye raise the house!"

"I'm more likely to level you. From this distance there's no chance that I would miss. The truth this time, if you please, Frankston."

He cast a fearful glance down the hallway toward Lane's door. "Please, ma'am! I dare not wake Mr. Fairchild."

"Then you had best speak softly and fast."

"The victuals be for my master. He, ah, sometimes fergets to eat during the day. Gets involved in his experiments, you know, ma'am, and—"

"Frankston," Jenna interrupted, "you try my patience. Your master dines with us at every meal. Perhaps it would speed matters if I wake Mr. Fairchild." Keeping the pistol aimed at the valet, she took a step toward Lane's door.

"Nay, ma'am, please!" he cried in an urgent undertone. "I'll tell ye everything. Only don't be waking that one." After another quick glance down the hallway, he continued, "The tray *is* for my master. He's so caught up in his work, he don't notice much when he eats, so I try to feed him summat between mealtimes, so's he won't eat as much then. You see, I takes care of his supplies, and over the last months, I been noticing some of his chemicals disappearing. And my master, he's been having powerful pains in his stomach ever since your husband died. So I've started fixing him food with my own hands."

That instinctive foreboding tightened in Jenna's gut. "Just what are you implying?"

"I don't know nothing fer sure, my lady—and what court would listen to the likes of me speaking against a nob? But Mr. Fairchild there—" he jerked his chin toward Lane's door "—he didn't never like my master, and since Mr. Bayard's come into the title, he likes him even less. A cold, calculating man he is, that Mr. Fairchild. I wouldn't put it past him to be poisoning my master, just so's he can be viscount instead."

The implications of having Lane possibly scheming to do away with Bayard made her dizzy. Taking a deep breath to clear her head, she motioned Frankston away. "Very well, you may go now."

"Thank'ee, my lady. You be careful of Mr. Fairchild."

She nodded, then watched as he scuttled down the hallway and disappeared into the darkness, the candle casting an eerie flickering glow as he went. Slowly she backed into her room, heart pounding and hands shaking.

"Did you hear, Sancha?" she whispered after she'd closed and relatched the door.

"*Si,* mistress," the maid replied. "Sit here. I will get you sherry."

After lighting a single candle, she poured a glass and

brought it to Jenna, who gratefully sipped its fiery warmth. ''What does it mean, do you think?'' Sancha asked.

''I'm not sure—I shall have to consider all the details.'' But even as she took another sip, she recalled a number of occasions upon which Lane had demonstrated a thinly disguised contempt of his odd, self-absorbed cousin, who seemed to have neither interest in the title nor, in Lane's opinion, the manners and bearing to make him worthy of carrying so great an honor.

Was his contempt virulent enough to prompt him to attempt murder?

And if he had committed himself to so heinous a course, would he not hasten to remove any other impediment that might stand between himself and the prize—including her unborn child?

The testimony she'd forced out of Frankston provided no more actual proof than she and Nelthorpe had already accumulated. But whether Lane was correct in warning her against Bayard and Frankston, or the valet correct in warning her against Lane, she now had enough circumstantial evidence to feel justified in leaving Fairchild House.

Under the guise of assisting Lady Charlotte in her Christmas preparations, she and Sancha would quit her cousin's house tomorrow morning.

After finishing the sherry and briefly explaining to Sancha what she intended—a decision of which Sancha heartily approved—Jenna went back to bed, the pistol once more on the pillow next to her.

Heavens, she thought with grim humor, and she'd thought upon the end of the war to have left behind her forever the days of sleeping with a weapon by her side!

But when in danger on the continent, she'd had Garrett to consult with and assist her. Resolutely she banished the ache of missing him—and a longing for the dark-haired, gray-eyed man who'd succeeded him in watching over her.

Her sleep no more restful than before, it seemed she had hardly shut her eyes when once again, some muffled sound jerked her awake.

This time, the footfalls were more purposeful—and they stopped just outside her chamber. Before she could do more than grab her pistol and pivot toward the entry, a thin metallic noise rattled the lock and the door swung open.

CHAPTER TWENTY-TWO

TONY HAD TO INSINUATE himself into three ton parties that night before he finally tracked down Lucinda Blaine. He'd been warmed that Jenna seemed concerned for his safety—even if, he admitted with a sigh, that concern probably stemmed more from not wanting his death or injury on her conscience than any exceptional fondness for his person. Not wishing to add to her worries, he'd let her think he'd agreed to her request that he not pursue the countess. But with Jenna's safety still in jeopardy, he intended to ruthlessly track down every potential foe.

He stood now observing the woman he'd idly pursued before leaving for the Peninsula. In her early twenties, with the bloom of youth still upon a skin cleverly augmented by expensive cosmetics, the countess was perhaps more strikingly attractive than he remembered, if no longer presenting an aura of virginal innocence.

Not that Lucinda Blaine had ever been truly innocent. From her debut in the ton, she'd known she'd wanted the most elevated title her looks and her father's maneuvering could buy. Loving a second son like Garrett Fairchild—if love him she ever had—would not have swayed that purpose.

With Garrett off to the army and the earl's heirloom ring upon her finger, she'd quickly tired of her aging husband. Rumor had already linked her with several reckless ton bachelors when she'd embarked upon that flirtation with Tony. Despite their contretemps in the park a few days ago, he expected she might be susceptible to flattery from an old admirer, especially if preceded by an abject apology and a little groveling.

To protect Jenna, Tony was fully prepared to grovel.

Given the size of her court and his weak leg, it took him some time to muscle a spot amid the circle of swains surrounding Lucinda Blaine. Once propped against a convenient pillar, he fixed what he hoped was a look of soulful admiration on his face and waited.

A few moments later, she scanned a restless eye over the crowd, first passing by him, then returning to focus with amused recognition. ''Why, Anthony Nelthorpe, what brings you here? I thought you were far too preoccupied by good deeds to bother with pleasure.''

''Simply doing my duty to assist the widow of a fellow officer, my lady,'' Tony replied, limping over to kiss the hand she offered. ''Alas, too often for a soldier's liking, duty must take precedence over pleasure—and,'' he added with a silent apology to Jenna, ''one's own preference.''

She made a self-satisfied murmur. ''Given the prudish prune of a widow you were assisting, I'm sure there *wasn't* any pleasure.'' She smiled as several of her courtiers tittered. ''Which is only what you deserve for being so ill-advised in your choice of…friends.''

''I protest, dear lady! Never did I mean to slight you. If it appears I did, you have my deepest apologies.''

''Confess, my lord, you come here only because, I hear, your virtuous widow dismissed you.'' She shook her head in mock-pity. ''Such is the reward of benevolence.''

''But benevolence is not always a mistake. If you will only, in your mercy, forgive my maladroit behavior, I promise to demonstrate my most *ardent* contrition.''

''La, Tony Nelthorpe, you were ever a honey-tongued

rascal.'' She leaned closer to tap him with her fan. ''*Very* honey-tongued, as I recall,'' she added for his ears alone. ''Whatever am I to do with you?''

''As you so generously offered, let us renew old bonds—and explore new ones. Leave this dull party and come have supper with me.''

''What's this?'' inserted Wardsworth, one of the courtiers loitering beside her. ''You can't carry off the belle of the evening, Nelthorpe! Not sporting!''

''Ah, but Wardsworth, you gentlemen have been able to worship at her feet these past three years. 'Tis only fitting that those of us off doing valiant service for our nation should now have a chance. A gracious boon granted—'' he turned to Lucinda ''—to one of the victors of war.''

''Now, why should I grant you such a boon?'' she asked, her gaze playing down his person to linger at his groin.

He let his eyes follow the path hers had taken. ''That the conquerors might demonstrate the vigor that made them victorious?'' he suggested.

She giggled. ''Naughty boy! But we have many vigorous men here—who have not been so fickle in their loyalties.''

''Ah, but you have suffered their faces—and their technique—times out of mind. I offer the benefits of novelty…and foreign experience.''

A spark of interest lit in her eyes. ''Does—foreign experience—enhance one's enjoyment?''

He shrugged and gave her a lazy smile. ''Have dinner with me and you can decide.'' He held out his arm.

She tapped a finger against her lips, considering, prurient curiosity apparently warring with the desire to punish him for his lapse in slighting her earlier. Tony knew he dare add nothing else, lest he seem too suspiciously eager.

Fortunately her three-parts-castaway swain intervened at that moment. "Nay, you mustn't!" Wardsworth objected, grabbing the countess's hand to prevent her placing it in Nelthorpe's. "You cannot leave us just because this latecomer offers you a few pretty words."

With a contemptuous glance, the countess shook off his touch. "You are wrong, Wardsworth. I do whatever pleases me. Besides, gentlemen..." She raised her voice to carry across the assembled group. "'Tis but my patriotic duty!"

"So, Tony Nelthorpe—" she placed her hand on his arm with the graciousness of a sovereign awarding a great beneficence "—show me what you will."

"As you command, goddess," he replied, hoping what he intended to demonstrate would move her profoundly, though not in the manner she so obviously expected.

A SHORT TIME LATER, Tony led Lucinda Blaine through the portal of a handsome townhouse a few blocks away that, anticipating the success of his gambit, he'd arranged with an obliging fellow officer to borrow for the evening.

How much keener his anticipation would be, he thought with a sigh, if it were Jenna he had coaxed across such a threshold! But the quest that brought him here was more imperative, if much less enjoyable.

Fortunately, Lucinda had rebuffed the attempt to kiss her he felt obliged to make once they'd entered the hackney that conveyed them here. Doubtless intending to heighten his anticipation, she'd told him he owed her a fine dinner before they had any more *intimate* conversation.

But after they arrived and she'd refreshed herself, in the process dampening her gown to make her vaunted charms even more blatant, she apparently decided Nelthorpe deserved a taste of the pleasures to come.

After seating herself on the sofa, she patted the place beside her. "Come closer, my lord. One does not hold congress with one's friends at such a distance."

He couldn't deny that his body had risen in response to the voluptuous figure displayed by the wetted silk, despite his adverse opinion of its wearer. After her display of vanity and her treatment of Jenna, he'd as soon bed a slug.

Still, wanting to take no chances that lust might overpower good sense, he smilingly declined. "'Tis better to gaze from a distance."

"Is it?" she replied, her playful tones chilling.

"Yes, my goddess. The sages of the east proclaim that viewing without touching fires the appetite and gives greater endurance to the performance."

"I see," she said, somewhat mollified. Then, a hot light coming into her eye, she reached toward his trouser flap. "That being the case, shouldn't I—"

"No!" he cried, blocking her hand. "While, ah, gazing upon the charms of his lady strengthens the man," he improvised rapidly, "speculating about her courtier's attributes enflames the lady."

"Indeed? Well, if that's what the sages of the east say." After appearing to give the matter a little thought, her expression brightened. "It is rather titillating to contemplate. You promise I'll not be disappointed?"

"You may be many things afterward, my lady, but not that," he affirmed somewhat grimly.

Servants appeared with food and wine. Seeming content with his explanation for the moment, Lucinda let him ply her with champagne while she talked about her activities in London during the years he'd been gone. By the time he led her back to the events surrounding Garrett's death and his and Jenna's arrival back in London, she was more than a little tipsy.

"As you guessed, I did have hopes of seducing the widow," he admitted. "But my patient assistance in her projects led nowhere. She's still too distraught over her husband's death to succumb, even to one of my vaunted skill, and the matter grew even more hopeless after she lost the child."

"Such a tragedy," Lucinda said, but with a little giggle that belied the sympathetic words.

"Have you no empathy for a woman in mourning?"

"Well, why should I? Everyone else is fawning over her—ah, that charade of pity at Garrett's services! I lost just as much, nay even more, but no one is holding my hand and offering platitudes. He loved me, after all! She should never have married him, and if she lost everything, 'tis what she deserved."

"Harsh words. One might even suspect you wished her to have an accident."

Lucinda sniffed. "I—" she made a vague gesture, nearly upsetting her wineglass "—am not hypocrite enough to pretend I wished her well."

Tony captured the stemware and handed it back to her. "Some think it might not have been an accident."

Lucinda straightened, needing a moment to focus on him. "Indeed? Why would anyone think that?"

Nelthorpe shrugged. "There's talk that the head groom might have mounted her on an unpredictable horse and deliberately refrained from acquainting her with its habits. It seems someone suspects something, for that individual, who was discharged over the incident and is the only witness who would know the truth of it, just met with an untimely accident himself."

Wetting her lips, Lucinda put down her wineglass. "An…an accident?"

"Yes. It looks as if someone is tying up loose ends. The man was shot once through the heart."

"Shot!" she gasped. "But killing him was never part of—" she cried, before halting in midsentence to clap a hand over her mouth. "I...I think I must go, Tony," she said a moment later, her voice shaky. "I feel quite unwell."

You heartless, scheming bitch, Tony swore silently, cold rage hardening his resolve. "I don't doubt it. But you will remain here until you tell me everything you know about that incident."

Her dilated eyes widened further. "You...you are still working with her."

"Ever the clever one, my angel. So you will understand when I warn you that I don't intend to release you until you tell me everything you know."

"I—I don't know anything. You will take me home at once, or...or my husband shall pursue you and call you out."

"If your husband wished to call out every man who'd trifled with you, he'd be a very busy fellow."

With a hiccupping sob, she pulled a handkerchief from her reticule. "How could I ever have thought you charming? You are h-horrid!"

Tony seized her chin and forced it up. "Yes, I am horrid. I've just spent three years at war, a rather horrid business. Coming upon troopers being tortured by guerrillas, I've learned more than just the love secrets of the east. Should you decide not to confide in me, I might be forced to demonstrate some of my new skills."

At that, the countess's defiance crumbled. In halting, sob-marked sentences, she told of her long liaison with Lane Fairchild, who, noting her resentment when Jenna Fairchild returned to London and her outrage when she was informed that her lover's widow carried his child, suggested that a little accident might soothe much of her distress.

It wasn't as if she'd truly done anything wrong, she insisted. As Lane had explained it, all she need do was bribe the groom to change horses and hold his tongue. It had been in God's hands whether Hetty's mare trotted placidly or bolted.

Dismissing that rationalization with the contempt it deserved, Tony questioned her further, but she seemed to have no idea what Lane Fairchild would gain from such a plan, beyond the satisfaction of gratifying his mistress. Switching topics, he then forced her, with bitter resentment, to admit that though she had entreated Garrett to visit her when he'd been in London the previous March gathering troops, he had politely declined.

Concluding that he'd learned all he could from her, he sent a servant to summon a hackney.

"I never wish to see you again, Tony Nelthorpe," she said sullenly as he assisted her into the vehicle.

"Given that groom's untimely demise, I would suggest that if you wish to live to see anyone, you make immediate plans to depart London. Preferably to pay a very long visit to a suitably distant friend."

After letting that recommendation register in her wine-soaked wits, he closed the door behind her and watched the vehicle set off into the lightening dawn.

As he collected his belongings and tipped the curious staff, he reviewed the scene again, a little ashamed of his extortion tactics but nonetheless satisfied with the results. He couldn't help wondering, however, how Jenna might have reacted to similar coercion.

As she had once before, she would probably have remained defiant in the face of all his threats. Then while distracting him by feigning collapse, she'd have bashed him with the wine bottle and escaped into the night.

"You're in love with her, too, aren't you?" Lucinda Blaine had accused. "Why? She's not even beautiful!"

"She has a beauty of soul and character that will endure long after yours has faded," he'd told her.

But only if Jenna lived long enough. There being no question now that she was in danger—and from whom, he could not afford to wait until socially acceptable calling hours.

He must sneak into Fairchild House and warn her at once.

HAD JENNA'S CHAMBER WINDOW not faced over the street, Tony might have attempted to avoid the possibility of encountering servants by climbing up to it, painful as that might have proved with his stiff knee. Instead, drawing upon skills of stealth developed over a misspent young manhood, he used his knife blade to pick the lock of the back gate and the kitchen entry, then tiptoed through the deserted house up to Jenna's chamber.

'Twas many years since he'd crept into a lady's bedchamber while her household slept. Before, it had been almost a game, the danger of discovery amplifying his anticipation of the pleasure to come. Though his mission this time was far too serious for sport, still the idea of slipping to Jenna's bedside and gazing upon her with her hair unbound, her body cloaked only in the fine linen of a night rail, caused his mouth to dry as his mind filled with images of how he might stroke her to wakefulness, had only the peril not been so great.

Forcing his thoughts from those tantalizing possibilities, he primed himself to enter. He'd need to wake her gently, so she did not become frightened and cry out. He'd not be able to get her away safely if she caused an uproar or was paralyzed with fright.

Taking a deep breath to keep his hand steady, he

picked the final lock, pushed open the door and stepped in.

In the next, confusing instant he saw Sancha, outlined by moonlight as she poised to throw her knife, and Jenna holding a pistol aimed at his heart.

FOR AN INSTANT, NONE OF THEM moved. Then, shaken by the knowledge that she'd come within a hairbreadth of firing on him, Jenna gasped, "Nelthorpe!"

"What in the world are you doing here?" she whispered, motioning him closer as she set down her weapon. "Sancha, close the door and stand guard by it, please."

She slid from the bed and took a chair, indicating that he take the one adjacent. "You're lucky I didn't shoot you through the heart. Honestly, this must be the most outrageous thing you've ever done!"

"Then you've led too sheltered a life," he drawled, his features silvered by moonlight. "I've done things a deal more outrageous, I assure you. But I didn't sneak in here just to broaden your education. Tonight I induced Lucinda Blaine to admit that she paid the groom to sabotage your ride—on the recommendation of Lane Fairchild. Who most probably arranged to fire upon you and dispatch the groom."

"And who also may or may not be attempting to poison Bayard and win the title for himself," she informed him. "Or so Bayard's valet, at gunpoint, was made to confess."

"God in heaven!" After following that exclamation with several muffled curses, he sprang up from his chair. "Then surely now you understand how imperative it is that you quit this house. Sancha, pack only those necessaries you can fit in a bandbox and we shall leave at once."

"And go where?" Jenna demanded.

"To Lady Charlotte's, I suppose. You did speak with her, didn't you?"

"Yes, but I'll not venture there until a reasonable hour of the morning. Don't scold me for being foolish," she said, holding up a hand to forestall his protest. "As you have seen, both Sancha and I are armed and watchful. Besides, though I no longer deny Lane threatens me, as exacting as he is about the honor of the family name, I don't think he would attempt to murder me at Fairchild House. Such a death would be much too difficult to conceal or explain."

"An interesting theory, but one I wouldn't wish to put to the test. Leave now, Jenna."

She shook her head. "'Tis nearly dawn. As soon as Sancha and I can depart with any semblance of normalcy, we shall proceed straight to Lady Charlotte's."

"Thanks be to God!" he said fervently. "Though I still cannot approve the delay."

"Don't think I am not deeply appreciative of your concern—and your efforts on my behalf, but 'tis not your decision to approve. Indeed, I am almost tempted to remain in spite of what we've discovered." *Garrett would not run away with the murderer of his child unpunished,* she thought. "We still have no proof that Lane attempted to harm me—only the suppositions of a valet and a faithless jade. If we could force him to take some further action—"

"Absolutely not, Jenna! I won't let you risk it."

"Then how shall we ever bring him to justice—or protect Bayard, for that matter?"

"Jenna, get dressed and, Sancha, start packing. We can argue strategy to your heart's content—once you are safely out of this house."

"Very well, we shall plan later. But I will not leave the house until morning. If I do, Lane will surely know that I am suspicious of him, and become so careful that we may never be able to prove his guilt.''

In the thin moonlight he studied her face and seemed to realize she would not be budged. ''Morning, then,'' he agreed with a sigh. ''But I'll not leave until dawn breaks. Three can keep watch better than two.''

''No, you must go at once! The longer you remain, the greater the risk of some servant—or even Lane himself—becoming aware of your presence. Which, in addition to the scandal, would be just as plain an indication of my suspicions as if I fled in the night.''

Nelthorpe proving as stubborn as she, they argued the matter until Sancha prosaically observed that if he didn't leave soon, the disagreement would be moot.

''Please, Tony,'' Jenna whispered, risking the jolt of awareness that always shook her when she touched him to take his hand. ''Please, though you cannot like it, let me do this my way.''

After a start of surprise, he gripped her fingers fiercely, his jaw working as he gazed at their joined hands. ''All right, Jenna. Your way. But for God's sake and mine, be careful!''

''I will. Meet me at Lady Charlotte's later and we shall plan what to do next. Now, use your vast experience to good advantage and creep back out of here undetected.''

He gave her fingers another hard squeeze before releasing them, then stood, hesitating as if he wished to say something more.

In the end, with a ''God be with you,'' he limped out.

Over the next few hours as the new day brightened, having given up the fruitless effort to sleep, Jenna dressed and discussed strategy with Sancha. By morning, they'd decided to modify the plan.

They would leave together, but not with a bandbox—an irregular item that would surely be noticed and cause speculation among the staff. Having agreed that, not knowing the extent of the conspiracy, it would not be wise to trust the grooms or any of the staff, they would announce they wished to take a morning walk.

Once safely away from the house, they would hail a hackney to convey Jenna to Lady Charlotte's house. Sancha would return to Fairchild House with a tale of having met Lady Charlotte in the park, after which her mistress had been invited back to breakfast. During the meal, while discussing her imminent departure to spend the holidays at her country house, Lady Charlotte had begged Jenna to accompany her, and at length, her mistress agreed. Sancha was to pack her trunks and return with them.

Though Jenna was pleased with the plan, the wait for full morning light seemed endless, both she and Sancha starting at every small noise. Her nerves were worn raw when at last, they descended the stairs, her back prickling with a sense of threat as they walked away from the house.

They halted a block away, Jenna's breath as shallow as if she'd run every step. *"Madre de Dios!"* Sancha said with a triumphant chuckle. "Mistress, we have done it!"

A few moments later, she helped hand Jenna into a hackney. "Come quickly, Sancha," Jenna murmured, giving the maid a hug. "I will not rest easy until you too are safely out of Fairchild House."

"Nay, my lady, the plan is sound, nor am I in danger. I will pack quickly and join you soon."

Jenna nodded and, after giving the driver her direction, settled back against the squabs, her mind moving forward to the next challenge.

How could they prove Lane Fairchild's part in this?

After reviewing all her dealings with him since arriving in London, she had to admit it still seemed incredible.

His concern for her welfare, unless he was the most skilled actor she'd ever met, appeared genuine. That Lucinda Blaine had bribed the groom to change horses, on Lane's recommendation, was the only fact definitely linking him to the events—assuming they could trust Lucinda's word.

Frankston's belief that he intended to dispose of his cousin was unproven speculation, though a speculation that made the shot fired at her and the groom's fatal accident fit into some logical order.

Though free for the moment from menace, a shiver traveled down her spine. Had Lane truly designed this elaborate scheme? Was he capable of murder? Or might someone else be responsible?

She was still mulling over that disturbing question when it suddenly occurred to her that by now, she should have reached Lady Charlotte's. Had the driver not understood her directions?

She banged on the forward wall. When the vehicle did not slow, she banged again, then reached over to put up the window shade, latched to keep out the morning chill, so she might determine their location.

Only to find the curtain nailed into place.

For a shocked second she sat immobile. Then, dread gathering in the pit of her stomach, she seized the door handle.

She wasn't surprised to discover that it, too, was bolted shut.

CHAPTER TWENTY-THREE

PANIC SWEPT THROUGH HER, swiftly succeeded by a rage that tempered her fear. After a few moments speculating about how their plan had gone awry, she set her mind to determining what she would do when the carriage arrived at whatever destination to which she was being taken.

Her abduction could, she decided, be an advantage, for whoever had arranged it was likely responsible for all the rest. If she were lucky enough to be able to face the perpetrator, rather than being held or dispatched by hirelings, she would discover the true face of her enemy.

It must be either Bayard or Lane. Having caused her pain and cost her Garrett's child, Lucinda Blaine would have little to gain by killing her. Indeed, she would probably prefer Jenna alive, her grief-stricken presence among the ton a constant reminder of Lucinda's cleverness in punishing the woman she held responsible for ''stealing'' the man she claimed to have loved.

Bayard or Lane? The new viscount would appear to have had the most to gain. She'd not searched to discover whether the tray Frankston had carried that night held something more lethal than food. Both Bayard and his valet were odd enough that she had no real grasp of how vile a crime they might be capable of committing.

Setting her mouth in a determined line, she patted the pistol in her reticule and adjusted the knife in her half-boot. Whomever—Bayard or Frankston or Lane—she encountered once freed from this prison would find her much more difficult to eliminate than her unborn child.

Despite her perilous position, with a soldier's appreciation for resting when he could before the battle to come, she dozed. So when the vehicle finally halted, she was not perfectly sure how long they'd traveled.

She could make a break immediately when the door was opened. But she had only one shot in the pistol and her knife would not prove adequate against a crowd of brigands. Better to wait, assess the odds against her, and pray she found another chance.

And to improve that possibility, better to appear the terrified, trembling female they were no doubt expecting.

So when the door was opened, she shrank back. "What is the meaning of this outrage? Where are we?"

"Get out with ye now, so's I kin get back to Lunnon," the driver replied, motioning to her.

"You will return me immediately," she said, ending on a frightened squeak that belied that demand.

"Nay, the gent only paid me to transport ye here. Out, or I'll have to pull ye out."

"Don't you dare touch me," she said, clutching her reticule and feeling for the grip of her pistol. Avoiding the man's hand, she swung down, scanning the scene outside.

They had stopped before a well-kept country manor bordered by a small wood that obscured the drive as it stretched away from the house. Allowing an occupant to hear approaching vehicles before those within it could observe him.

In addition to the hackney driver, two burly men approached from the house, their mounts tethered nearby. Even if she made a dash for the box and tried to drive away, on horseback they would swiftly overtake the carriage.

No, for the moment she must acquiesce. "Who are you?" she asked. "You—you had better do me no harm or my cousin, Viscount Fairchild, will see you hang!"

One of the men laughed. "Feisty little filly, ain't she?" he asked the other as he paced closer.

She backed away with a strangled sob. "P-please, I beg you, do not h-hurt me!"

"No need to turn on the waterworks," he said, stepping by her to pay the driver, who quickly remounted the box and set his team in motion. "Ye'll be safe here. Fact is, yer cousin hired us to protect ye. 'Twas why he had you removed from London, he said."

"Why did my cousin say nothing to me of this?"

"Didn't want to frighten you, I suppose. Come in, now. Inside there's food and a woman to wait on ye."

"When will I see my cousin?"

"I expect he'll be along directly," the man replied.

Which cousin? Jenna wondered as she followed him. Had she been sent here in someone's misguided attempt at protection—or so she might fall victim to a conveniently fatal accident, far from the interested gaze of the ton?

Far from the friends who might help her. Like Nelthorpe, she thought despairingly, whom she had forced from her side.

For a moment, panic seized her, but once again she called on anger to loosen its grip.

It appeared she would not be bound or molested. She would have time before her cousin—whichever cousin—arrived to assess her surroundings, the number and intent of her captors. And to prepare for the confrontation to come.

About midafternoon, as near as she could tell by the position of the sun outside the room to which they conveyed her, a knock sounded at the door. A moment later, Lane Fairchild strode in.

"Jenna, you are safe," he cried, advancing toward her. "And not too frightened, I hope. I apologize for removing you so...abruptly from London, but given the doubts you'd expressed about Bayard, I dared not let you remain. Should he have learned of your suspicions, I fear he might have made another attempt to do away with you."

"So the accident was *his* doing! How can you be sure?"

"'Tis true, I'm afraid. I've just returned from tracking down the groom I'd dismissed. Under threat of the magistrate, he confessed that Bayard paid him to change you to a horse he felt certain would unseat you."

Except, Nelthorpe had told her, the man had been dead for more than two weeks.

A coldness settled in her bones. *Liar, liar,* she thought contemptuously. *Just what other lies will you spin to try to tangle me in your web?*

"But that's dreadful! What are we to do?"

He stepped closer and took her hands. It required every ounce of her soldier's discipline not to snatch them away when he raised them for a fervent kiss.

"I know 'tis still so soon, but will you not grant me the privilege of protecting you forever? With us wed, I would be much better able to safeguard you. Together we could work to insure Bayard was held accountable for his dastardly acts, perhaps even force him to quietly renounce the title and live in exile where he could no longer threaten you."

"You think you could manage that?" she asked, wondering how he'd planned to frame his hapless cousin.

"One way or another. Ah, the future we could have! Garrett chose wisely when he selected you to be his viscountess. Together, we can maintain the prestige and honor the ancient name of the Fairchild deserves.''

Lane was clever—so very clever. Had she not already discovered enough to see through his deception, she might well have been taken in by his accusations against Bayard.

But he had underestimated both her will to uncover the truth and, she thought, her eyes dropping to her reticule, her ability to resist.

''Flattered as I must continue to be by your regard, cousin, as you say, 'tis still too soon for me to think of marrying again,'' she said, pulling her hands free.

Lane gave her a deprecating smile. ''I trust in time to inspire in you a tenderness as deep as that which I cherish toward you. I surely hope so, for in my haste to secure your safety, I'm afraid I've forced your hand. Cousin I may be, but once it becomes known that you are here in my company, you will be ruined if we do not marry.''

She shrugged. ''As I have no desire to cut a dash among the ton, I care little for that.''

''Now I know you're upset, or you'd not be talking such nonsense,'' he said patronizingly. ''Once you are calm again, you'll realize you cannot risk exposing the Fairchild name to scandal.''

''Cousin, I'm afraid I care as little for the 'honor' of the Fairchild name as Bayard.''

Lane's smile grew strained. ''Why not rest now? I'll rouse you shortly, and trust by then you will be reasonable again. Indeed, I am counting upon it, for I brought a special license with me and have summoned a vicar to attend us in an hour. I apologize again for the haste, but I promise, you may have a wedding dinner in London afterward that is as lavish as you could desire.''

She stared at him, amazed that he could possibly misinterpret her refusal. ''Cousin, I have no intention of marrying you, in an hour—or ever. Would it not be even more an affront to the honor of the Fairchilds to have me repudiate you before the vicar?''

His smile vanished altogether. ''I'm beginning to lose patience with these missish megrims, Jenna. Reconciled to it or not, in an hour we will wed. If you choose to resist, those two stout fellows below will assist you, even repeat the vows, if necessary.''

''I can't believe any vicar would officiate at such a farce!''

''Not marry me to my poor widowed cousin who is so deranged by grief that I fear for her sanity? Whom I am marrying so I may assume responsibility for her care—in the best of asylums, if necessary? And who is being very well paid for his trouble?'' He shook his head gently, smiling once more. ''I don't believe so. If you need more convincing, perhaps I should summon my assistants now.''

All at once she had a terrifying vision of what it appeared he was planning: to marry her, by force if necessary, declare her mentally incompetent if she resisted him and thus seize from her legal control over both her person—and her fortune.

If he were about to summon his thugs, she could wait no longer, hoping for a better chance for escape. She must deal with Lane now, before he brought in reinforcements.

Seeking to disconcert him while she determined how best to evade him, she said, ''So I'm to be shuttled off to an insane asylum, rather than poisoned like Bayard?''

He looked surprised for an instant before that smile returned to his lips. ''I thought you might have puzzled that out. Or been alerted by his clumsy valet—who, by the way, suffered a tragic fall down the back stairs this morning. 'Twas why I knew the wedding must be now.

Can't have you going to the authorities with some wild story of intrigue and ruining all my plans.''

''To murder my child, finish off Bayard and seize my fortune?''

He held up his hands. ''I did no murder. Nor did I have any hand in arranging the accident.''

''But you put Lucinda Blaine up to it.''

He shook his head gently. ''If Garrett had lived, none of these tawdry actions would have been necessary. He was an exemplary Fairchild, fully worthy of bearing the name. But after his death, I could not tolerate the idea of Bayard as viscount, dragging the family honor into the dust with his odd behavior and bizarre schemes.''

''So you decided to poison him?'' she asked, not bothering to conceal the revulsion in her voice.

''A sad task, but necessary. By the time I learned you were with child, I had become…reconciled to taking over the mantle myself. After all, 'twas no guarantee your son would have been as worthy as I of carrying on the honors. Nor could I allow you, my dear, to dispose of your person and your fortune outside the family—or squander your money assisting a pack of indigent vagrants.''

While he talked, Jenna covertly scanned the room. She dare not descend the stairs, where his two cohorts might capture her. Soon after her arrival, she'd seen out her window that the large wisteria had been trained against the wall, its sturdy branches growing up and around the ledge. If she could divert or immobilize Lane, she might scramble down it and make a break for the woods.

''So you tried to shoot me at Richmond Hill?'' she asked, edging closer to the window.

''Had I wished to kill you, my dear Jenna, you would be dead. The shot was merely a warning—to frighten off the ubiquitous escort of that coward Anthony Nelthorpe.

No, I envision you by my side, helping me maintain the grandeur of the Fairchilds.''

Jenna felt behind her for her reticule. Under no circumstances did she intend to be coerced into delivering herself into the power of the man who'd set Lucinda Blaine to murder her child. Backing toward the window, she pulled the pistol from her reticule. ''I believe I'd rather die first.''

Lane shook his head. ''Jenna, Jenna, that was most unwise. I might have to gratify your wish.'' With a sigh, he removed a pistol from his own pocket and leveled it.

NEAR NOON, A GLASS OF SHERRY untasted at his side, Tony sat tapping his foot in Lady Charlotte's front parlor. What could be keeping them? he wondered for the thousandth time. He was about to abandon stealth and go to fetch Jenna himself when a maid entered to tell them Sancha just arrived at the servants' entrance, accompanied by a large trunk.

Cursing a woman's need to have to carry all her fripperies with her, Tony silently seconded Lady Charlotte's order that Sancha be shown up directly.

A few moments later, the maid hurried in. ''Mistress, all is ready!'' she exclaimed, then halted, gazing around the room in confusion. ''My mistress has been shown to a chamber?'' she asked Lady Charlotte. ''Why then did you summon me?''

Tony's heart plunged to his boots. Before he could question Sancha, Lady Charlotte, her face looking equally stricken, said, ''Lady Fairchild is not here. We thought you were to come together.''

''*Madre de Dios,* this cannot be!'' Sancha cried. ''I myself put her in a hackney three hours ago!''

Anguish scouring him, Tony jumped to his feet. *Three hours.* Somehow, Lane must have learned of their suspicions—and captured Jenna. And they had no idea even in which direction she'd been taken.

"Three hours!" Lady Charlotte exclaimed, echoing his thoughts. "How do we begin to try tracking her?"

Telling himself to calm, Tony started pacing. He must think clearly, devise a workable plan.

At that moment, another knock sounded and Tony's pulses leapt. *Dear Lord, let it be Jenna,* he prayed, *even if I will strangle her afterward for changing our plan and scaring us half to death.*

But the figure that stood upon the threshold when the door opened was not Jenna Fairchild, but Lord Riverton.

"Mark!" Lady Charlotte cried, running to him. "Thank God you are here! The most dreadful thing has happened."

"Jenna left London this morning in a hired vehicle?"

Shocked, Tony stopped pacing. "How did you know?"

"Come with me, all of you. I'll explain as we go."

After hurrying them to a traveling barouche that stood before the townhouse, horses at the ready, Lord Riverton gave orders to the driver and joined them in the coach.

"Tell me everything!" Tony demanded.

"First, let me explain that, on behalf of our government, for a number of years I have concerned myself with matters of…security."

A spy, Tony translated. A quick glance at Lady Charlotte showed her face registered no surprise. *She knows,* he realized.

"When Charlotte confided to me Jenna's suspicions concerning her accident, I was sufficiently alarmed to take the liberty of establishing a surveillance over her."

Bow Street? Tony wondered.

"Unfortunately," Lord Riverton continued with an expression of disgust, "I did not convey to my assistants the gravity of my concern, for they did not notify me until after my meeting a short while ago that they'd observed Jenna entering a hackney—which sped her out of London. I assume by your distress that she did not leave willingly.''

''You know where they've taken her?'' Tony broke in.

''I've had a man trailing the carriage, yes, and expect to hear from him shortly. The coach took the Great North Road. There's a tavern just outside the city where he will have left word for me.''

''Then let us spring the horses,'' Lady Charlotte said.

Lord Riverton gripped her hand. ''So we shall, as soon as we leave the city. We will get her back safely.''

Though Tony had kept his own counsel while he waited with Lady Charlotte for Jenna's arrival, under the circumstances it only seemed prudent to share the information he'd gathered. After listening to the whole, Lady Charlotte gasped, ''Mark, they intend to harm her!''

''We don't know that,'' Riverton said soothingly. ''The sudden disappearance of a peer's widow would not go unnoticed, making it much more difficult for someone to profit from arranging her demise, as her abductor must surely realize.''

Tony had a sudden image of Jenna rising from her bed, pistol trained on his chest. With just such skill and daring had she dealt with his threat long ago. For the first time since he'd heard of her disappearance, a small bubble of hope buoyed his spirits.

''Her abductor will find Jenna Fairchild is not so easily dispatched,'' he said to Lady Charlotte.

Riverton gave him a long look. ''Then may she shoot straight,'' he replied.

To Tony's relief, at the inn they found Riverton's agent waiting. He had indeed trailed the hackney, to a manor not far north of their current location, he told them. Leaving Sancha and Lady Charlotte, over their strenuous objections, at the inn for safety, Riverton gathered Tony and his men and headed there on horseback.

The afternoon light was dimming when at last they reached a winding carriage road. "We'll leave the horses here, approach the house from the shadow of the woods," Riverton told him. "I'll have my men creep in to ascertain her position and then bring her out."

"No!" Tony said urgently. "Let me help. I'll go mad if I can't do something, and I know a bit about creeping into houses."

Riverton studied him. "You will follow my orders."

Tony nodded.

"Come along, then."

After a nerve-straining interval advancing through the woods, they reached the manor, where a dark-clad man slipped up to inform Riverton he'd observed three menservants, a handful of maids and a lady, who'd been seen at the window of an upper chamber at the back of the manor. A well-dressed gentleman had arrived and joined her a short time ago.

Riverton motioned them to follow. As they rounded the corner, Tony's breath froze and his heart skipped a beat.

Framed by the window, Jenna stood facing Lane Fairchild—both with pistols raised.

CHAPTER TWENTY-FOUR

"UP THE STAIRS!" Riverton ordered his men, who set off at a run.

"Too late," Tony told him. "She's close enough to the window to escape, but she needs a diversion—*now.*"

Without waiting for Riverton to reply, Tony launched himself toward a thick growth of wisteria that trailed up the wall and framed the window. Willing his knee to cooperate, he climbed swiftly upward until he paused, his body parallel to the window, one foot braced at the ledge's outermost edge. Then he pried free a sturdy branch and swung himself through the casement, booted feet first.

The window shattering before him in a hail of glass and splintered wood, he staggered to a landing between Jenna and Lane—as both discharged their pistols.

A searing tongue of flame blasted through his shoulder. Praying his rash action had saved rather than condemned her, he spun backward into darkness.

AFTER DINNER TEN DAYS LATER, Tony limped up the stairs to his bedchamber, glad of the returning strength that made such simple movement possible. After awakening the day after Jenna's rescue from a hazy, pain-filled daze to see her face hovering over his, feel her hands wiping his brow, he'd made rapid progress toward recovery. But like a man who has supported a burden for so long that when it is lifted, he is more disoriented than relieved, he could not decide what he should do now that Jenna was no longer in danger.

Lane Fairchild was dead, she'd told him, her aim under pressure being better and her finger on the trigger faster than her cousin's—fortunately, she'd scolded him, else she might have blown a hole through his back rather than Fairchild's chest. In a final twist of irony, she added, the local magistrate had promised to put abroad the story that Lane had died in a hunting accident—so as not to tarnish the Fairchild name.

Over the days of his convalescence at Lady Charlotte's country house outside London, where they'd brought him after the incident, Jenna tended him faithfully, seeming to enjoy his company, even with the physical pull that still buzzed between them despite his injuries.

He was terribly tempted to accept Lady Charlotte's invitation and linger on for the holidays, to tease and cajole Jenna with enough evidence of his continuing need for character improvement that he persuaded her to renew the bargain she'd tried to repudiate. He no longer questioned the certainty of loving her or the knowledge that each day together was, for him, a gift.

But it was also torment. Torn between wishing he'd spoken to her the words of love that had trembled on his lips that night in her moonlit bedchamber and believing it wiser that he'd kept silent, he knew he soon must leave.

Not that he wanted to. He thirsted for her touch, her smile, her laughter like a badly wounded soldier in the wake of a battle craves water. She'd brought into his life a dimension of joy and peace he'd never known, and he desperately wanted to hang on to it.

He would be good for her, he tried to convince himself, amuse her, challenge her reforming abilities, and bring her limitless pleasure.

Add the power of a declaration of love to the gratitude

she'd already voiced about his rescue, and he might be able to talk her into marrying him, binding her sweet courage and passion to him forever. But he didn't really want her to marry him out of gratitude, did he?

With a sigh, he had to admit he was still enough of a rogue that he'd take her on any terms he could get.

But with the danger past, she no longer needed a rogue. He couldn't seem to force from his head Colonel Vernier's disparaging final words: if he truly cared for Jenna, he would walk away and leave her to a better man.

He had to admit that in reputation, character, wealth—everything except love for her—the colonel was superior.

He thought, too, of Miss Sweet, who'd begged him to redeem the sins of the father by becoming the man she'd hoped he might be.

Could he do that without a heart? For if he walked away from Jenna, he'd leave that in her keeping.

The ache settled deep within him at the certainty of what he must choose. If he were ever to break away from his father's pattern of selfishness, 'twas time to begin. Christmas was almost upon them. Tomorrow he'd seek out his hostess, express his gratitude, and leave.

The season of miracles, he'd once called it. But though he knew he was making progress in putting his wastrel's life behind him, even the holy season wasn't miraculous enough to turn Tony Nelthorpe overnight into the caliber of man Jenna Fairchild deserved.

Knowing his only partly reformed character would never withstand the temptation to stay if he had to say goodbye to Jenna in person, he decided to borrow her tactics and leave her a note. Which he would compose—tomorrow.

Stifling the clamor of his protesting heart, he turned his thoughts to where he would go. London? But the thought of encountering his father didn't appeal.

Hunsdon, perhaps. 'Twas also time he began learning to manage the estates his old comrade's father, Banker Harris, had salvaged for him. And perhaps eventually, if the adage that virtue was its own reward had any truth, he'd find a measure of solace for his lonely soul.

EARLY THE FOLLOWING MORNING Jenna answered a rap at her chamber door to find Lady Charlotte on the threshold. Wondering what news would have brought her friend to her room before breakfast, she ushered her in.

"Jenna, Nelthorpe just came to bid me goodbye," Lady Charlotte said, taking the chair Jenna offered. "He insists that he must depart this morning as soon as he completes packing. Something about pressing business awaiting him at Hunsdon. Did he mention this to you?"

An unpleasant tightness squeezed Jenna's chest. "No. He didn't say a word about leaving."

Lady Charlotte watched Jenna's face. "If you mean to do anything about it, I advise you to make haste. I've had the staff delay finding him a trunk, but that will not slow him for long." She swept Jenna into an impulsive hug. "You have more courage than I, dear friend. Use it."

After Lady Charlotte went out, on legs gone suddenly weak Jenna stumbled back to her chair. What *did* she mean to do about Anthony Nelthorpe?

Perhaps it was good that he was leaving. She had grown quite attached to seeing him every day. She wasn't sure she had the strength of mind, in the wake of her recent ordeal, to demand that he go.

Once he left, she could rebuild the serenity that had shattered while she'd watched in horror as he took a bullet meant for her. She could return to the business of purchasing property for the soldiers, anticipate the return of the eminently more suitable Colonel Vernier.

Except, as perfection sometimes does, Vernier inspired

her to admiration but not to affection. She enjoyed his company, but did not pine for it. She found him attractive, but experienced no unquenchable desire to touch, taste and explore him.

Unladylike reactions, those latter. But honest ones.

She now knew Tony Nelthorpe was far from as venal as she'd once thought him, though admittedly a man who could sneak into ladies bedchambers, deceive country people with Banbury lies, and threaten a peer's wife was not the sort of upright man Garrett would choose for her. But as many imperfections as she'd recently uncovered in her own character, who was she to cast stones?

Perhaps her greatest flaw was in believing she could master this weakness for Nelthorpe's company and his caresses. If she were to stop denying the truth and allow herself to consider the possibility of a legitimate relationship between them, that weakness would become not a flaw but a bond. Based on what happened between them whenever he was near, a powerful one.

Besides, this was not Garrett's choice, was it?

Follow your heart, my darling, she seemed to hear Garrett say.

A deep sense of peace settled over her, dissolving the guilt that had pressed heavy at her chest each previous time she'd considered a future beyond Garrett. *Thank you, my love,* she whispered back.

What did her heart desire?

'Twas still too soon after Garrett's death to know for sure. Should she eventually choose Nelthorpe, she might not occupy a high position or conduct herself always with propriety, but she'd never be bored. He was likely to challenge, amuse and keep her deliciously satisfied for a lifetime.

And though he was a far better man than she'd once

thought, he had the potential to become even better—with a little work by a determined woman.

TONY SAT AT THE DESK in his bedchamber, crumpling his latest effort at penning Jenna a farewell note. Faith, if he didn't finish one soon, he might as well wait until tomorrow to leave.

Squelching the insidious temptation to do just that, as he dipped the quill again, a knock sounded at the door.

Probably someone with a trunk—at last. Bidding the servant enter, he looked up—to see Jenna Fairchild on the threshold.

Heart suddenly pounding, he set the pen down so quickly, he nearly upset the inkwell.

"Jenna!" he cried. Suddenly recalling the proprieties, he added, "What are you doing here?"

She walked in and shut the door. "You were going to leave without saying goodbye."

If I had to face you, I'd never leave. He couldn't tell her that, of course, so instead he stuttered, "I, ah, was just writing you a note."

She shook her head reprovingly. "How very rude and unappreciative. Sometimes I almost despair of making something of you. But I did promise."

He tamped down a wild flash of hope. "I thought we'd agreed that bargain was over."

"One can't renege on a promise."

He looked away from her, willing himself to remain resolute. "It would be wiser. Seeing me would...complicate matters. Besides, I can't, as you well know, promise not to tempt you into something you may later regret."

"Isn't it my choice whether to risk that?"

You don't know what you risk! Desperately he put up a hand to keep her from coming closer. "Please, don't make this any harder. I can only scrounge so much courage.''

Ignoring his appeal, she approached the desk. ''What, you—one of the heroes of Waterloo?''

She was at the edge of the desk now, oh, so close, his fingers itched to touch her face, her hair, run a fingertip along those lips. Her honeysuckle fragrance filled his head, making coherent thought almost impossible.

He curled his fists around the chair arms to keep from reaching for her. ''I'm not a hero, as you well know. Not like Garrett—or Vernier.''

''Did you not do your duty, just as they did? Stand by your men and bring them through? There's as much nobility in that as in winning medals or mention in the dispatches.''

Him, noble. He stifled the urge to laugh. Did she not know how close he was to chucking nobility and dragging her into his arms?

Then the thought flashed into his head. *Tell her the whole. Admit to her what you've never dared admit to any living soul. You'll have no need then to be noble, for she'll look at you with contempt.*

Though she would never know it, 'twould be the most heroic thing he ever did—sacrificing what little esteem he'd earned in her eyes and pushing her toward someone better in such a way that she would never look back.

I can do it, Miss Sweet.

''A hero, am I? Shall I tell you how this 'hero,' after that first ghastly battle at Badajoz, cast up his accounts before every engagement? That only the dread of being humiliated before my men kept me in the saddle, moving forward? That at Waterloo, faced with the mass of D'Erlon's corps, I would have wheeled my horse and fled, but my knees were too weak. 'Twas my mount, better trained than I, who answered the charge.''

Too ashamed to look at her, sure she'd already turned to leave, the sound of her voice startled him. "But once you charged, you did valiant work. I found you on the field, remember. I saw the enemy dead all around you."

Bleeding inside at the memories, he made himself continue. "I couldn't even lift my saber until a lancer lashed out at my horse. Balthasar didn't deserve to die, so I fended him off. I praised heaven when recall sounded, but—but the regiment didn't heed it! I would have gone back, but then—oh God, then they were all over Kit, pulling him off his horse, and I couldn't just watch and do nothing. And then those two lancers and a cuirassier went after Kendrick and—"

Shaking uncontrollably now, he made himself stop. "Lord, Lord, I shouldn't be telling you this!"

Her voice fierce, she seized his arm. "Who else could you tell? I've walked the fields after a battle. I know what war means. I asked Papa once how he could bring himself to fight. He told me those who didn't fear war's horror were either madmen or fools. Fear keeps you alive, he said."

Tony laughed without mirth. "It did that, if barely. But I did nothing compared to Vernier. Standing at the gates of Hougoumont, fighting back wave after wave of attackers!"

"You don't think he was afraid?"

"No!"

"How do you know? Men never talk of such things. Papa only spoke of it to me because I was so distraught."

She had the right of it there, he realized. Before a battle, there was talk of tactics, encouragement, bravado. But no one spoke of fear.

Only madmen and fools aren't afraid, her father had said. A man who had survived far more battles than Tony.

He wasn't sure how long they both remained immobile

while he gathered his composure. As his breathing steadied, wonder and gratitude infused him that, after he'd confessed his most shameful secret, she'd stood by and gripped his hand instead of turning from him in revulsion.

"A man needn't be perfect to be honorable. He need only keep trying to improve. But then again," Jenna said, releasing his fingers, "if you think yourself so inferior, you might be right. I certainly could detail a number of serious flaws."

Tony would have resigned himself to an onslaught of criticism, except that she accompanied her words by sliding the hand that had been holding his up his waistcoat. He gasped a breath, his chest, and other things, swelling.

"S-such as," he replied shakily.

"Creeping into bedchambers in the dead of night."

"That could get one shot."

"Climbing up innocent wisteria vines."

"Very hard on the knees."

"Seducing a willing widow and then thrusting her into the arms of a rival, as if she were no more to him than a casual tryst in the shrubbery."

"'Twas an attempt to be noble!" he protested.

"Craven," she pronounced. "Craven and exceedingly foolish."

"Foolish," he agreed, resistance weakening as she sat herself on the desk in front of him.

"Such serious flaws," she murmured, leaning toward him, "will require much work and attention to amend. I shall have to be very diligent."

He tried to ignore her lips drifting closer, the warm breath that brushed his skin. Through the increasing sensual haze flickered the image of Miss Sweet. "I did promise to try harder."

"Indeed, you said you would go to great lengths. Ah," she whispered, glancing down, "I see that you have."

Allowing her to proceed any further was madness. But all thought of asking her to stop evaporated when she reached down to trace one finger along the uncomfortably constraining fabric of his trouser flap.

Groaning, he closed his eyes, clutching the chair arms ever more tightly lest he succumb to the now-raging desire to drag her to the bed.

To his consternation, at his groan, she ceased stroking him and drew back. "But I forget, you are still recovering. Did I cause your shoulder pain?"

"No! Though I swear, if you do not immediately resume your ministrations, I'm certain to suffer a relapse."

She laughed deep in her throat. "What would you have me do, then?"

Love me forever. Not wishing to scare her off, he bit back those words and said instead, "Pray continue your instruction in whatever way pleases you."

Bliss returned as she moved her hand back to cover him. "Oh, I plan to have you please me mightily. But you're a hard man, Tony Nelthorpe. It shall take much time and effort to soften you."

"Mold me as you will, lady."

Obligingly, as he closed his eyes, savoring each millimeter of motion, she shaped him again with her fingertips. "Such deficiencies, my lord," she chided after a moment.

"Deficiencies?" he gasped, his eyes popping open.

"In courtesy," she murmured, her expression grave. "A desk is a very uncomfortable surface upon which to…instruct. Shall we continue this session over there?" Gesturing to the bed, she slipped down from her perch and walked toward it.

Not sure this wasn't all some fantastic dream, he limped after her.

He could scarcely believe she meant to lie with him in

the guest chamber of her friend's house, in full daylight when a servant with coffee or clean linen—or the requested trunk—might at any moment knock at his door.

Yet at the same time, her boldness inflamed him such that, mad as it was to indulge in this, he couldn't have made himself call a halt if all the members of Parliament were about to arrive for a session here in this very room.

A step away from the bed, she paused with a frown. "One's belongings, sir," she said, indicating the folded garments he'd stacked there, "belong in one's wardrobe, not strewn about one's bed."

With two strokes of his hand he sent the whole collection to the floor. "Indeed, you are correct. I shall remedy that deficiency—later," he concluded, drawing her up for a kiss.

She responded avidly, her fingers biting into his shoulders, her tongue seeking his. Seeming fired with the same impatience that consumed him, without breaking their kiss, she urged him onto the bed, pushed him back against the pillows.

He was well and truly lost now. Ah, that this time, heaven would not end in her regret!

Knowing it was unlikely he'd be able to entice her to a second, more leisurely loving, he wanted to slow the pace, prolong and savor every moment. But even as her tongue caressed his, her fingers clawed open the buttons of his breeches.

They both shuddered at the touch of her hand to his naked skin. With a murmur of approval, she deftly eased his erection free and before he could move or think, took him in her mouth. Though he desperately wanted to touch and taste her in return, all thought dissolved at the first velvet stroke of her tongue.

Using lips and teeth and tongue, she moved up and down his length, taking him deep, sliding him almost free, nibbling at the exquisitely sensitive tip. Just when he thought he could stave off completion no longer, she released him and scrambled onto the bed.

"Love me," she gasped, her breathing frantic and her eyes wild. "Love me, Tony." Lifting her skirts, she straddled him, thrust downward to take him deep within her.

He shuddered, his whole body trembling as he hovered at the sharp edge of pleasure so intense it was nearly pain. Ah, how he longed to bare her breasts, feel the softness of her naked skin under his hands while she rocked into him! Yet there was a naughty, erotic excitement to this clandestine coupling in the bright morning light, both of them almost completely clothed.

After pulling her face close enough to kiss, he struggled through the layers of skirt and shift until his hands reached the smooth skin of her buttocks. Then, clutching her close and praying he would last long enough to pleasure her, he let her ride him as she would.

Her breaths accelerated with the thrust of her hips until, far too soon, her fingers clenched on his shoulders. Opening his mouth to swallow her cry, he let himself catapult with her into the abyss.

Timeless, weightless, they clung together, suspended in bliss as ancient as mankind, as fresh as the new morning. His one thought as slowly the sensations softened, faded, was a fervent hope that this time, she would wake without tears.

A few moments later, still within the circle of his arms, she pushed up on her elbow. Her gaze scanned the garments he'd been packing, now scattered about the floor. "Ah, Tony," she whispered, her eyes imploring, "you won't really leave me, will you?"

She was not going to banish him. She wanted him here.

At that realization, joy expanded his chest, clogged in his throat so that he had to struggle for speech.

"Never!" he said at last, drawing her back into his embrace.

For another few moments they lay quietly, Tony drinking in the wonder of her warm breath against his chin. "I suppose," she said at last, pushing to a sitting position, "I can inform Lady Charlotte you'll not be needing that trunk."

"Did you come here this morning to seduce me into staying?" he asked with a smile.

"No! Well, perhaps. Oh, I don't know!" Her cheeks coloring, she looked away. "I only knew I did not want you to go. You'll stay for Christmas? Help me afterward with purchasing the property and resettling the soldiers?"

"I must begin setting my own estate to rights, but yes, I shall help you with whatever you wish." He made himself inspect her face. "You are sure you want that?"

She gazed back steadily, her certainty unquestionable. "I do."

"Then," he said slowly, teetering between caution and fondest hope, "you must...care for me, at least a little."

She sighed, her lips quirking into a rueful grin. "I do care—far more than I would like. Since I don't seem to have much control over the emotion, I've decided to stop trying to resist or explain it away and just accept it."

Before he could bring order to the muddle of shock, relief and exuberant gladness her admission evoked, she reached out to gently touch his cheek. "I don't know yet where my feelings will lead. Sometimes it seems I will never cease mourning, never escape the grief and regret for what will never be. It's selfish, I know, to ask you to dance attendance on me when I can offer—"

"No!" he interrupted, seizing her hand. "I am happy

to help you. Besides, there's the matter of my character to finish reforming."

"Then we still have a bargain?"

Tenderly he smoothed the hair at the nape of her neck. "It appears we do."

EPILOGUE

THE PLEASANT JULY SUNSHINE warming her face, Jenna stood before a small stone building, gazing down at the fields and dwellings she now called home. Below her stretched meadows of gently-waving grain, the harvest from which would later fill the storehouse behind her. The wooded crest to her right was crowned by a spacious manor house built of the same stone, stables and outbuildings clustered behind it; across the fields to her left, workmen labored to complete the new school which, after the harvest, would fill with the children of the workers and the war orphans Evers and Sergeant Anston had collected.

Thanks to Lady Charlotte's help in recruiting employers, the first of the widows who had begun training last winter under Sancha's watchful eye would soon leave to take up positions as housekeepers, cooks and seamstresses. Lady Charlotte had also insisted on collecting subscriptions to help defray the cost of the school construction and to pay the salary of the headmaster she'd employed. All in all, Jenna had good reason to feel satisfied with the work of the last six months.

Somewhat to her surprise, after having lived such a vagabond existence all her life, she had discovered she loved her quiet, settled days as mistress of a country estate on the Hampshire downs. From the moment the agent had led her through it, Farrendean House had seemed like an old friend. She'd made an offer to purchase the property on the spot, removing here immediately after the holiday festivities at Lady Charlotte's.

In the intervening months, the sense of purpose she'd found in offering a haven to lives blighted, like hers, by the war had gradually helped fill the terrible emptiness that had tortured her after losing Garrett. The long rides through Farrendean's rolling hills and meadows soothed her restlessness of soul, gradually strengthening the tentative sense of peace she'd felt last Christmas when she'd first given herself permission to move forward into a life without him.

She'd known last spring that she had chosen the right direction when she journeyed to London for supplies and encountered Colonel Vernier, in the capital briefly for consultations about his ongoing diplomatic mission. Not only did she feel no envy at being fixed in rural England while he moved in the glittering international arena of Vienna, she had felt for him personally only respect and warm admiration. Without a qualm she gently turned down his request to call on her.

Upon the anniversary last month of the great battle, she'd refused all invitations to the various memorial services and come instead up here. Alone with her memories, she'd gazed out across the vista of fields, a view very similar to that from the cemetery above the Waterloo plain where Garrett lay. Acceptance of her losses that dreadful day settling deep into her soul, she'd descended the hill knowing she was ready not just to go on with her life, but to risk sharing it.

Casting a glance down the farm road to find it still deserted, she sighed. If only she could be as certain about Nelthorpe's inclinations as she was about her own.

He'd been a solid supporting presence these past months, encouraging, offering counsel on her purchase of the estate and its supplies, teasing her out of lassitude when recurrent sadness ambushed her. He alternately amused and exasperated her, impressed her with the diligence with which he'd thrown himself into learning the business of estate management, moved her to chastise him when he tried to distract her to drive or ride instead of work. He challenged her intellect with his wit, soothed her lonely spirit with his friendship, and had generally made himself so indispensable to her well-being that she could no longer imagine a future without him.

In short, though her feelings for Tony Nelthorpe were in many ways different from the almost hero-worship she'd felt for her husband, she knew she had come to love him.

She was not at all sure how he felt about her.

Somewhat to her chagrin, he'd readily agreed to the one caveat she'd added to their original bargain: that he refrain from attempting to seduce her. Of course, given that she'd all but compelled him to take her on two previous occasions, his ability to tempt her was moot. Though occasionally lackadaisical about other things, since the New Year he'd shown an all-too-assiduous sense of responsibility in refraining from encouraging her to any further intimate contact.

Indeed, aside from taking her hand to help her in and out of the carriage, or giving her a leg up into the saddle upon occasion, he'd scarcely touched her since their last kiss under the mistletoe just before Christmas. Despite her having offered him several excellent opportunities to repeat that gesture on his last several visits, he seemed perfectly content to continue in his avuncular, elder-brother role.

Perhaps, having twice had his fill, he no longer desired her? At Christmas she'd practically begged him to continue their relationship. Perhaps he merely felt obligated to watch over the grieving widow who'd saved his life until she found her feet again. After all, he'd never offered more than companionship—never even hinted at cherishing for her emotions warmer than friendship.

Knowing she might drive herself to distraction with such doubts and speculations, she'd decided to ask him to meet her here in this secluded place, where servants, workers and household staff were unlikely to interrupt them. Rather than agonize over the matter any longer, better to baldly inquire about his feelings and discover straightaway whether she'd pierced together her shattered heart only to break it again over a man who didn't really want her.

A flicker of movement caught her eye. Joy and nervousness warred in her breast as she watched Tony Nelthorpe round the bend in the lane. Taking a deep breath, she advanced to meet him.

"Jenna, you're looking as lovely as this sunny afternoon," he said, kissing the hands she offered. "Rested and refreshed! Evers must be finding fewer recruits to occupy you."

She took his arm, an automatic zing of awareness shocking through her. Surely he still felt it, too!

"Yes, we've had only a handful of soldiers and one more widow arrive since your last visit," she replied, guiding him toward the stone storehouse. "Your spring planting has prospered, I trust?"

"As yours has, I see," he said, nodding toward the fields below them. "A pretty site, this. You asked me to meet you here to admire the view?"

"It is lovely, isn't it? But you must be hot after that long walk up. Come, let's get out of the sun. I've brought some wine."

Did she only imagine his minute hesitation on the threshold, as if troubled when he noted the deserted building's relative isolation? "That would be most refreshing,'' he said an instant later, following her into the cool dimness within.

She let him gaze around as she poured wine from the basket she'd carried up. Primitive but solidly built, the one-room storehouse was unfurnished, its single small window looking out over the vista of hill and meadow.

''Does the place remind you of somewhere?'' she asked after a moment.

Nelthorpe gave a short laugh, the tips of his ears reddening. ''It does rather bring to mind that abandoned monastery outside the walls of Badajoz.''

''Where you lured me under false pretenses, then tried to seduce me? Threatening, I recall, not to allow me to leave until I succumbed to your advances?''

Nelthorpe groaned. ''What an arrogant, chuckleheaded coxcomb I was! Still following the sage advice of that great arbiter of correctness, my father, who'd preached that a woman rebuffed a man's advances only as a sap to her conscience. That she really wanted him to take her, despite any protests to the contrary.''

Jenna laughed. ''I dispelled that illusion rather pointedly.''

''I've got the scar to prove it,'' he acknowledged with a rueful grin. ''I couldn't have been more shocked—I was so presumptuously sure you wanted me as I wanted you!''

This was her opening, Jenna thought. Gathering her courage, she said, ''I did want you. I just didn't know it yet. I…I still want you.''

He jerked his gaze back to her face, the sudden blaze in his eyes mitigating her uncertainty. An instant later, however, he tightened his hands into fists and stepped away.

''I thought we'd already decided that would be… unwise.''

She stepped after him, took his arm and made herself continue. ''Do you no longer want me?''

His fists flexed, unflexed, as if he could not decide whether to leave her hand on his arm or brush it away. Finally, he left it, covered it gently with his own. ''You know I do,'' he said gruffly. ''But the result of indulging that desire might be a child, and I couldn't risk that. You are honorable to your bones! I would expire of frustration before I would place you in a position where doing what was right compelled you to accept something you didn't want, weren't ready for.''

''And if I were to tell you that I am now ready?''

Once again he snapped his gaze back to her. ''Are you implying what I think you're implying?'' he demanded, studying her face.

''Let me say it plainly. I love you, Tony Nelthorpe. Once, another world and time ago, we came together to a room like this and you asked me to marry you, threatening to detain me until I was fit to be no man's wife but yours. I wish more than anything for you to ask me again, but this time there must be no coercion. Don't offer out of gratitude for my saving your life, or pity for the widow left alone. Don't offer even out of passion for a wanton who cannot seem to resist your advances. Offer only if you love me, Tony. Only love can insure you are meant to be no woman's husband but mine.'' Her courage beginning to falter, her voice wobbled as she asked, ''D-do you love me, Tony Nelthorpe?''

For long, nerve-shredding moments he simply stared at her. Her face was flaming in chagrin, her heart lacerating in anguished disappointment, when finally he stuttered, ''L-look in my waistcoat pocket.''

''Your waistcoat pocket?''

He grabbed her hand and thrust it inside his jacket. ''Here.''

For half an instant she wondered if he wanted her once again to seduce him, until her fingers touched folded paper. At his curt nod, she drew it out.

"Read it."

Still baffled, she unfolded the document—and discovered it to be a special license, permitting one Anthony Nelthorpe to wed one Jenna Montague Fairchild at a place of their convenience, any time within the next three months. The paper was dated June 25—the anniversary of Waterloo.

Incredulous, she looked back up at him. "But we've met three times since you obtained this! Why have you said nothing?"

"I sensed—I hoped—that you had at last recovered from your grief, but every time I thought to propose, my courage failed me. I was terrified you might dismiss my pretensions as contemptuously as you did that day in Badajoz, or be so insulted by my unworthy offer that you banished me. I lost you once. Difficult as it was to be with you as a friend when I wanted so much more, I could better stand that than the thought of losing you forever."

He seized her hands, still holding the special license, and kissed them fervently. "I love you, Jenna! And though a lifetime might not be enough for you to remake me into the kind of man you deserve, will you marry me anyway? Will you love and cherish and mold me for the rest of my days?"

He loved her. After the anguish and despair of the last year, she could hardly allow herself to believe it. A fierce joy welled up, swelling her chest, making her throat ache and bringing the sting of tears to her eyes. "I will," she replied, her voice unsteady. "Indeed, I suspect a lifetime will be just long enough." Clutching the special license in one hand, she threw herself into his embrace.

Forrester Square
LEGACIES. LIES. LOVE.